TH
QUANTUM
GRAIL

A NOVEL

J.D.
REDVALE

GOTHAM
BOOKWORKS

Copyright © 2024 by J.D. Redvale

Cover design by James T. Egan of Bookfly Design.

All rights reserved.

No part of this book may be reproduced in any form or by any electronic or mechanical means, including information storage and retrieval systems, without written permission from the author, except for the use of brief quotations in a book review.

The characters and events portrayed in this book are fictitious or are used fictitiously. Any similarity to real persons, living or dead, is purely coincidental and not intended by the author.

Paperback ISBN: 979-8-9909738-1-7

Hardback ISBN: 979-8-9909738-2-4

Ebook ISBN: 979-8-9909738-0-0

jdredvale.com

gothambookworks.com

For Joel—the kindest soul I've ever known.

The world you know is already gone.

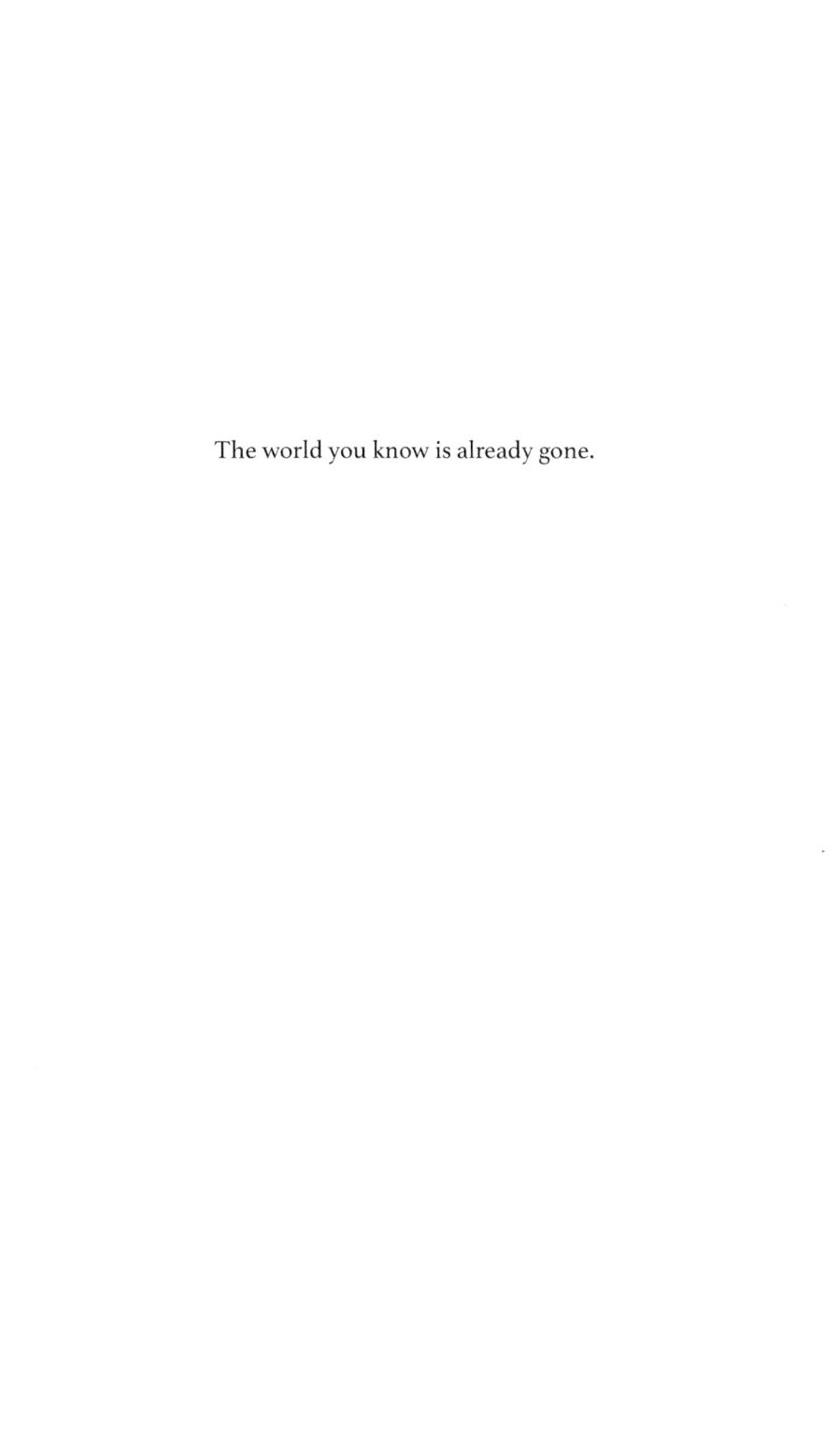

1

The projector screen was awash in green hues of night vision footage. Captured through his helmet camera, the video showed the soldier weaving through narrow hallways with a Heckler & Koch HK416 rifle. Like the nose of a hound, the gun's muzzle methodically homed in around every corner. Smooth and steady. Until it recoiled with a flash.

More flashes erupted on the left edge of the screen, as another soldier's rifle briefly entered the camera's field of view. After a short pause, the movement through the hallway resumed. Sprawled bodies emerged from the shadows: three men in paramilitary uniforms, each with a bullet hole in his forehead.

The soldier continued past them, arriving at a hulking door that resembled the wall of a shipping container. He checked the doorknob. Locked. Within seconds, a shotgun entered the frame, pointing at the knob. A strobe of light, and the soldier burst through the door, his camera revealing more paramilitary men—hunkered down behind a wall of screaming children.

The footage froze, and lights in the room came on.

Holding the projector remote, Captain John Mitcham

stepped next to the screen, turning his attention to the twelve men in the audience. After eight years of standing on this side of the quaint auditorium, he had developed a calcified ambivalence toward the days when he'd been in their seat. The men hailed from every corner of the country. They checked off most ethnic and socioeconomic backgrounds. They were a motley assortment of life, and the world's most skilled purveyors of death. They were assault squadron members of SEAL Team Six.

"Clearly an extreme encounter of civilian hostages," said John, his eyes sweeping over the paused footage of nine boys being used as shields. "Although a prevalent pattern in the Babil Province at the time." He turned to the SEALs, studying their faces as they studied the screen.

At forty-five, John was old enough to be the father of half of the men facing him. Even though his disciplined physique was comparable to theirs, the age difference was accentuated by John's skin, weathered by far more deployments where the sun and wind were as hostile as the targets. And as far as targets were concerned, John's eyes finally locked on his current mark.

"Officer Moynihan."

"Sir," answered a stout man in the front row whose hair was the color of ash. His colleagues called him Hoosier, even though he was from Iowa, not Indiana—an inside joke John was not privy to.

"Given the mission intel and rules of engagement, assess the situation and lead us through next steps."

Moynihan's intense blue eyes probed the frozen footage.

"Sir, intel stated low likelihood of civilian presence, but ROE dictate to prioritize avoiding civilian casualties. Contingency course of action would be immediate withdrawal. P-5 to P-2, directly to LZ for exfil."

John had once been good at hiding his disappointment, but

whatever showed on his face made Moynihan shift slightly in his seat.

"Am I wrong, sir?"

John forced a reassuring nod. "You are correct." He gestured to the screen. "Unless anyone has anything to add, let's finish the video and analyze the withdrawal."

"Sir, those children are as good as dead."

John swiftly turned toward Petty Officer Third Class Alex Romero. The SEALs called him Bronx, a more fitting nickname considering he'd grown up three blocks from Yankee Stadium.

"Officer Romero, please elaborate."

"Sir... the cuts on the children's heads and their black clothing are part of a customary ritual for commemorating the Day of Ashura. Which means these kids are Shiites, not Sunnis. This coincides with the intel report of Shiite abductions in the area. The report also notes that the death rate after abduction in the Babil Province is over ninety-eight percent."

In all the years of John showing the footage, Romero was only the third SEAL ever to have memorized a seemingly trivial detail of the fourteen-page intel report, pair it with scattered supplemental training on Iraq's political and cultural dynamics, and have the confidence to voice his observation. For that, he was rewarded with a follow-up question.

"Based on this, what is your assessment of the appropriate course of action?" said John.

The furrows forming in Romero's brow seemed like the result of tectonic plates grinding against each other inside his head. He stared so deeply at the nine frightened boys that John was sure he would reach his hand out to them at any moment. But then his eyes sagged with the rest of his expression, and John knew what he would say before he ever said it.

"I agree with Hoosier, sir. Withdrawal and extraction."

There it was. The only correct answer. Orders were orders,

and moral ambiguities had no place on the battlefield. And so, John decided not to muddy the water any further. He omitted that three days after the withdrawal, each boy was strapped with fifteen pounds of C-4 explosive and sent to the largest farmers' market in the city of Karbala. A single-point detonator. One hundred eighty-seven casualties.

He also omitted that he was the soldier in the video, haunted by a recurring nightmare of nine children begging him not to let them die.

2

At half past seven, John checked his watch for the twelfth time in the last hour. By this point the whispering of other patrons at Terra Vinoteca was raking his ears. Their darting eyes had lost all subtlety half an hour ago, when the pressure to finally order something made John choose a bottle of Chianti, which the young waitress brought with two stemmed glasses. The look of pity on her face was now spreading among the rest of the staff. Even the line cooks threw glances across the counter at the lonesome man whose date had never shown up.

After she served *Eggplant Parmigiana for Two* to the elderly couple two tables over, the waitress turned to John. Despite her best efforts, the smile she gave him slowly deflated into something bordering on a grimace. She fidgeted with her hands as she approached.

"Sir, would you like more bread?"

Considering John had only broken off a small piece of the complimentary ciabatta, it was clear she had run out of questions to ask. *The wine is good,* he had assured her. *No, it's not a special occasion. Why yes, it is a scorcher out there. What were the specials again?*

John decided to take mercy on her. "No, thank you. Just the check."

"You've barely taken a sip of your wine. I can take it off the bill."

"No, that's all right."

"Are you sure?"

"Only under the condition you donate the bottle to the staff after their shift."

The waitress smiled at that and turned away. John took out his phone, and just then the waitress spun back, as though a brilliant idea had crossed her mind.

"You know, dating is hard. At any age. I know a great dating app…"

Her voice trailed off as her eyes settled on John's flip phone. She stared at it as though a prehistoric relic had just been unearthed.

A sigh escaped her mouth. "I'll be right back with the check."

After she put ten feet of distance between them, John flipped his phone open. The last four unanswered texts he'd sent read like phases of grief: denial, anger, bargaining, depression. The only one left was *acceptance*, and John's thumbs clunked away:

> Claire, I understand if you changed your mind. I even understand not wanting to talk. When you feel |

John stopped typing with the realization he didn't really know what he wanted to convey. Was there even a combination of words that would make a difference? What was the right thing to do in a situation like this? Because what the patrons and staff at the trendiest new restaurant in Alexandria, Virginia, didn't know was that the man with the archaic phone and untouched bottle of wine had been stood up by his own wife.

3

"Claire, I... I am following everything we talked about. I am giving you the space. But it's been five days. This radio silence, it worries me. I just want to make sure you're okay. Please, let me know."

"If you are satisfied with your message, press one. To record—"
"Message deleted. To record a messa—"
"Claire..."
"Message deleted."

John snapped his phone shut and set it on his office desk, next to the picture of Jenny two days after her nineteenth birthday. Her smile bright as a glacier. Hair unruly in the Montauk wind. Left arm wrapped around Claire, right around John. The flash of perfection and happiness and all that was good with the world. Had been good.

John's right hand began shaking. He took solace that no one was around to see it. He anchored it to the desk, then used his left to press the red button on the landline phone.

"Mrs. Simasek, please reschedule the rest of my meetings today. Whatever works."

"Yes, Captain Mitcham."

As John eased his Chevy Tahoe into the cul-de-sac, his heart rate went up. A soldier should not break protocol. Nor should a husband separated from his wife break the rules of separation. But the what-if scenarios were tearing through his imagination. What if Claire had fallen down the stairs? What if she'd decided to hurt herself? What if there had been a gas leak? The cruel infinity of unlikely possibilities, easily dispelled with the likeliest: his wife wanted nothing to do with him.

John tensed at the sight of Claire's car in the driveway—it appeared she'd come home early from the hospital. He had imagined having the tactical advantage of sitting on the front steps as she pulled into the driveway. But now he had to entertain the likely possibility that their conversation would unfold through a half-open door, as though John were a Jehovah's Witness or a salesman. Then again, he *was* preaching love and selling reconciliation.

Pushing aside his pessimism, John edged up to Claire's car, shut off the engine, and promptly climbed out. He resisted the urge to veer off the walkway and pick up the scattered newspapers on the front lawn. By the time he rang the doorbell, his memorized speech was nothing but fragments of a once-solved puzzle. All his deployments throughout the world's most hostile places, yet it was his front yard in Arlington that struck the most fear into him.

He rang the doorbell two more times, but Clare did not answer. It dawned on John that he hadn't even considered this scenario. His wife could simply not open the door at all. His hand hesitantly floated to the illuminated button once more, as though it were a fragment of hot coal.

"She's not home," said a nasal voice.

John closed his eyes, then slowly opened them and turned to the right.

Barry stood at the border of their yards, wearing the same straw fedora he'd worn when he welcomed John and Claire to the neighborhood eight years ago.

John skipped the pleasantries. "Her car is in the driveway."

Shaking his head with a sigh, Barry sauntered into John's yard.

"I hate that you have to find out this way. Claire left almost a week ago."

"Left?"

"I saw a moving van pull out of the driveway. One of those rentals."

John felt a hot stone plunge into his gut. His thoughts trampled over each other.

"It can't be," was all that came out of his mouth.

"Look, John..." Barry adjusted his fedora as if the words he was looking for would fall out of it. "When people go through what you and Claire went through, sometimes a fresh start is the only way. How many times has she mentioned that everything around here reminds her of Jenny?"

Barry was the kind of neighbor who knew what everyone had said, even though they had never said it to him. Which is why of all the people to break to John that Claire had left, it being the neighborhood's gossip mayor added a distinct tinge of indignity. John wanted to tell him that he knew his wife better than anyone. That there had been other things Claire had said. That she would never just pack up and leave. Most of all, he wanted to grab that stupid fedora and toss it like a frisbee.

Instead, all he said was, "Thank you for your perspective, Barry. If you don't mind getting off the grass, we had the lawn care company fertilize it five days ago. Their van looks like 'one of those rentals.'"

4

John entered his house for the first time in six months. A part of him felt like an intruder. The other part felt like the last six months had been a dream.

Claire's keys hung on the wall, swelling his uncertainty. She was either in the house, or she'd left her keys because she'd left everything behind. More out of habit than reason, John hung his keys on the hook next to hers.

"Claire? Claire, it's me."

Silence. The air felt heavy with it.

John took off his shoes. Claire hated when he would forget.

He wasted no time climbing the foyer stairs, two steps at a time. Upstairs, the door to Jenny's room was wide open. John stopped in front of the doorway, looking inside as if the room's contents were museum artifacts encased in glass. The picture of Jenny in Montauk was sitting face down on the nightstand. Claire had said everything in life was inverted after her death; the pictures and keepsakes that had brought the most joy had become mementos of profound sorrow. But John still preferred sorrow over nothing at all.

He turned his eyes to the end of the hallway. The master

bedroom door was ajar. John strode to it and peeked through the opening.

"Claire?"

Silence. The worst kind of nothing at all.

He pushed the door all the way and took in the room. Bed made. Curtains drawn. Bathroom door was closed. With uneasy steps, John approached it and knocked. Unrelenting silence.

He twisted the knob. It gave so easily that the door opened, and John had to hold it from going farther. Most of his career had come down to encountering unspeakable horrors behind closed doors. He steadied himself and pushed this one open.

His eyes traveled over the beige tiles. Until they reached the bathtub.

With a quivering exhale, John found it empty.

Swiftly turning around, he swept across the bedroom and entered the walk-in closet. His eyes scanned every inch as he tried recalling what had been there before. He couldn't find Claire's favorite suitcase, and there was a handful of empty hangers. His jaw clenched.

After making sure Claire's wallet was not inside her nightstand, John came downstairs. As he stood in the hallway overlooking the living room, his gaze drifted to the kitchen bar on the other side. Even from this distance, the white envelope stuck out.

He approached it as if it were a land mine.

But landmines didn't have John's name written on it.

He took a deep breath and pulled the paper out of the envelope.

John,

There is not much I can write here that I haven't told you already. I gave it my all, and it wasn't good enough. I'm not sure what's next for me, but I know it can't be here. And it can't be with you. I hope you'll find a way to forgive me. Please take care of yourself.

Love,
Claire

John's hands began shaking. Not because of his condition. Not because he felt angry or hurt. Not even because his wife had left him. It was because after reading the last sentence, he knew Claire had not meant a word of her note. And she was in some horrible danger.

5

OCTOBER 7, 2001

The towers had fallen four weeks ago. Today, America was officially at war.

John took a sip of his coffee, his other hand holding Claire's. They sat mostly in silence, huddled around a small dining room table in a fittingly small apartment on the outskirts of Jacksonville, North Carolina. It was the twenty-third year and first deployment of John's life.

He was one of the last members of the Twenty-Sixth Marine Expeditionary Unit to be summoned to Marine Corps Base Camp Lejeune. The Twenty-Sixth would reinforce the Fifteenth in conducting an amphibious assault a hundred miles from Kandahar—and would be some of the first American soldiers to fight on land in Afghanistan. It all sounded serious and dangerous, and Claire's face showed it.

"I packed an extra toothbrush," she said.

John smiled, but he understood what she really meant. *We have no idea how long you'll be gone.* She stood up and started toward John's rucksack on the floor.

"Let me make sure you have enough—"

"Claire, it's fine," said John, not letting go of her hand. "Just sit with me, honey. I only have a minute left."

Almost reluctantly, Claire sat back down. John understood this too: it was easier to run around than sit and let the mind do the running.

Claire sat, adjusting the wedding ring that was two sizes too big. After September 11, she and John both knew they had little time. They had gotten married a week later. A private ceremony inside a small chapel in Durham, North Carolina. *We'll do a proper wedding when I get back,* John had said. But now, looking at Claire, he was questioning the wisdom of getting married at all—and the real possibility of making her a widow.

"It's gonna be fine. I promise I'll be careful."

Claire let out a sound between a sigh and a scoff, and John felt silly for saying it. She had enough family members in the military to know *careful* had little to do with survival.

John checked his watch.

"I have to go," he said and squeezed her hand.

As he put on his rucksack, a part of him felt like a boy on the first day of school.

Claire walked him to the door, and once he stood in the hallway and she remained inside the apartment, it finally felt real to John. He did his best to project calm.

"I'll be back before you know it. You just take care of yourself."

"Don't say that."

"Say what?"

"To take care of myself."

This John did not understand.

"Claire, I don't…"

She cupped his face and looked him in the eye.

"Those were the last words my father said to me the day he took his life."

John was momentarily stunned. He and Claire had talked about her father's suicide plenty before, but she'd never mentioned this detail.

"Honey, I'm really sorry."

Claire cracked a surprising smile.

"It's all right. You didn't know. But let's never use that phrase."

"Never," echoed John. "Understanding new husband is understanding."

This made Claire smile even more. But a streaming tear betrayed her facade.

"Come back to me."

"I'll swim across the ocean if I have to," said John, and kissed his wife of three weeks goodbye.

6

PRESENT DAY: JUNE 24, 2024

Barry opened his front door with a smirk.

"John, no need to apologize. Emotions got the best of y—"

"I need every detail about the van you saw leave my driveway."

White cargo van. Roughly twenty feet long. No lettering or logo of any kind. Only distinguishable feature was a dent on the left side, its shape resembling an upside-down checkmark. With a cup of coffee in his hand, Barry had watched through his living room window as the van pulled out of John's driveway around eight a.m. last Wednesday. It was now Monday.

Five days late with details as insipid as the van itself. John knew he couldn't go to the police with this. Not with Claire's note. He had swept the house and outside perimeter for footprints. Nothing. He had searched Claire's car twice for clues. All he'd found were items that stabbed his heart. Claire's favorite cinnamon mints. Too many depleted packs of tissues. John genuinely wondered how many tears it had taken Claire to go through them. The one item he couldn't seem to put down was Claire's hospital badge.

Slumped at the wheel of his Tahoe, John cradled it with both palms. The badge looked fairly new, but Claire's photo had been clearly reused. Her picture was from years ago, when she had her hair shoulder length. It had probably been taken on her first day at the VA hospital. Back when she had just quit her psychiatric practice to devote her expertise to men and women who needed her help the most. People whose traumas on the battlefield followed them home. People who had a hard time assimilating to civilian life. People like John.

No matter how many times John had brought up the notion that Claire started working with veterans to better help him, she denied it. But she readily admitted it helped her better understand him. John had put up an impermeable wall, according to the many psychiatrists who had tried breaking through it. There was a running joke between him and Claire that he was purposely pissing off every psychiatrist in town until Claire would be the only one left to treat him.

As challenging as those years had been—as John transitioned from active duty to an instructor role—he now looked back with nothing but fondness. That was the power of photos. They were rectangles of nostalgia that reminded John that life would never be as good as it once had been. Eight years had passed since Claire's picture was snapped at the VA hospital, but it felt to John as though it were a lifetime ago, and another life altogether.

His hands cupped the hospital badge so tightly that it twisted into an arch, elongating the lettering below Claire's picture. John's eyes suddenly narrowed. He realized for the first time that the place of employment below Claire's name was not the VA hospital. It was something called Franklin Medical Center.

John pulled into the parking lot of a nondescript commercial complex. He would've been hard pressed to tell it apart from any other dotting the I-66 corridor of Fairfax County. He followed signs for Franklin Medical Center and parked in the first available spot. With a peculiar sense of unease, John took in the beige three-story building. Had he and Claire really grown apart so much that he didn't even know her place of employment? Was he already an estranged relic of Claire's past?

John shook off the thought, climbed out of the car, and strode to the entrance.

The doors slid apart, the smell of antiseptic immediately thick around him. It wasn't the VA hospital, but it was still a hospital. John approached the young woman sitting behind the lobby's reception desk, scrolling through her phone.

"Excuse me, I need to speak with someone about Claire Mitcham."

The receptionist pointed her eyes upward.

"Are you a patient?"

"I'm her husband."

Her lower lip dropped at the same time as the hand holding her cell. She finally gathered herself and keyed a few buttons on the landline phone.

"Dr. Edwards, could you please come to the front desk?"

7

Sitting across Dr. Edwards's desk, John scanned the myriad of pictures on the wall behind him. Claire was in three of them, seemingly joyful, with the rest of the psychiatric staff that had once worked out of the VA hospital.

"Yeah," said Dr. Edwards with a deflated breath. "They moved us from the VA to this building about five months ago, after the last round of budget cuts. I thought Claire would've told you."

"She and I are ... taking some time apart."

"That makes sense."

"Excuse me?"

Dr. Edwards pushed the bridge of his glasses, his face pinched with sudden unease.

"Mr. Mitcham, she changed her emergency contact from you to her mother."

That one stung. Especially considering Claire's mother was battling the early stages of dementia. John understood Claire needing separation, but this felt borderline punitive.

"We called her mother on Wednesday, the day she didn't show up."

John genuinely doubted that Claire's mother remembered receiving that call.

"When was the last time you or someone on the staff talked to her?"

"Last Tuesday."

"Anything unusual you can recall?"

"No. Not that day. And the next, she doesn't show up."

It seemed as though Dr. Edwards was going to say more, but he stopped talking, then pushed the bridge of his glasses once more. *He's nervous.* John could have this effect on people—that much he knew. Yet he had interacted with Dr. Edwards plenty of times during the holiday parties Claire had dragged him to over the years, and John couldn't recall ever seeing the man fidget with his glasses like this.

"Dr. Edwards, is there anything else you can tell me?"

Dr. Edwards cleared his throat. "I'm afraid not."

John held the man's gaze long enough to search his eyes for a clue. All he found was a dead end.

"All right," said John with a heavy sigh. "If you hear anything, please call me immediately."

"Of course." Dr. Edwards stood up and ironed his white coat with his palms. "Let me walk you out."

"That's all right. I've already taken up enough of your time."

"No bother at all. You've caught me on a light day."

The way Dr. Edwards phrased his words made John sink back into the chair.

"Mr. Mitcham?"

John rubbed his chin for a moment. "Earlier, you said *that day*."

Dr. Edwards tilted his head. "Not sure I follow."

"When I asked you if there was anything unusual you can recall about the last time you spoke to Claire, you said, 'Not that day.'"

"And?"

"What about any other day?"

"I'm not sure what you're getting at."

To be frank, John didn't quite know either. He would've let the matter go, except Dr. Edwards pushed the bridge of his glasses for the third time.

John finally surmised what was behind the nervous gesture. Dr. Edwards knew information about Claire, perhaps something she'd shared with him in confidence, but he was uncomfortable disclosing it given that Claire and John were separated. A psychiatrist by the book. John almost admired his stance.

John's eyes drifted back to the wall blanketed with Dr. Edwards's pictures. It was practically a chronological panorama of the man's life, running left to right. Graduation photos, residency pictures, poses with colleagues and in front of the world's famous landmarks. But glaringly missing from the wall was a family. Dr. Edwards was a man married to his job. He ran one of the largest psychiatric practices in the country and took his profession as seriously as John took his military service. He insisted that John call him Dr. Edwards, though John had never reciprocated with insistence on being called Captain. So how could John expect a man this rigid in his principles to bend?

"Have you ever come close?" said John, his gaze still on the wall.

"Pardon?"

"Getting married?"

Dr. Edwards turned toward the wall, as though searching for a moment in time when a wedding photo might have had a chance of being hung there. He slowly sat back into his chair, studying John with an expression that resembled pity.

"No."

John let out another heavy sigh, gathering the right words.

"I understand you are respecting Claire's privacy. I really do.

She and I are separated, but I know something that leads me to believe she is in great danger. I assure you that sharing whatever it is you know is more important than respecting her wishes."

Dr. Edwards went still. His hand reached toward his face, and John was sure he was going to push that damn bridge of his glasses once more. But instead he took the glasses off and set them on the desk with a trembling hand.

"Mr. Mitcham... it's not her wishes I can't go against."

Fear. John had seen plenty of it on the battlefield, in the eyes of soldiers and civilians alike. But he had never witnessed the kind of terror he saw in Dr. Edwards's eyes in civilian life. John leaned in, his voice a razor.

"Whose then?"

"I'm not sure. They... they took statements, looked at the security footage, all that. They told me I am under no circumstances allowed to discuss with anyone."

John's bewildered curiosity rose with shivers up his spine. "Security footage?"

"Oh, John..." said Dr. Edwards, his lower lip quivering.

For the first time ever, he addressed John by his first name. It disquieted him.

John's left eye twitched once. He had developed the response early in his career, when a situation called for emotional detachment. A coping mechanism for the brutal realities of warfare.

"Show me the security footage."

8

The security monitor was replaying a video of four men standing in a designated smoking area, a few yards from the main entrance of Franklin Medical Center. Two were smoking cigarettes, one was vaping, and the fourth had his hands in his pockets.

"All four are Claire's patients," said Dr. Edwards, gesturing at the screen. "They did this every morning they'd come here, twice a week. Just hang outside for a bit before coming in."

Before John could ask a question, a white van pulled up next to the men. The side door slid open, spilling six figures wearing balaclavas and SWAT-style gear. Even from the grainy footage, John could tell they were holding AK-47 rifles. They loaded Claire's patients into the van with military precision, the entire ordeal taking no more than eight seconds before the van peeled off. But not before John caught the dent in the shape of an upside-down checkmark.

A rush of blood swarmed his head.

"It happened so fast we didn't even realize it," said the security guard as he paused the footage.

"We?" said John, glancing at the cell phone on the guard's desk. "What screen were you watching at the time?"

"Mr. Mitcham, please," Dr. Edwards interjected. "This is not a high-security facility. We have guards for when patients get physical inside, not... this."

John was still processing *this*. It felt surreal, as though he'd just watched footage from one of his missions abroad. How could *this* happen in the suburbia of Fairfax, Virginia, mere miles from the nation's capital? He turned to Dr. Edwards.

"When *did* you realize what had happened?"

"Well, we started calling the patients when they didn't show. But when Claire didn't show up, either, we knew something wasn't right. The following day we started getting calls from the soldiers' commanding officers. We were about to call the police when they showed up."

"They?"

"At first it was a couple of case workers from the VA. But then, I don't know what agency they were from, but they flashed TS/SCI clearances, and the case workers left immediately."

"Then what?"

"They asked questions, looked at the same footage as you, and told us to delete it."

"Why haven't you?"

"The system automatically wipes it after a week. We have no control over it to prevent tampering. All we can do is have the system preserve the footage—and I assure you, Mr. Mitcham, this is getting deleted on Wednesday."

The fear resurfacing in Dr. Edwards's eyes made John's imagination run wild over the conversation that had involved someone holding the highest national security clearance.

"What questions did they ask?"

"You know I can't tell you that."

John considered that for a moment.

"No. But you can play the video of when they came in."

Dr. Edwards shook his head with a sigh.

"Pull up the lobby footage from Thursday at two thirty p.m."

The guard clicked on a folder and selected a video file from among a dozen. John trained his eyes on the screen with intensity he'd once reserved only for mission intel.

Three men in suits entered the lobby. John knew they were former military just by their movement through the perimeter. Two of them approached the case workers immediately, while the third said a few words to the receptionist. As she picked up the phone, the man scanned the entire lobby with surgical focus.

"Pause right there," said John.

The guard clicked a button, and John brought his eyes closer to the monitor.

"Can you zoom in?"

"Not really. I can enlarge the video a bit, but that's about it."

"Do it."

With a few clicks, the face of the man in the lobby took up most of the screen.

John clenched both of his fists.

9

At 6:09 p.m. on Tuesday, Mason Hartwell walked into his two-story house in the Pine Hills neighborhood of Arlington, Virginia. Crossing the foyer, he noticed from the corner of his eye that the desk lamp in his office was turned on. He distinctly remembered it being off when he'd left the house that morning.

"Bonnie? Are you home?"

He shook his head and strode into his office, mumbling about the virtues of not wasting energy before he shut off the lamp. He then shut his eyes, lowering his head with an exhale.

"She's not home yet," said John. "We have fifteen minutes."

Mason opened his eyes and lifted his chin. He steeled himself before turning toward the chair in the corner.

"Hello, John."

"Have a seat, Mason."

―――

Mason unbuttoned the only buttoned button of his suit jacket, then sat in the plush leather chair behind a large oak desk.

"You forgot to set your alarm," said John. He gave the front yard a perfunctory glance. "Then again, who would worry about an alarm in a neighborhood like this." His eyes locked on Mason's. "The CIA must be paying well these days."

After holding John's gaze for a few seconds, Mason retorted, "It's not my fault you chose to stay with the navy, schlepping down to Virginia Beach to give lectures at Dam Neck. I know they can't be paying you well if you're supplementing your income by showing field agents how to hold a nine-millimeter." Mason planted his forearms on the desk. "I'm going to assume you have some evidence that Claire was abducted as well? Because we suspect she might've just... you know."

"Don't bring my personal life into this."

"John, just because you and I haven't spoken in years doesn't mean that Claire and Bonnie still don't talk every month. It tore me apart to get the play-by-play of your separation."

"So torn you couldn't even bother to call an old friend to check in?"

Mason's forearms retreated from the desk, slumping into his lap.

"I'm sorry. You're right. I should've..." A raspy sigh came out of his throat. "Life just... believe me, I've been dealing with my own shit."

John carefully took in Mason for the first time since he'd sat down. Bruise-colored bags puffed under his eyes. Patches of hair were so unkempt they resembled tumbleweed. His navy SEAL physique was long gone. Judging by the draping sleeves of his custom-tailored suit, he was shedding weight at a rapid clip. For a man approaching fifty, Mason looked at least a decade older. He was dealing with shit all right, and John was about to add more to the pile and another five years to his appearance.

"A neighbor saw the same van pull out of my driveway."

Mason leaned the chair back and bit his fist. His sigh was a borderline whimper.

John allowed time for the reality to settle in before speaking.

"Why don't we start from the beginning, and you tell me why my wife's patients are, I can only assume, your operatives. Then you can connect the dots for me about how Claire would have anything to do with ... whatever it is you're doing at Langley these days."

Mason was shaking his head with an expression so absent that John wondered if he'd even heard him. He finally composed himself and leaned forward.

"Claire has over thirty active patients, and I can assure you my guys aren't the only CIA agents she sees. Heck, I went down her list and recognized two names from the FBI and this clown I know at DOD. All current or former military with more issues than *Times* magazine. It's a town full of PTSD and only so many psychiatrists to go around. You know this, John." He began rubbing his temples like a man exorcising his own traumas. "As for the rest, you know I can't talk about that."

"Of course you can."

Mason scoffed. "Don't be ridiculous."

"Don't be *what*?"

"John, I don't know what you thought was going to happen here today, but I'm not committing a federal crime by disclosing classified information to you. The Espionage Act might not mean much to you, but I swore an oath—"

"If you bring 'my country' speech into this, I'm going to drag you up and down the street until the police show up. Cut the bullshit, Mason. My wife is a civilian, and the only oath I care about is the one you swore to me."

Heavy silence fell over the room. John noticed mist forming in Mason's eyes and wondered if he'd gone too far.

"John ... if I haven't thanked you enough..."

"I don't want you to thank me. I want you to do right by me."

Mason stood up and walked over to the window. He was

looking over the perfectly manicured lawn set beneath arching magnolia trees. But John knew he was far away and long ago.

"Bonnie and I still talk a lot about that. How lucky we are to have all this. How none of it would be here if you hadn't carried me out of that ditch." He turned to John. "I have dreams that I'm still in Iraq. Like I never left."

The last words bored into John, softening his posture. Only a soldier could truly understand another soldier's nightmares bleeding into reality.

Mason cleared his throat and walked to the liquor cabinet. He picked out a bottle of Lagavulin 16 and pinched two whisky glasses between his fingers.

"No, thank you," said John.

Mason poured two fingers' worth into both glasses and held one in front of John.

"Just hold it in your hand so that I don't feel like I'm drinking alone."

John took it with reluctance induced by melancholy, his mind swirling with one of the happiest memories of his life.

10

OCTOBER 5, 1999

The bar reeked of booze and bluster. John's Naval Academy friends couldn't have asked for better on his twenty-first birthday.

It was the third establishment they'd escorted him into this evening, but the mission remained the same: John needed to convince women to write their name and number on his underwear. Landlines, cell phone numbers, beeper digits; it didn't matter. It would take a total of twenty-one names and numbers —a pair for each year of John's life—until they would mercifully let him stop embarrassing himself.

Fortunately, most women found the combination of John's six-foot-two frame and shy face endearing, which had so far resulted in fifteen pairs of names and numbers Sharpied onto his tighty-whities. Some of the numbers were likely fake, but John's friends didn't hold it against him.

"Come on, Casanova, these two look good," said Andrew Connolley, John's best and drunkest friend, pointing to the two young women sitting at the corner of the bar.

John shouldered his way through the forest of testosterone

and planted himself close enough to catch the women's attention.

"Excuse me," he began. "I'm really sorry to bother you, but—"

"Do you need a whole entourage to talk to us?" said the red-haired woman on the right.

John looked over his shoulder. The grins of his midshipmen made them look like a cackle of hyenas. "Back up," he said. They moved by less than an inch. John shook his head and turned back to the ladies.

"No, see, it's my birthday, and they have to verify that you would be willing to write your name and number on my underwear."

John had barely finished the sentence before the women burst into laughter.

"That is the lamest pickup line I've ever heard," said the blonde with butterfly clips in her hair.

"No, I'm serious."

"Show me your underwear," said the redhead. For the first time, John noticed her emerald eyes. It took John significant willpower to break eye contact and pull a corner of his underwear above the waistline of his jeans.

"Oh my God," said Butterfly Clips, laughing hysterically. She seemed a few drinks in.

The two girls conferred privately through whispers walled by cupped hands around their ears. Finally, Emerald Eyes turned to John.

"Here are your two options. You can have my friend write her name and number and be on your way. Or, you can go to the restroom, throw your underwear into the trash, and come here and try to earn my number. No guarantees."

John looked into her eyes and made the easiest decision of his life. "I'll be right back."

A wave of shouts and boos slammed into him as he turned around, every one of his friends calling some form of shit—bullshit, horseshit, and even a *Fuck this shit*. John knew he would pay dearly at the dorms later, but he couldn't care less as he made his way to the restroom.

By the time he returned as a future commando going commando, the cackle of hyenas had lived up to the short attention span of its species, moving down the bar to take shots. John composed himself in front of Emerald Eyes and said the wittiest opening line he'd managed to come up with.

"Midshipman John Mitcham, reporting for duty."

It sounded awful compared to how he'd imagined it.

But Emerald Eyes brightened.

"I'm Claire."

The sound of her name created an involuntary smile on John's face.

"This is my friend Bonnie. She's going to join your midshipmen for a shot while you shoot yours with me."

Bonnie gave a coy smile as she stood up and walked away, gravitating toward Andrew, who appeared to be on her level of intoxication. *Birds of a feather,* thought John, taking a seat in Bonnie's chair.

"How many names did you have to give up for me?" asked Claire.

"Fifteen. I would've given up a million." *Smooth, John. Smooth. Keep going.*

"A million?" Claire grinned. "You don't even know me."

"I know you're the only one who told me to take off my underwear."

"Is that all it takes?"

"No. It also helps having the prettiest eyes I've ever seen."

Claire rolled those pretty eyes at that, but she couldn't suppress a smile. "I hope these cheesy lines get better."

"They do, the more you drink. Guaranteed."

"All right, birthday boy, what are we having?"

"Lady's choice."

Claire threw a glance at Bonnie and the midshipmen.

"Looks like they are pounding cheap bourbon. But since it's your birthday and I take pride in my Scottish heritage, I'm going to treat you to a proper birthday whisky."

She waved the bartender over.

"Two glasses of Lagavulin Sixteen. Neat."

John's mouth was agape. The contrast between Claire's gentle expression and fervent disposition was more intoxicating than the alcohol.

"I'm gonna have to put a ring on it," he quipped. "Will three carats suffice?"

Claire laughed. This time she did not roll her pretty eyes.

"I'll settle for two. Save a carat for our honeymoon."

"Pragmatic future wife is pragmatic," said John and clinked his glass of single malt Scotch whisky against hers. "Cheers."

"Happy birthday, John Mitcham."

Years later, whenever John would tell his version of the story, he insisted he was only half kidding about proposing to Claire Elspeth Stewart.

11

Mason tilted his head and drained all the whisky from his glass. He promptly refilled it. *Liquid courage,* thought John. This was going to be bad.

"The project is called the Quantum Grail," said Mason. "Under the initiative of catching up to China on the cyberwarfare front, we built a quantum supercomputer. I won't bore you with the physics of it, but just imagine a computer more powerful than every other in the world, combined. The applications are limitless. Hacking, code breaking, outcome simulation, you name it. This was our silver bullet if there ever was one."

"Was?"

Mason took another healthy swallow of golden brown.

"Six months ago, the facility housing the machine caught fire and burned down. Luckily no one was there at the time, so no casualties. The investigation determined the cause of fire to be a faulty circuit breaker. But something was off. There should've been components that survived the flames. They simply weren't there."

John already knew where this was going, but he let Mason finish his whisky and his soliloquy.

"About a month ago, we detected Quantum Grail's binary signature across the web. The machine does this to ingest data it needs to start simulations, test for system weaknesses, calibrate hacking algorithms. Basically booting into operation mode. At that point there was no doubt left that someone had stolen the parts and reassembled the Grail."

"Someone?" John's whisky glass squeaked under his grip. "Those were Kalashnikov rifles I saw in the security footage."

"I know what they are, John. We found the van abandoned off the highway, eleven miles north. It was stolen the night before the abductions, license plates swapped, the whole vehicle wiped down to the last hair follicle. This has the Russian FSB written all over it."

John couldn't suppress a rueful laugh.

"Let me get this straight. You built a weapon to combat the Chinese government. But now the Russians stole it, and are going to do *what*? Use it against us? Trade with China for some missiles? Hell, they don't even need to bomb Ukraine. They can just hack their entire power grid and freeze the country into submission. How the fuck did you let this happen, Mason?"

Mason seemed to have run out of words. And thirst for whisky. The look in his eyes was one John had seen before—on poor schmucks leaving a Las Vegas casino, wondering how they'd lost it all.

John stood up and dragged the chair to the back of Mason's desk.

"Why would they kidnap Claire?"

"If I had to guess—"

"You're not guessing. You already know, so just spill it."

"The four men they loaded into the van are all Grail operators. They will need them to learn how to fully work the machine. These guys have been Claire's patients for years. I doubt any of them can function without seeing her twice a week. And it wasn't just her patients they kidnapped. Eight other operators are missing. Basically the entire team."

John absorbed it all, shaking his head with incredulity.

"How can so many men with severe trauma work on a CIA project like this?"

"John, all due respect, these men are damaged, not irredeemable. They are all capable and good at what they do."

"Don't put words into my mouth. A soldier who honorably served this country is the furthest thing from irredeemable. And calling them *damaged* reminds me that you were never exactly a mental health advocate, so I do wonder, where does your sudden altruism stem from?"

Mason clasped his hands and rubbed his thumbs before answering.

"The funding for this project wasn't exactly optimal..."

"Ahh, there it is. You couldn't afford to hire from within, so you went bargain shopping at the VA hospital. Un-fucking-believable. And now you've dragged Claire into a shitstorm that might end up in history books."

"John, it's easy to just sit there and berate me but—"

"*Easy?* They will put a bullet into my wife's head the moment they're able to operate that thing themselves."

"We won't let that happen. We'll find out exactly where they are and send an extraction team."

"How? These guys could be in Siberia by now."

"They don't know the Grail is sending out the signature pattern. We can follow the trail to figure out its exact location."

"Mason, you just admitted they've abducted all of your operators. Who is even left to follow the trail?"

"The only person who can. She wrote the Grail's operating system."

"Another stray from the VA hospital?"

"Far from it. Although she has her own set of issues, let me tell you."

"Who is she?"

Mason looked out the window, as if searching for an escape route. But there was only John, and the last card Mason had left to show him.

12

JULY 14, 2021

THE WASHINGTON ENQUIRER
Nia Banks, Notorious Hacker, Arrested

FBI Deputy Alan Frost called a press conference at 1:05 p.m. EST to announce the capture of the world's most infamous hacker, Nia Banks. The arrest in the Cayman Islands marked the end of a manhunt that had lasted over three years and spanned four continents. Frost acknowledged multiple domestic and international agencies were involved but declined to name them explicitly.

A native of Chicago, Illinois, Banks first came on the FBI's radar after hacking the IRS in 2017. Only eighteen at the time, she was subsequently linked to previous hackings of multiple US banks between 2014 and 2016. In 2018, she left a trail of cyber thefts across some of the largest government contractors, which pushed her to the number one spot on the FBI's most wanted list.

Banks's most notorious hack occurred in 2019, when she stole over $200 million from LIS, a publicly traded hedge fund accused of insider trading. Through a complex web of shell accounts, Banks deposited the money into various charities worldwide, much of which remains unretrieved to this day. Banks left a daring signature by hacking into Wall Street and changing the *LIS* stock ticker symbol to *LIES*, prompting many in the media to dub her as the Robin Hood of Wall Street.

As the pandemic swept across the globe in 2020, Banks remained relatively quiet. Her only publicly known hack came at the expense of the FBI when she changed her picture on the most wanted list to that of Carmen Sandiego. The theatrics cemented Banks as the most daring hacker in the world, intensifying the search by law enforcement agencies. It is still unclear what ultimately led to her arrest, although analysts have pointed out that her cross-country movement became severely limited by the pandemic.

Banks is scheduled for extradition to the United States within twenty-four hours and will be arraigned in the Southern District of New York, where she will face charges of federal computer hacking, bank fraud, wire fraud, wire fraud conspiracy, and money laundering.

13

"Is this also part of your newfound altruism, Mason?"

"She's paying her debts in exchange for a reduced sentence. I am hardly the only one using her services. She's been burning the midnight oil for the FBI and NSA, and those are just the ones I know about."

John looked through the window, his contemplative gaze drifting aimlessly.

"So this is what it comes down to. My wife's life is in the hands of a former most wanted criminal." He turned to Mason with a stone-cold look. "I need to meet her."

"You know even I can't make that happen. She's walled off inside a safe house, and you don't have a security clearance to get anywhere near it. If she was just a CIA asset, I'd be able to pull some strings, but I can't push this past other agencies."

"I've trained many of their agents on how to handle a firearm."

"I know, John. But it doesn't work like that."

"No. It doesn't. You can get my wife kidnapped, and I can just pray it all works out." John glanced through the window again. "Speaking of wives, yours is home. Safe and sound."

"John... you have my word I will—"

"Don't give me your word, Mason. It'll sting less when you disappoint me."

"John, please."

John stood up and set his glass on the desk.

"Here, finish your whisky while I show myself out the back. Give my best to Bonnie."

14

NOVEMBER 18, 2023

John drizzled honey into a mug of steaming ginger turmeric tea. He stirred until honey and tea became one, then brought the mug to Claire at the dining table.

"Thank you," she said, wrapping her hands around the mug.

"I'm going to rake the yard," said John.

Claire took a sip. "You raked it three days ago."

"It stormed last night."

Claire threw a glance at the backyard, where John could have counted the fallen leaves on his fingers.

"John, if you're going to make up an excuse not to talk, at least make it a believable one."

"It's not an excuse. We talked for over half an hour. What more is there to talk about?"

"Are you seriously asking me that question?"

John let out a deflating sigh. *Here we go.* He plopped into the chair across from Claire. "Honey, we keep talking about the same things. We went over every recent interaction we've had with Jenny ten times over. Analyzed and scrutinized every little thing she said, or did, or we said, or didn't say, or did, or haven't done, should've done… Claire, I don't see how this is productive. None of it has brought us closer to closure."

"But yardwork will?"

"No, I… I'm just saying, we keep rehashing the same questions that have no answers. At some point we just have to move on."

"Move on…"

"Yes. Accept and move on. We can't fix the past, and nothing we say at this table will change that."

Claire set her mug down without taking her eyes off John.

"Do you even hear yourself? Fix? Move on?"

"You know what I mean."

"I know exactly what you mean. That's the problem. You're treating our daughter's suicide the way you treat a flat tire. This is not about fixing things. It's about understanding them. You think losing yourself in work and errands is moving on? It's not, John. You're just running away. Sweeping your feelings under the rug while you vacuum it. Eventually that pile will get so big under the rug that you won't be able to stand on it. So cut your bullshit and talk to me."

Silence settled heavy over the dining room.

Nothing broke it until John rubbed the five o'clock shadow on his face and said, "Claire, the only running I've ever done in my life was back to you after my missions."

"This is not one of your missions. It happened to both of us."

"I understand that."

"Do you?"

"I do, Claire. But you know me better than anyone. I'm only good at fixing things. And there is nothing to fix here."

John was sure Claire was about to speak, but she remained quiet. A subtle smile formed on her face. It looked to John like she finally understood where he was coming from. A breakthrough after all the table talks and couples therapy sessions. He stood up, walked over to her, and kissed her on the forehead.

"I'll be in the yard. Done in time for dinner, scout's honor."

Claire nodded and squeezed his hand.

John stepped into the cool autumn afternoon and promptly strode to the toolshed.

The raking took longer than expected. The storm had scattered just a few leaves, but it had also left countless pine cones and small branches.

This made John assess the state of the trees in the backyard. He didn't like what he saw. A large dead branch—the main culprit of the mess John had just raked—was hanging too close to the roof. Waiting for a tree-removal company posed a risk. Plus, why pay for a service he was perfectly capable of performing himself. *Let's get to work, Mitcham.*

The branch never stood a chance. John first climbed the tree and tied its dead appendage with rope. He could've tied those knots underwater—which he had done during Basic Underwater Demolition / SEAL training exercises. He further used his rope skills to harness himself to the trunk of the tree and saw off the branch. Once John was back on the ground, it was simply a matter of gradually loosening the rope that suspended the branch. He gently lowered it to the ground, avoiding any contact with the house.

John neatly sawed the branch into sections, chopped those into small pieces with an axe, loaded them into paper bags designated for yard trimmings, and took the bags to the curb. The city would collect them on Tuesday, and that would be that. Mission accomplished. Problem fixed. And with time to spare, John realized after checking his watch.

Claire had already put dinner on the table by the time he had taken a shower and walked into the dining room. Meat lasagna. His favorite. He gave her a smile as she hung up her cell phone.

"Who was that?" said John.

"Just Bonnie."

"Oh yeah? How's she doing?"

"Good. She's good."

John took his seat and wasted no time serving healthy portions of lasagna to Claire and himself. They talked about Bonnie for a bit. How Mason was so overworked these days, she barely saw him. But they mainly talked about the little things. The regular things. Things that made John finally feel a semblance of normalcy after Jenny's death. As sad and devastated as John was, the conversation gave him hope that there was a path to a time when his pain wouldn't be debilitating. He and Claire would learn to live a new normal, whatever that might look like.

Claire dabbed her lips with a napkin and took a sip of water.

"John..."

"Yes, honey."

"I think we should take time apart."

15

The headstone was the color of the slate sky that hung above it.

John never understood why he and Claire had picked this granite for Jenny's grave. It had seemed lighter at the time, or perhaps their world had been so dark that they couldn't tell shades apart.

The yellow bouquet in John's hand felt like a torch in the gloom as he laid it against the stone. But that torch would gutter out, too, dark and rotted as all that dies.

Yet the weeds seemed eternal. They had sprouted across the grave again, unyielding and indifferent. The longer John observed them, the more they felt like a rash in the back of his mind. He planted his knees and ripped out a clump of pigweed from the upper right corner. Half of it stubbornly remained rooted into the soil. *Rip.* Still a few left. *Rip.* There.

He moved onto the clusters tracing the right edge. *Rip.* How did they grow so fast? *Rip.* Why did they live, while all beautiful things died? *Rip.* If John could just pull out enough, the grave would be pristine again. *Rip.* And that would be better. *Rip, rip.* A step in the right direction. *Rip, rip.* Today the weeds, tomorrow the possibility of Claire coming back. *Rip, rip.* Could he rip out enough to salvage his marriage? *Rip, rip, rip.* How many weeds and deeds for Jenny to tap him on the shoulder, alive and well with a smile that conquered the world. *Rip, rip, rip. Fix it, John. FIX IT—*

A raindrop fell onto his wrist, halting his frenzied reverie.

But it wasn't raining.

John wiped his eyes with the back of his hand, releasing the torn weeds into the breeze. Yet it wasn't just the weeds that drifted away. A feeling was leaving him, though he couldn't quite place it. He sat down and leaned against the side of Jenny's headstone.

"Oh, baby girl. How did we get here?"

John truly did not know. But he knew there was no going back.

Out on the horizon, a fissure of lightning split the sky.

16

John was driving the third rental in as many days, tailing Mason's car. He had already figured out where the safe house was. Sloppy. That was the word to describe Mason. He always had been. Even back in Iraq. But now, he was borderline unhinged. Going through two packs of cigarettes a day. Weeks away from being reamed by committees in Washington, his entire life reduced to one epic failure. How could John trust a man in this condition and that predicament to find Claire? John was practically doing him a mercy.

John was inside the fifth rental in as many days, parked on the side of a street, peering through binoculars. Two thousand yards away, a man wearing a black suit and sunglasses exited a black SUV in front of an inconspicuous house in an inconspicuous neighborhood in the rolling hills of Northern Virginia. He exchanged a few words with another man in a suit and sunglasses, who then climbed into the passenger seat of the SUV. As the car glided away, John put down the binoculars and picked up a legal pad. The opened page was a grid of names, dates, times, and notes. In the row labeled *Lefty Subtle-Limp*, John scribbled *1200*.

John entered his vacation cabin near Shenandoah River State Park. He strode past family photos on the walls into the dining area, and pushed the dining table against the wall. He rolled up the rug, revealing a false floor. It took a considerable effort on his part to open the latched door. Inside the cavity was an array of military-grade equipment, meticulously arranged. Noveske 10.5-inch NSR-equipped carbine. McMillan TAC-338 sniper rifle. SIG Sauer P226 pistol. IBA bullet-resistant outer tactical vest. Ammunition. Cartridges. The smell of alloy.

John was sitting at the dining room table awash with maps and hand-drawn schematic diagrams. He marked an *X* on an intersection. Punched keys on an eight-digit calculator. Added to the notes on the pad.

John stood outside the cabin, presiding over a bonfire. He tossed maps, diagrams, papers into the flames. Finally, his wallet.

17

America was celebrating its birthday.

The residents of Sterling, Virginia, had already teased out intermittent fireworks, a mere prelude to the 9:25 p.m. festivities. When the clock struck the proper hour, the rapture of booms, pops, cracks, sizzles, lights, and colors filled the night.

Amid all the commotion, only one person could distinguish the sound of three sniper bullets being fired. The third finally hit the target, ripping open the discharge hose of an AC condenser unit belonging to an inconspicuous house in an inconspicuous neighborhood in the rolling hills of Northern Virginia.

———

At forty-seven minutes past noon on the sultry fifth of July, John pulled up in front of 1145 Willow Lane—a bland, single-story brick ranch that had the quality of a bunker. Wearing a navy coverall with a pinned name tag that read *Patrick Wiedman*, he climbed out of the cargo van, whose exterior was covered with the blue-red signage of NoVa

Superior HVAC: "Service you can rely on. People you can trust."

Before closing the driver door, John glanced through the intermittent slits of the van's partition wall, taking in the ankles of Patrick Wiedman—no doubt a fine HVAC technician who was now lying tied, gagged, and covered in a convenient nook in the back of the van. The nook and the van's retrofitted walls provided plenty of soundproofing in the unlikely event Patrick lost his mind and decided to make noise. But John deemed Wiedman to be a reasonable man who wouldn't risk getting shot —an empty threat John had made and of which he was not proud—which is why he had the decency to leave the front windows half-open to allow for a breeze to enter the van.

As John turned the corner around the back of the vehicle, he was met by agent Lefty Subtle-Limp.

"You're late."

John attempted his most defusing smile. "Ran into traffic."

Lefty said nothing. His black suit was clearly absorbing the sun like a magnet, his unbuttoned-by-three-buttons shirt soaked with sweat. He walked with the slightest of limps and positioned himself ten feet away from the back of the van.

John swung open the double doors. He pulled down the portable ramp, climbed into the van, and came back wheeling a hand truck loaded with a large yellow bin. "I need to go inside first to inspect the thermostat," he said with a nod toward the front door of the house.

"The thermostat is fine. The AC is off, and we already know the issue. Let's get going."

John let out a heavy sigh. Backpedaling into the driveway, he registered a black SUV parked twenty yards up the street.

By the time he reached the AC condenser, he was sweating himself. Laying down the hand truck horizontally, John crouched and pretended to assess the unit. He wondered whether, in his younger days, it would've taken him three tries with a sniper to hit the hose from four hundred yards.

"Oh yeah, the discharge hose popped," he confirmed. "I'm going to need to check inside the unit to make sure the compressor didn't blow out."

"Do what you have to do, but make it quick," said Lefty, beads of sweat gliding down his jaw.

John wasted no time flipping the AC disconnect switch, popping open the bin, and grabbing a toolbox along with a new hose. It took him three minutes to swap it, two less than the first time he'd done it with his own AC unit last summer. He then unscrewed the unit's access panel and acted out another assessment.

"The compressor looks good, but you're going to need a refrigerant refill."

Lefty's rigid face gave the indication he cared little for what John said and more for studying what John did. John had to soften him up.

"Don't worry, I'll fix you up good. It'll feel like a snowy Alaska winter in there."

Lefty's face relaxed, the corners of his lips twitching with the onset of a smile, as if he were envisioning the crystal snowflakes soothing his hot skin. That was the peril of a wandering mind: paint a man a picture that comforts his ills, and he'll make it come alive with the yearnings of his imagination.

Would Lefty have otherwise questioned the sheer size of the cylinder tank John pulled out of the bin? Would he have wondered why no lettering of any kind was on it? Even if Lefty didn't know anything about AC units, would he have found it odd that John connected the tank directly into the compressor?

John smiled and flipped back the disconnect switch. "The thermostat needs to be turned on." He glanced at the undersized, open window above the AC unit. "Make sure all the windows are closed."

Lefty brought the wrist microphone to his lips. "Camelot, this is Merlin. Turn it on and close the windows."

Within seconds, a pair of hands slid the window shut, and the unit thrummed to life. With a continuous hiss, the compressor eagerly inhaled the contents of the gray, eighty-five-pound portable tank.

"Give it about five minutes," said John.

They waited in silence. Until Lefty cocked his head.

"You look familiar."

John's throat tightened. His mind cycled through the faces of countless agents he had trained over the years. No. Unlikely. John wanted to believe he was memorable enough that Lefty would've recognized him right away.

"I service this area a lot."

Lefty gave nothing away from behind the sunglasses. But his posture gave John the sense he was about to reach inside his jacket, where his handgun was holstered. John felt his heartbeat rising. "Check now," he said with his most casual tone.

Slowly, Lefty tore his shades away from John and spoke into the microphone. "Camelot, are we good?" He waited. "Camelot, status?" He shook his wrist. "This thing," he muttered to himself. "Camelot. Do you copy?" Finally, he shook his head. "For fuck's sake."

"Stay here," he said to John and marched off.

With laser-sharp glances at Lefty's receding back, John crouched by the bin and unwrapped a white towel. Staring back at him was a gas mask. He picked it up, unearthing a SIG Sauer P226 pistol.

18

John slid the pistol into the shoulder holster under his coverall. As Lefty disappeared behind the front-right corner of the house, John strapped on the gas mask and leaped on top of the AC unit, his fist wrapped inside the white towel. He halted himself midpunch, realizing whoever had closed the window hadn't locked it.

He propped the window open and lifted himself by the sill, wriggling through the casing until he fell onto the floor and rolled. He pulled out his gun and scanned the small storage room. Nothing but piled boxes of nonperishable food.

Gun leading the way, John swept into the clearing in the middle of the house. It really was a bunker, the whole structure gutted and fortified. He counted five agents sprawled on the floor just as he heard the front door being unlocked. *Lefty.*

John dragged away the only agent who would be visible from the hallway, mere milliseconds before he heard the door swing open.

"You assholes playing cards while I'm out there sweating balls?" shouted Lefty.

John leaned his back against the wall around the corner of

the hallway. His heart hammered twice for every one of Lefty's footsteps. *Thud-thud-clomp, thud-thud-clomp, thud-thud-clomp...*

"I swear, if my chip stack looks short—"

Lefty froze at the doorway, absorbing his colleagues sprawled in the kitchen just as John pointed the gun at his face.

"Slowly take out your firearm and place it on the ground."

Lefty tilted his head at John, struggling to process.

"Are there two of you?"

"No. I'm a unique Alaskan snowflake. Slowly put the gun on the ground."

Lefty considered for a moment before reaching into his jacket.

"Stop," barked John. "I know you're left handed, which means you're reaching with your right for the emergency transponder. You have five seconds to put your gun down before I put a bullet in you."

"All right, all right. Easy."

Lefty slowly took out his gun and slid it across the floor, John's eyes flickering toward it—

In a flash, Lefty lunged, grabbing John's wrist, pointing the gun away as he slammed him into a wall. All of John's half-forgotten training melted into a magma of panic. Years of instructing instead of doing had dulled his combat readiness, but his survival instinct propelled him into a savage maneuver—while Lefty burrowed his fingers into John's wrists to wrestle the gun away, John slid right and drove his foot into Lefty's limping knee.

The cry that came out of the man stirred battlefield memories inside John.

Lefty slumped to the floor, clutching his knee and bellowing. With heavy breaths through the mask, John regained himself and crouched. He took out Lefty's transponder from the holster and tossed it. Then he retrofitted himself with Lefty's earpiece and wrist microphone.

"Surgically repaired?" asked John, placing a palm over Lefty's hands that held his knee as though they were keeping it intact.

Lefty either nodded in answer or his head bobbed from pain.

"Iraq or Afghanistan?"

The question took Lefty by surprise.

"Afghanistan."

John shook his head. He took in the room of unconscious people, guilt rising from his core. How many of them had served? He finally turned to Lefty.

"Captain John Mitcham. Former SEAL Team Six and Twenty-Sixth Marine Expeditionary Unit."

Lefty went wide eyed. "Shit, man. I knew you looked familiar." He seemed to suck in air to suppress his pain. "Sergeant Rob Kowalski, One Hundred Seventy-Third Airborne."

A sad smile washed over John's face. Such a simple declaration—rank, name, unit—yet it never ceased to amaze him how quickly the words tore down walls between two strangers. His guilt swelled.

"Rob, I'm not proud of what I've done. My retribution will come in due time. But I don't want anyone else to get hurt today. So I need you to think of your colleagues and their families." He unclipped a set of keys from Rob's waist. "You can tell me which key and which door. Or I can figure it out myself. But if that takes too long and your colleagues start waking up, I might have to resort to actions both of us will dream about for the rest of our lives. Do you understand?"

Rob looked toward a corner. His eyelids were getting heavy. The sleeping gas was taking effect, though John doubted it would knock him out at this point. Rob finally looked back at John with a resignation that clenched John's chest.

"Maybe this is my retribution," said Lefty, managing half a smile. "Middle key. Gray metal door."

John nodded. He took out a voice recorder and a piece of paper from his pocket.

"There is one last thing I need you to do for me." He unfolded the paper in front of Rob's eyes. "Read this aloud."

Rob squinted at the paper as John brought the recorder to his mouth. He read aloud, "Bird Watcher, this is Merlin. Work complete. He's coming around the corner."

John pocketed the voice recorder and took out a heavy-duty zip tie. He placed a hand on Rob's shoulder and looked the man in the eye.

"I'm sorry, Sergeant. A sinner like me could never be your retribution."

After tying Rob's hands behind his back, John ran through the rear hallway and exited into the backyard, scanning the perimeter before turning a hard right around the side of the house. He dropped to his knees by the toolbox and took out a straight pick, puncturing intermittent holes into the bin's lid. He then emptied and closed the bin, placed it on the hand truck, and wheeled it around the back and into the house.

Much of his navy coverall was already a few shades darker from sweat. But when John unlocked and swung open the fortified steel door, the sight of stairs leading down to a basement spiked his sweat glands into overdrive. "Shit."

Drawing his gun, John carefully threaded down the stairs, halting at the landing to take in the room. Like the roots of a weeping willow, cords ran from every outlet of every concrete wall, feeding into a swirling trunk that branched off into laptops, desktops, monitors, server racks, and blinking devices John knew nothing about.

At the center of it all, slumped unconscious in a chair behind an oversize desk, was Nia Banks.

19

Her braided hair was tied in a ponytail that hung over her left shoulder. She'd taken off her T-shirt before the gas had knocked her out, which left her wearing a tank top over a sports bra, running shorts, and Chuck Taylor high-top sneakers so pristinely white that John doubted she'd ever left this house. A slender frame and gentle face made her look younger than any of the recent pictures John had found of her online. Her old FBI's Most Wanted profile listed her at five-foot-five, but that was generous by at least an inch. John had prepared himself for one of the world's most dangerous criminals, but Nia Banks looked more like a kid.

John lifted her from the chair with a grunt—she was an adult all right—and carried her up the stairs with considerable effort. Carefully laying her in the yellow bin, he maneuvered her to the side into something resembling a fetal position.

He bolted down the stairs again and ripped every computer out of its power outlet. Three laptops and two desktop units were cradled in his arms as he ran upstairs. He wedged each around Nia inside the bin like a puzzle board. All those server racks remained in the basement, but there was no room left in the bin. *Please let this be enough.*

He closed the bin, grabbed the handles of the dolly, and wheeled it toward the rear hallway. Nearly hyperventilating under the mask, heat gripping his throat, John wondered how much better he would've fared during his active-duty days. He'd kept up with most of his daily PT regimen—five hundred yards of breaststroke in the pool, mile-and-a-half runs under ten minutes, fifty push-ups under two minutes, fifty sit-ups as well—but no matter how much you sharpened a blade, Father Time still made it rust.

Before reaching the back hallway, John threw a parting look at Sergeant Rob Kowalski, who had joined his colleagues in the Sevoflurane-induced doldrum. John had underestimated the potency of the anesthetic, much like he'd underestimated the physical toll the heat would take on him. Backing through the exit door, he barreled into the hot July afternoon, wasting no time tossing the gas mask.

Sucking air, he pulled the hand truck around the side of the house and stopped at the AC unit, desperately trying to catch his breath. He took the voice recorder out of his pocket and pressed the second channel button on the wrist microphone. With the click of a button, the recording of Sergeant Rob Kowalski, 173rd Airborne, played into the mic. John then waited. It could've been seconds, but he felt like the heat was melting time itself.

"Copy, Merlin," John finally heard in Rob's earpiece. "We'll look for him at the front."

John exhaled a sigh of relief and tossed his earpiece and wrist microphone. He lifted the hand truck and pushed forward.

Only after his feet touched the driveway did John realize that, deep down, he hadn't really believed he would get this far. It was a long-shot mission, a stupid, risky plan, and yet, here he was, feet away from the van. Summoning all his calm, he opened the van's back doors, pulled down the ramp, and wheeled the hand truck in, then laid it on the floor.

As he pushed in the ramp and closed up the van, his hands began shaking.

Please, not now...

John climbed into the front seat and started the engine, anchoring his trembling hands to the wheel. He put the gear in reverse and his foot on the gas pedal.

The van swayed as he backed it into the driveway. Gear into drive, foot on the gas pedal again. He pulled out of the driveway, barely prying his eyes away from the side-view mirror. The house and the black SUV shrank with each second, collapsing into a singular point in the square horizon.

It felt as though it wasn't the van moving him, but rather a force pulling everything away, sucking from under him the canvas of his life and all that had taken him a lifetime to paint.

20

Nia stirred to life with a muffled groan. Lying on the couch, she turned to the side, her right hand slapping the coffee table. This made her eyes open.

Sitting in a chair across the table, John observed her pupils for signs of adverse reaction to the sleeping gas. They seemed normal. She blinked twice, then jerked, slowly lifting herself upright. Languor gave way to confusion.

"Wha..." she muttered, the remainder of the word lost in her cracking voice.

"There's a glass of water on the end table," said John.

Nia turned to it, staring with daze and suspicion.

"You've inhaled an anesthetic and need to hydrate."

She threw a bewildered glance at John before picking up the glass and bringing it to her lips. The first few gulps came slowly, but then she tipped the glass and drained it. John took the pitcher of water from the table and poured it full again.

She didn't take her eyes off his face, as if desperately trying to remember him from somewhere.

"Who are you?" The question spurred her to look around the room. "What is this?"

"Let's give it more time for the anesthetic to wear off so that I don't have to repeat myself."

Begrudgingly, she sank into the couch and resumed sipping her water. They waited in silence. With each passing minute, the furrows in her brow grew deeper, her stare sharper. Finally, she took the pitcher and refilled her glass. John nodded and cleared his throat.

"My name is John Mitcham. We are in a townhouse in Georgetown."

"What? How?"

"Earlier today, I extracted you and most of your computers from the safe house."

"Extracted? Are you with the CIA?"

"No."

Nia's free hand gripped the couch seat, as though bracing herself against being swept away. The glass in her other hand trembled as she set it on the table.

"Relax, Nia. I'm not going to hurt you."

She shook her head with such incredulity that it made John doubt she'd even fully heard him, let alone believed him.

"What happened to the agents?"

"Same thing that happened to you. They inhaled the Sevoflurane I pumped into the AC vents and passed out. You're the only one that got a ride out of it."

"What do you want from me?"

"I want you to hear my proposal. If by the end of it you feel you'd be better off doing what you've been doing, I will drop you off at the nearest police station, and that will be the last time you'll ever see me."

Nia finally decompressed. She leaned back, her shoulders sinking below her neckline.

"Okay."

From his shirt chest pocket, John took out the picture of him,

Claire, and Jenny in Montauk and slid it across the table. Always best to put a human face to a story.

"My wife, Claire, has been abducted by the same people who stole the Quantum Grail operators. She's an innocent bystander, caught up in clandestine warfare. All I ask from you is to do what you've already agreed to do. Follow the Grail's binary signature to locate it. Once I confirm it, I will give you the one thing the government is not willing to give you. Your freedom."

John stopped there, carefully studying Nia's expression while waiting for a response. If there were traces of the sleeping gas still inside her, they could not dull the sharpness of her narrowing eyes.

"Why would you extract me if you already knew they had me looking for the Grail?"

John didn't bother suppressing the smirk twisting his lips.

"Nia, let me tell you what's going to happen in the coming weeks. Mason will be paraded in front of half a dozen oversight committees. He will be stripped of his duties, titles, and rank. And that's his best-case scenario. The CIA will put another deputy in charge, and every one of that person's actions will be scrutinized by politicians in Washington, bogged down by the quicksand of bureaucracy and finger-pointing. All the while, my wife will wither away in some horrible place. Until the day she becomes expendable." John clenched his fist, producing a chorus of cracking knuckles. "I'm not going to let that happen."

21

Nia scoffed. "Some foreign country or god-knows-what crime syndicate stole CIA's top secret cyberweapon, abducted a bunch of people associated with it, and you're going to just roll in there and extract your wife? Okay, Rambo."

John found the response amusing. He eased back in the chair.

"I won't be alone."

"What?"

"A few friends will join me."

"Friends?"

"Friends."

"Uh-huh..." Nia studied John curiously. "These friends must be as crazy as you are."

"They make me look like the Dalai Lama."

Nia laughed at that. John took it as a good sign to close the deal.

"Look, the arrangement I am proposing is straightforward. You find the Quantum Grail. All indications are that it's somewhere in Russia. I will find a way to get us there. Once we confirm its location, I call in the cavalry, and you and I shake hands and part ways."

"You're going to leave me in Russia?"

"You've evaded authorities across four continents. Something tells me you'll be just fine."

Nia acknowledged the point with a grin. Her eyes began drifting around the living room. She took in the tall windows, the ten-foot ceiling, art deco crown molding, marble fireplace, the entire room flowing into an oversize kitchen.

"Did you say we're in Georgetown?"

"Yes."

"That's literally across the river from the CIA headquarters."

"Precisely."

"You really are out of your mind. Agents could storm this place any minute."

"Right now they are following the trails I left that indicate the logical escape as far away from here as possible."

"Trails?"

"A certain HVAC technician was tied to the driver seat of his van, which gave him a front-row view of watching me get into a red Dodge Durango and peel off west on I-29. I won't bore you with the details of other cars I switched that indicate my movement could've been west, south, or north. The point is that multiple agencies have no doubt already allocated heavy resources on traffic cameras leading out of neighboring states. Every airport and border patrol station in the country has our names and pictures. The wider they cast the net, the better."

John could practically see a light in Nia's eyes, as though a thrill she had not felt in a long time was coming alive. She turned her head toward the windows again, the last of the setting sun filtering through the curtains and bathing her face.

"Not exactly the most inconspicuous neighborhood."

"This street is known in DC circles as Mistress Row. Care to guess why?"

Nia thought about it for a mere second before letting out a snicker. "Because politicians bring their side squeezes here?"

"Politicians, diplomats, military brass, you name it. People who need absolute privacy and don't pry into their neighbors' lives. The townhouses on this block are more often empty than not." John leaned in again, pausing for extra effect before letting the next words roll off his tongue. "And they all have *excellent* Wi-Fi."

Abracadabra. Nia went still. Her eyes brimmed with alertness. Eagerness. Almost a kind of predatory quality. It reminded John of highly trained soldiers before a mission. Nia seemed frozen in time. What was she calculating behind those big eyes? Suddenly, she snapped into motion.

"Is there anything to eat? I'm famished."

―――

Froot Loops and chocolate chip Pop-Tarts. That was what she'd chosen over a perfectly good frozen lasagna. *To each their own*, thought John, picking through layers of dough, watching from across the dining table as Nia devoured the last of the Pop-Tart. She continued the next phase of her feast by pouring almond milk over dyed cereal, dug her spoon into the bowl, and shoveled in an alarming pile of sugar-refined corn.

"So whose place is this anyway?" she said through a crunching mouthful.

"Some weasel on a diplomatic mission in Congo. What he's really doing is making sure the cobalt mines keep pumping most of the mineral to us and not China. We have this place and his Range Rover for two months."

"How do you know all this?"

"I've been in this town for too long."

"What does that mean?"

"It means I've attended too many fundraisers where drunken dignitaries spill unsolicited secrets." John stabbed his lasagna with disgust. "Look, Nia, I need an answer. Every passing minute is one less I have to save my wife."

Nia threw her spoon into the bowl and tore off a sheet of paper towel. She dabbed the corners of her mouth before neatly folding it in front of her.

"Pretend you're me. Why should I believe you'll let me go if I find the Grail?"

She had a point. If John had a good answer, it eluded him.

"You're right. You don't know me, and you shouldn't trust me. But we do have something in common. Our mutual disdain for the CIA."

"Do we?"

"I should think so. They turned you into an indentured servant and allowed my wife to become a hostage. For years I've slugged through the world's most hostile places, watching my Teammates die for questionable motives backed by shoddy intelligence, all courtesy of the CIA. Do you really think I would give them the satisfaction of getting you back?"

Nia held John's gaze for a while before grabbing her spoon and swirling the now-soggy cereal around the bowl.

"And what if I can't find the Grail?"

"Why wouldn't you?"

"I've never even seen it."

"What?"

Then Nia said, casually as a greeting, "Truth be told, I'm not sure it even exists."

22

John calmly placed his fork on the table, the gesture a veneer over the heat spiking inside him.

"Let's start from the beginning. You wrote the operating system for the Grail. So how could you have never seen it?"

Nia rolled her eyes. It reminded John of Jenny anytime he'd inquired about some boy, or a party, or why she was hanging out with that Amanda girl.

"Do I really need to explain cloud computing to you?"

"No, I've had enough patronizing for one day."

"Oh, good."

"So if the Grail was in the cloud, why would you doubt its existence?"

Nia paused to think. She pushed the bowl of cereal to the side, as though her next words would need the space.

"What do you know about quantum computers?"

John blinked as though the question was a rhetorical one.

Nia sighed. "All right. Let's start with the fact that no one has ever successfully built one before. Silicon Valley has been trying for decades, with very limited progress. The issue is the quantum error correction—"

"Nia, Nia, stop. I changed my mind. Please patronize me and explain as if I were a child."

"Most children can understand this, so I'll patronize you like the middle-aged man that you are."

Another snarky comment, straight from Jenny's playbook. It was like the two had colluded. Nia grabbed the box of Froot Loops and poured a pile of cereal in front of her.

"Okay, look..." Her nimble fingers started sliding only yellow and red loops out of the pile, arranging them into a single line: yellow, red, yellow, red, yellow, yellow, yellow, yellow. "Every computer in the world, cell phones, laptops, servers, they all store information inside tiny little capacitors called bits by either charging them with electricity or not charging. Just like a switch. On or off. One or zero."

She pointed to the first Froot Loop in the line: "Yellow is off."

Second: "Red is on."

Third: "Yellow, off."

Fourth: "Red, on."

Fifth through eighth: "Off, off, off, off."

"A computer would read this entire sequence of bits as zeros and ones and translate it into capital letter *P*. *P* for 'patronizing.'" She winked at John. "You follow so far?"

John nodded with an inadvertent smile.

"Good. But quantum computers operate on a subatomic scale using principles of quantum mechanics. Instead of storing ones and zeros into little capacitors, they store them into something like an electron. You can change the electron from one state to another by firing a laser into it. Pretty cool, eh?"

"Pretty cool," echoed John. In truth, he found it more cool that Nia was able to convey the concept without him knowing anything about electrons or subatomic particles.

"Okay, now here is where stuff gets weird. If you shoot the laser at half strength, the electron enters a superposition of states, meaning it behaves as though it's both one *and* zero. On *and* off. That's why quantum computer bits are called qubits." She slid two more Froot Loops out of the pile and aligned them above the first one in the line representing the letter *P*. "So now the number of computations a quantum computer can simultaneously perform with qubits becomes two to the power of N." She slid two more loops to the second one in the line. Two more to the third, then fourth, fifth.

"Do you see? If this keeps going, it means a quantum computer can perform more calculations than there are known atoms in the universe!"

"Nia, all I'm hearing so far is how cool and powerful quantum computers are. What's the actual problem?"

"Right. The problem is a process called quantum decoherence. Everything is fine as long as the qubits remain isolated in their quantum world. But when we try to measure them to obtain their actual value, we can affect that value, which creates errors. The only way to reduce these errors is arranging the qubits into a specific scheme so that they remember their value. This quantum error correction requires building a massive system of chips, electronics, cables, cooling systems, we are talking about a small warehouse of some of the most complex machinery in the world."

Nia wiped away her Froot Loops bits and qubits.

"Forget about the fact that no one has successfully built it before, after decades of trying. Ask yourself, how could someone steal just a few components and re-create the whole machine in a matter of months?"

John sat in silence, absorbing it all.

"How long did it take them to build the Grail?"

"They started years before they made me work on it. I inherited a shitty custom programming language that I had to completely rewrite. Then I wrote the operating system. But all other programs that run on that operating system were written by someone else. I've never seen any of it. I couldn't even tell you what the damn thing does. I just know how to track its binary signature when it does it."

"Mason told me what it does. Hacking. Code breaking. All the worst capabilities that would allow the Russians to infiltrate nuclear power plants and defense systems."

"Those are hardly the worst. If they truly built a quantum computer, it could theoretically be powerful enough to gather and crunch enough data to simulate our reality."

"Not sure how that's worse than penetrating defense systems."

"Why waste time penetrating defense systems when you can know all its codes and who to manipulate to operate them?"

"How would that be possible?"

"That's what emulating our reality means. A true quantum computer could calculate the probability of outcomes with astonishing accuracy. Anything from the global fallout of assassinating a world leader, to how many goals Lionel Messi would score if he eats an extra apple a day, to what codes were selected for a nuclear missile and which schmucks will press its buttons when bribed or extorted."

"Nia, what are you telling me? That the Grail could predict the future?"

"I'm telling you it's theoretically possible. But it's so far-fetched, which is why I don't understand how they built it."

John stared at the scattered pile of cereal, lost in thoughts and colors. "I can't tell you how they've built it." He placed a single finger on a yellow Froot Loop. "But I can tell you with a high degree of certainty that along the way"—he slid the loop away from others—"someone leaked information about the Grail to the Russians." He slid another yellow out of the pile. "Could've been multiple people. Maybe some of the operators."

He paused for a bit, his eyes narrowing. He then placed his finger on a red Froot Loop and slid it to himself. "But if I had to guess, I think the leak came from someone more technical. A person who understands the inner workings of the machine. Do you know who was in charge of the hardware?"

"I wasn't allowed to meet anyone. Including the operators. I don't know... it just doesn't add up."

"Well," said John, picking up the red Froot Loop. "Only one way to figure it all out." He placed the red loop into his mouth and swallowed it like a pill. "You in or you out, Nia?"

Nia exhaled a tired sigh, her gaze hovering over the pile of Froot Loops. She plucked a blue one and popped it into her mouth.

"Where are my computers?"

23

John arranged a stack of laptops, a row of desktops, and a pile of clothes on the dining room table. It was the clothes that caught Nia's bemused attention.

"I went bargain shopping a few days ago," said John. "I tried to assess your size from online photos, then bought what I could, including a size bigger and smaller."

Nia rummaged through the pile, eventually excavating a pack of sports bras.

"I don't know much about ... all that," confessed John. "I just bought a bunch, so hopefully something fits."

Nia snickered her way through a head shake.

"Able to infiltrate a house full of federal agents, but he can barely make it out alive from the women's section."

Fed, showered, and clothed, Nia picked up a laptop from the table. She then smashed it on the kitchen floor.

John leaped from his chair. *"What the hell are you doing?"*

"Ensuring you still have a chance of finding your wife."

"By destroying your—"

"Relax, G. I. Joe. If I had turned on that laptop, agents would swarm this place within half an hour. You're lucky you didn't grab one of the external hard drives from the rack servers, because those have independent GPS trackers on them."

John slowly retreated back into the chair.

"Any other computers you plan on destroying I should know about?"

"No. Grab a broom and dustpan, and clean this while I set up. Teamwork."

This girl. Three hours from waking up scared shitless, now giving orders. John had to establish the chain of command. He cleared his throat and ... realized there was only one thing to say.

"All right."

Nia was up and running within five minutes.

"I'm missing a couple of cables, but this will do. You know the Wi-Fi password here?"

John shook his head.

"Wouldn't wanna make it too easy now, would we?" Nia muttered. "I'm going to have to write a few shell scripts from scratch. It might take a bit."

Just like that, Nia began, filling the room with the sound of spasmodic bursts of keystrokes, the occasional *click click click* of the mouse. Trails of white characters ran across black consoles. Soon, entire rivers of white streamed upward faster than John could read, their shifting hues emitting from the monitors and dancing across Nia's face. No matter how fast things moved on the screen, it didn't seem fast enough for Nia. She kept tapping her fingers impatiently, waiting for her code to execute.

The Quantum Grail 75

John sat quietly in the corner, admiring the maestro at the keyboard. He wasn't sure what he had expected, but it wasn't quite this. He'd watched movies and TV shows about hackers before, and they'd usually portrayed them confronting kinetic graphics and 3-D models. But Nia's domain was a two-dimensional affair of black and white, and far more nuanced. Quiet. Introspective. She would pause to think. And think. Rubbing her temples. Burying her head in her hands. Muttering to herself. Maybe admonishing?

Her efforts lasted an hour, and John started to get worried. He had told himself he wouldn't interrupt, but it was getting late in the evening, and maybe it was best to pick up again tomorrow.

"Proving stubborn?"

Nia flinched, turning to John as though she'd forgotten he was in the room. "Huh?"

"The Wi-Fi. Having trouble hacking it?"

"Oh... no. I hacked it a while ago. And all the others in the area that have full signal. I'm just writing a load balancer to make sure my computers are always using the fastest connection. Also spoofing my MAC addresses so that they look like computers that are already on the networks."

Load balancer. MAC addresses. Spoofing. John knew nothing about any of this. But even he understood quite well that the young lady in front of him had just plowed through multiple networks like a stroll through the cyber park.

"It's late," he said, rising from his chair. "Let's get a good night's sleep."

Almost reluctantly, Nia pried herself from the keyboard.

John walked her up the stairs to her bedroom. Standing at the doorway, he almost felt guilty uttering his next words.

"This door will be locked from the outside. You have a

private bathroom in there. If you need anything, knock on the wall behind your bed."

With a mixture of indignation and deflation on her face, it appeared to only then fully dawn on Nia: she'd exchanged a house in Northern Virginia for a townhouse in Georgetown, but she was still a prisoner.

John watched her face disappear as he shut the door. He inserted a screwdriver into the bowels of the exposed lock.

———

The scrambled eggs sizzled in the skillet. Nia watched them with a frown induced by John's insistence that there would be no sugar-refined anything eaten this morning.

It was time to plate. John poured the eggs evenly over four slightly toasted blue corn tortillas. Bits of roasted red peppers and white onions poked out of the eggs, but soon they were covered with freshly diced avocado and salsa verde. Finally, a garnish of cilantro. Voilà. Breakfast tacos. Jenny's favorite.

Truth be told they were the only decent breakfast dish John knew how to make. He'd always been more of a griller, but ever since Jenny had gone vegetarian her junior year of high school, John's prowess on the grill had become nearly obsolete.

John set a plate of steaming tacos on the kitchen bar in front of Nia and poured her a glass of pineapple-orange juice. Its sweetness would do well to counterbalance the salt-garlic-achiote spice mix.

Nia somewhat begrudgingly folded a taco and took a bite. Within seconds, her frown melted like the earthy, buttery oaxaca cheese John had melted into the eggs.

"Oh my God," she said before sinking her teeth into the taco again.

For the first time since he couldn't even remember, John's

smile rose from his gut. He watched Nia devour the blue-wrapped goodness with childlike enthusiasm, washing it down with gulps of sweet-tangy juice. She finally paused to catch her breath.

As John observed her, he became genuinely curious, and nudged his head at the cockpit of computers and monitors.

"So how did you get into all this anyway?"

24

APRIL 3, 2007

Nia heard the hooting and shouting before she even turned onto South Wabash Avenue—a typically quiet artery of the Washington Park neighborhood in Chicago's South Side.

She halted in her tracks and clutched her lunchbox, assessing carefully. Out in the distance, half a block away, a large group of people swarmed a front yard in a frenzy. She could go the next block over and walk down Michigan Avenue, but Mama said best to avoid it with all the drug dealers and whatnot. State Street was out of the question—two shootings there in the last month.

Decision time. After crossing to the other side of Wabash Avenue, Nia carefully treaded toward the unruly affair. Her backpack suddenly seemed heavier. Her legs stiffer. She could now make out some of the shouting. Swear words. Lots of *That's mine!* and *Leave it!* So many swear words.

Nia came close enough to see it was Ms. Young's house. Boarded up. Stapled with foreclosure signs. Furniture, electronics, clothes, all sorts of things were strewn across the front lawn, with people swarming over them like bees over flowers.

It had been half a year since Ms. Young had passed away. Her nephew, who'd been living with her, had not been seen or heard from in months. Rumors were his disappearance had been a drug deal gone bad. For all anyone knew, he could've been buried in an alley nearby.

When she reached the stretch of sidewalk across the street from the spectacle, Nia lowered her head and quickened her stride, hugging her lunchbox like a float in a wayward tide. Quiet as a mouse. But who would even hear her through all the shouting and fighting on the other side of the street.

"Fuck you, bitch!" was the last thing Nia heard before the boom of gunshots.

Her legs buckled, then seemed to run on their own as she ducked behind a car. Screams rained down on her, then more gunshots, and Nia curled into a ball, knees to chest, back to the car tire.

"Mama," she whimpered, her eyes shut so hard she thought she just might wish herself into her mother's arms. She dared to peer through her cracked eyelids for a split moment—shadows colliding all around her, people running manically in every direction, the world squeaking and crunching under their soles.

The chaos eventually receded into the distance, like a lucid dream. Crouched behind the car, Nia could now make out only two voices coming from across the street. Men.

"Help me pick this shit up."

"Nah man, get the radio."

"Put the radio on the couch, fool. We gotta get the fuck outta here."

Glass crunched, men groaned, and the couch began floating south on South Wabash Avenue. Soon there was nothing but silence. *Get up, Nia. Run home.*

But when Nia lifted the lunchbox she'd dropped after the boom of the first gunshot, she did not run. Instead, she turned toward Ms. Young's house. It almost looked unrecognizable, as though all the boards and signs and personal items had dropped from the sky. Miraculously, no one lay there, dead or wounded.

Nia crossed the street and scanned the debris on the front lawn. Not much was left except for knickknacks, old magazines, worn books, and broken pictures. So many black-and-white photos of Ms. Young and people who had once been in her life. An entire lifetime reduced to one afternoon of indignity.

Amid the puddles of gray mementos, there was a pop of color—a blue book with loud yellow lettering. For reasons Nia would never be able to explain for the rest of her life, she walked to it and crouched.

Pete Horton's Inside the PC—Seventh Edition

Nia flipped the cover and a chunk of opening pages.

How (Almost) Any Computer Works

Flipped again.

How Much Space Does Information Need?

Flipped again and again. Diagrams that looked like labyrinths, photos of transistors, paragraphs about bits, bytes, nybbles, hexadecimal, ASCII... there was a whole world out there, and it was real. She picked up the book, heavier than any other she'd ever held, and wedged it into her backpack.

Then Nia Banks—seven years and eight months old—ran. She never looked back.

25

John did the dishes as Nia did her work on the computers. Her story pressed heavy on him, and he, for the life of him, couldn't remember the first time he'd heard gunfire. Had it been when his father took him to the gun range in Akron, Ohio? But hadn't his childhood friend—Dylan what's his name—shot empty cans of Campbell soup in his backyard? Either one was a strikingly different introduction to firearms compared to that of a child dodging bullets in the South Side of Chicago.

"We are up and running," said Nia.

John placed the last plate on the rack to dry and sat in a chair.

"Meaning?"

"Meaning I'm running the program that will detect whenever the Grail fires off its binary signature."

"So now it's a waiting game?"

"Yes. Days. Could be weeks. Even months. We have no control over whoever is operating it. The last signature was detected ten days ago, but it didn't last long enough for me to pinpoint its location. I've optimized the tracking algorithm, so it should do better next time."

"Good. Because we're going to get a head start."

"What does that mean?"

The more John smiled and said nothing, the more uneasy Nia seemed.

"You want me to do *what*?"

"Nothing you haven't done before, Nia."

"I'm not sure you realize what you're asking."

"I am asking you to do the same thing the FBI and CIA are doing with us right now—scouring every plausible DOT camera footage, hoping to catch a glimpse of us. I just want to track the van from a couple of weeks ago. The Russians stole it the night before the abductions, then swapped it for another vehicle. If we follow the van, we might come across other suspicious-looking vehicles in the area around that time. Maybe we see something the agencies missed."

"Oh yeah, I'm sure we'll catch something entire teams of highly trained operatives haven't."

"They have strength in numbers, but we have another advantage. No one to answer to."

"I don't even know what that means."

"It means that they are bogged down by red tape. Getting access to public footage from dozens of municipalities is a bureaucratic nightmare. You don't have that problem."

"You think it's all so easy, don't you? Hacking into all these systems."

"I didn't say it was easy."

"It's damn near impossible."

"So you can't do it?"

The lightning in Nia's eyes returned. "I can do anything."

There it was. The bravado that had fueled her to the top of the FBI's Most Wanted list.

"Good to know," John said with a defusing smile. But Nia was not placated in the least; her chest was heaving, no doubt to keep up with the adrenaline rushing through her. So that was her button. Tell her she couldn't do something. It made sense. A kid who'd made it out of one of the most violent places in the country and become the de facto queen of the cyberworld. Who could tell her what she could and couldn't do?

John sat down with a growing unease that he'd taken it too far. Had gone about it the wrong way. Like so many times with Jenny. *Haven't you learned anything, John? Course correct.*

"Look, Nia. You don't have to do it. But the sooner we find the Grail, the sooner you'll be rid of me."

This realization seemed to finally sway Nia. She sat down in her cockpit, looking over her equipment as though assessing it for the job.

"What exactly would we even be looking for?"

"I just need a face. One good face."

"A face?"

"Infiltrating foreign soil. Stealing a top secret weapon. Abducting multiple targets and smuggling them out of the country... the number of people in the world capable and brazen enough to pull this off is smaller than you think. And they needed cooperation from someone on the inside. I just need one recognizable face to track down and make them squeal."

John leaned forward.

"Nia, as good as you are at what you do, I am just as good at tracking people down and making them squeal. You find me a face, and we may not even need the Grail's binary signature."

Nia stared into John's eyes, but John could not translate her expression. With a workmanlike tone, she said, "Put on a pot of coffee."

26

On day one of *Operation Find Me Face I Can Make Squeal* (named by Nia and frowned upon by John), Nia phished IT emails of the Virginia Department of Transportation, Fairfax County Police Department, Virginia State Police, and Arlington Police Department. She gained system admin access with frightening speed, and John learned that the easiest thing to hack was people.

Nia then compiled all traffic camera footage from the day of the abductions. She pored over it with John, starting with the footage of cameras closest to John's neighborhood. They got an immediate hit. At 8:05 a.m., the van crossed the intersection of South Glebe and Columbia Pike. John and Nia followed it all the way to Franklin Medical Center, then to an exit off I-66.

Food consumed: grilled chicken and vegetables, leftover lasagna.

On day two, Nia confirmed the van was abandoned out of sight of cameras. Three vehicles that had left the area emerged as likely suspects: a semitrailer truck, an RV, another van.

Nia hacked the Department of Motor Vehicles, cross-referencing plates and police reports. The RV came in clean, belonging to a law-abiding retiree who'd driven the vehicle to Virginia Beach—where he was still vacationing, according to his granddaughter's Instagram account.

The van came in hot with a filed theft report—Bingo!—and Nia tracked its path west on I-66. She hacked more traffic camera footage, all of it dead-ending into the arrest of the drivers—two Guatemalan immigrants—in Morgantown, West Virginia. John admonished himself for not recognizing right away that the van had been a decoy, the immigrants likely paid by the Russians to drive in the opposite direction.

Food consumed: sausage biscuits, grilled salmon and asparagus, frozen dinners (but the good, organic kind with couscous).

On day three, Nia tracked the path of the "plates clean" semitrailer truck: it drove east on I-66; looped with I-495; up I-270; continued on I-70 after Frederick, Maryland; exited onto MD-66; took a right on MD-64; crossed into Pennsylvania; passed through Waynesboro; and disappeared in Mont Alto State Park, which was adjacent to Caledonia State Park, which flowed into the vastness of Michaux State Forest.

"Phew, what a ride," said Nia.

"For them or us?" quipped John, his eyes fatigued after two hours of staring at the monitors.

"Both," said Nia.

She dug through local police reports, coming across one about a truck driver found shot at the wheel off a backroad inside the park. At least seven possible roads led out, all in different directions, rendering the diameter of traffic cameras roughly equal to the square acreage of New York City.

"That's a huge perimeter," said John.

"No kidding," confirmed Nia.

She tallied the number of suspected vehicles around that time: 117, give or take a dozen.

"Shit," said John.

Nia just rubbed her temples.

Food consumed: french toast, vegetable casserole, more organic frozen dinners.

Day four started with John saying, "C'mon, we can do this," and Nia saying, "Let's think." She focused on the three biggest roads, and only vans and large SUVs, which dropped the number of possible vehicles below a hundred.

"We're getting closer, no?" said John, mainly to convince himself.

His conviction fully eroded after it took Nia most of the day just to rule out two vans.

"At this pace we'll be here for fifty days," he said and regretted it immediately upon seeing Nia's dejected face.

"Can we take a walk around the neighborhood so that I can clear my head?" she eventually asked.

"Out of the question," said John.

Nia spent the rest of the day pacing around the living room, thinking, which yielded nothing.

Food consumed: eggs sunny-side up, leftover casserole, frozen dinners (not the healthy kind).

On day five, Nia was back at ruling out vehicles, an exercise in futility. John contemplated driving to Mont Alto State Park to search for clues. A silly thought and a dangerous plan—if one could even call it a plan.

Food consumed: sugar-refined cereal for Nia, eggs and bacon for John, frozen meals for lunch and dinner.

———

On day six, John told Nia to stop.

A sense of deflation settled over the townhouse like invisible pollen, infiltrating John's sinuses, tightening fibers around his skull. He kept repeating *It can't possibly end like this*, but each passing minute seemed to prove him wrong. Nia stared absently into the wall for long periods of time, and John wondered what she could be thinking. *I was kidnapped by a fool* became his favorite answer to mock himself.

Food consumed: indiscriminate amounts of high-fructose corn syrup cereal for Nia, the last of the eggs for John, cold cuts, raw peppers (already going soft), popcorn, more goddamn frozen dinners.

27

According to the book of Genesis, God had created the Earth in six days. John had lost his faith many moons ago, but even as a child being forced by his mother to attend Sunday service, he'd never taken this particular verse of the Bible literally. So why then, after the sixth day of their search, did John keep recalling the verse, when he and Nia had created nothing?

It seemed to him that vestiges of childhood always manifested in his moments of failure. As he poured freshly brewed coffee into a mug, he wondered what childhood memories might be percolating inside Nia. She stared blankly at the monitors, as though her only hope remained in detecting the Grail's binary signature.

"Here," said John, handing her the mug.

She took it, barely looking at him. She also barely took a sip before setting it down.

"Look, I know you think hackers are hermits, but we need the sun like the rest of humanity. Just walk with me for fifteen minutes around the block so that my skin absorbs some vitamin D, and I'll be as good as new."

"Nia, it's not a matter of choice. We can't risk being seen."

"You said these townhouses are mostly empty."

"They are. They all also have outdoor security cameras that are periodically checked by owners from the comfort of their cell phones. We can't just—"

Nia suddenly buried her face into her palms. John couldn't tell if she was sobbing or laughing hysterically. *I'm losing her.* But when Nia revealed her face, her smile was as wide as John had ever seen it.

"Of course," she said, placing a hand on John's shoulder. "How did I not think of it sooner?"

"Think of what?"

"The residential cameras."

"What about them?"

"Most home security companies store footage in the cloud for thirty days. We still have time."

John understood where she was going with this but doubted the plausibility.

"How in the world are you going to figure out which houses in the area have security cameras, let alone ones that store footage?"

Nia appeared insulted by John's question. Of course. *I can do anything* was her rallying cry.

"I'll hack into all the major security companies, search for all homes in the relevant zip codes, and obtain their footage. Easy-peasy."

———

It had not been easy-peasy.

The last of the sunlight was sinking behind the row of townhouses across the street, and Nia was just now getting access to the internal databases of home security companies. Unlike the state agencies and municipalities, it turned out that security companies actually had good security. In the end, none were a match for Nia, who now had a list of twelve houses pulled up as she downloaded their outdoor security footage from the day of the abductions.

John made himself useful by plugging each address into Google Maps, creating a reasonably small perimeter to track vehicles. Now it was all up to finding footage from outdoor cameras that captured parts of a major street—preferably a busy one. This narrowed down the list to only seven cameras. The endeavor looked bleak already.

The semitrailer truck had turned right on PA-233, but there was no footage from any stretch of that road. The footage from surrounding roads showed no truck. The logical question became, what vehicles were seen leaving the area that had not been seen entering it around that time? Surprisingly, there seemed to be only eleven. Seven sedans, one pickup truck, and three oversize SUVs—two gray, one black. John started getting tingles up his spine.

All three SUVs had gone opposite directions. Of course they had. Splitting up was the smart thing to do. With a hunch and nothing else, John told Nia to track the black SUV. His heart seemed to be racing to the beat of Nia's keystrokes. She plowed through the footage from Pennsylvania Department of Transportation and three major security companies serving homes and small businesses, until she found the recording they were looking for.

At a mom-and-pop gas station outside of DuBois, Pennsylvania, the black Chevy Suburban stopped for gas. Exiting the driver's seat was a man who scanned the surroundings. John did not recognize him. Another man climbed out of the passenger seat. John pointed to him on the screen, an unsettling sensation beginning to brew in his stomach.

"Is there another camera that can give me a closeup of his face?"

Nia obliged with keystrokes and mouse clicks, pulling up the footage from inside the gas station. The man walked in and strode his way to the restroom. Nia rewound and paused right at the moment he glanced toward the counter. She then zoomed into his face.

John felt as though the ground had shifted beneath him, adrenaline spiking through his body. He found the nearest chair to sit.

"Is he your inside man?" asked Nia.

John had to physically gather himself to answer.

"No. He's about as outside as it gets."

"You know him?"

"He is the leader of a Russian mercenary group. His name is Yuri Volkov."

Although John had lost his faith long ago, he conveniently never lost his belief that God found ways to punish him for prior deeds.

"I killed his brother."

28

MARCH 19, 2010

The trail of blood was wide as a paint roller.

In the main hallway of the compound, Senior Chief Petty Officer John Mitcham dragged the wounded Lieutenant Commander Aaron Bradley, gunshots ricocheting from around the corner. What had been a mission to capture a top Al-Qaeda commander had turned into a get-out-alive scramble for the Red Squadron of SEAL Team Six. How could the intel have been this bad?

Yes, Al-Qaeda's top brass was here. But so was Andrei Volkov, the most notorious arms dealer in the world. Expecting no more than twenty Al-Qaeda soldiers, John's squadron had walked into a hornet's nest of too-many-to-count Russians, their combat skills leaving no doubt that most were former special forces. How had intelligence gathering missed that this would be an arms deal? Volkov probably thought the SEALs were here for him. *What a fucking mess.*

John shouldered through a half-open door, sliding Bradley into the corner of a windowless room. Two SEALs followed him, Petty Officer First Class Kevin Jones and Petty Officer Second

Class Daniel Rodriguez. They both hauled a double-pedestal steel desk into the hallway and tipped it over. John watched through the doorway as they took cover and started returning fire. *What a mess.*

Bradley began to speak, but his first word sputtered into a cough of blood.

"Don't talk," said John. "We'll get you out of here. Choppers are on the way."

By this point in his life, John had seen too many dying men not to know Bradley wouldn't make it. The darkness of the blood indicated a hit to the liver, and the best John could do was comfort a friend in his last moments. Bradley would leave behind a wife and two daughters—Anna, ten years old and already great at playing piano, and six-year-old Sarah, her doodles of "Daddy being a brave soldier" likely the most vivid memories she would have of him.

And he would be dead for what? A botched mission predicated on last-minute intel from a supposedly reliable CIA source. The word *dispensable* was echoing between John's ears louder than the gunshots.

Three more SEALs came into the room.

"Shit, Bradley too?" said Petty Officer First Class Sam Luntz, staring at the blood of his squadron commander.

"Who else?" asked John.

"Harrison and Pacheco on Alpha Team. Both in the leg."

John spoke into the comm microphone.

"Chopper Three-Seven, this is Echo Zero-Two. We have three wounded. What's your time to intercept? Over."

"Echo Zero-Two, twenty-three mikes to LZ. Over."

"No way we can hold 'em for that long," said Luntz, stating the obvious.

Rodriguez took time from firing at the Russians from behind the steel desk and rushed into the room, toward Bradley. "Let me take a look at him," he said, pulling out supplies from his medical kit.

John was about to ask for a status update from Alpha Team guarding the perimeter, but Bradley spasmed violently. Then he went still. And that was it.

The suddenness caught John off guard. The unceremonious end. The indignity. Mostly the regret that he hadn't said a few meaningful words of closure to his friend. It all flipped a switch that had never been flipped before. Years later, John would try to convince himself that he'd been thinking of Claire and Jenny. That his next actions were fueled by the unrelenting resolve to get back to his family.

But stirring inside him was the sound of the piano under Anna's lithe fingers. Sarah's giggles as Bradley swayed her on his shoulders. A perfect, impromptu intermission to a backyard barbecue that had transpired only eight months ago. John could invoke God, country, or duty, but the truth was, he just wanted vengeance.

"Alpha Team, this is Echo Zero-Two. Set up claymores at P-1 and meet at P-3."

"Good copy, Echo Zero-Two."

When every member of Alpha Team was in the room, when each one of them had witnessed their beloved former commander dead in a pool of blood, John doled out assignments.

One SEAL to stay in the room with injured Harrison and Pacheco.

Two SEALs to guard the south side of the hallway.

Five SEALs to go full assault on the north side and create a decoy.

Everyone else would follow John into the underground tunnel—a risky maneuver through the artery below the courtyard that connected the two sides of the compound.

Once again, Luntz stated the obvious: "We would be walking straight into Volkov."

"We're going to cut off the head of the snake," said John. "They won't expect it."

With that, Alpha and Echo teams moved out.

After pushing aside an armoire in the adjacent room, John's group dropped in through a latched floor door—a secret entry point the intelligence gathering actually got right. Each man lowered the helmet-attached NODs down to his eyes, turning his vision from pitch black into a phosphorus green. John led the way as the SEALs snaked through the tunnel and passed under the courtyard, then arrived under the east building. Above them, faint shafts of light sliced through the floorboards. To their right, the tunnel forked into two. Al-Qaeda members were long gone in the labyrinth of caves inside the adjacent mountain.

John was the first to climb through the floor door, emerging into an oversize pantry.

The rest of the team followed. They spilled silently from the pantry and fanned out into the kitchen. Smooth and quiet.

Until they were not.

The air swelled with a deafening roar of rifles firing and men shouting. Bullets were exchanged in a massive dining hall meant for sharing food and pleasantries. Two SEALs down. Nine Russians. Before their comrades in the hallway—lured by the decoy—could get back to help, Senior Chief Petty Officer John Mitcham located Andrei Volkov hiding behind a pile of broken dining chairs, and put a bullet into his head.

John got his vengeance.

Anna and Sarah were still fatherless.

29

John's gaze was lost in the beige dolor of the dining room wall. Had he always hated dining rooms, or had it started with Andrei Volkov? John and Claire had been in the dining room when the paramedics took Jenny's body out of the house. Five months later, Claire had asked for their separation in the dining room. And now, on the biggest laptop monitor in the dining room, the face of Andrei Volkov's younger brother practically radiated with karmic justice.

Vengeance begets vengeance.

"It could be a coincidence," said Nia, not very convincingly.

John snapped from his reverie on dining rooms.

"Some things are too coincidental to be coincidences."

"So what, Yuri abducted the operators and decided to take Claire out of spite?"

"No. His objectives were the Grail, the operators, and Claire. But the Kremlin has half a dozen mercenaries who could've pulled it off. They offered it to Volkov knowing he would be extra motivated because it's personal." John sneered with disgust. "I held a sliver of hope that whoever abducted Claire might eventually release her because she's a civilian. But Yuri will shoot her with a smile on his face. And before he does that, he'll make sure she suffers."

Hot tingles of panic began crawling up John's body. He closed his eyes to calm himself, but all he saw on the backs of his eyelids were horrid images of Claire being tortured. He snapped his eyes open and took a deep breath, slowly resetting into mission mode. *Get it together, Mitcham.*

"How far can you track him?" he said, pointing at Yuri on the monitor.

"Probably up until he left the country. Maybe Canada if he crossed the border."

John checked his watch. It was nearing midnight.

"I can go for another hour," said Nia.

Realizing Nia was running dangerously low on fuel, John poured more Froot Loops into her snack bowl.

"Let me know if you need anything else."

At ten past midnight, Nia tracked Yuri Volkov to a small gas station in Middle-of-Nowhere, Pennsylvania. After that, there wasn't a trace of the SUV in any direction, as though it had vanished into thin air.

Given the day's revelations, the jarring dead-end didn't entirely surprise John. Of course a Russian mercenary would be skilled enough to cover his tracks. Had John really bought into the hubris of believing he would track down a terrorist who evaded intelligence agencies across entire continents?

"It doesn't make any sense," said Nia.

It made perfect sense to John. "Time to shut it down."

Nia rubbed her eyes and pushed aside the empty bowl. As John grabbed it to put it into the dishwasher, Nia produced a few parting mouse clicks, stubbornly cycling through recorded footage of the gas station. Watching her made John remember all the times he had to pry Jenny away from the computer because it had been past her bedtime.

Nia's whole body suddenly tilted toward the screens.

"Take a look at this?"

John bent down and took in the footage of a gray SUV at the gas station.

"That looks like one of the SUVs they used to split up at Mont Alto State Park."

"Exactly. On the day of the abductions. But look at the time stamp in this video."

John squinted to make out the date and time in the lower right corner.

He nearly dropped Nia's bowl.

"That's from two days ago."

30

John had lain in bed for six hours and slept for none.

The same questions kept echoing between his temples, their answers reduced to speculation at best and the unexplainable at worst. Why were Yuri's men still in the country? Maybe they weren't his men. But if they were, was Yuri with them? If so, why? He'd gotten the Grail, the operators, their shrink, his vengeance. Could Claire really be four hours away? John had to suppress the maddening urge to get into the car and drive off in the middle of the night.

By the time Nia took her shower in the morning, a stack of french toast and a cup of coffee were waiting for her on the kitchen bar. She consumed both eagerly while John consumed all the available footage from the gas station. Both gray SUVs had visited it multiple times in the last three weeks. Which meant Yuri's associates were likely stationed in the area.

After gulping down the last bite of french toast, Nia went to work. An hour later, she came up completely empty. The area was so rural and sparsely populated that there were no other cameras to be hacked. But this worked both ways: there were only seven houses within a reasonable distance of the gas station.

John plotted them on Google Maps. The house had to be secluded yet perched on high and clear ground to see anyone approaching. This reduced the likely candidates to two. But only one stood out to John: a ranch with a barn that resembled a small hangar.

"Is this where we part ways?" asked Nia.

John tore his eyes from the screen, befuddled by the question.

"You're coming with me."

Nia's face pinched with disappointment, which quickly gave way to anger.

"You said you wanted a face. I did my part."

"I said I need to make someone squeal. Until I have Claire's definitive whereabouts, your part of the deal is not done."

Nia threw her hands up, retreating into the living room. She paced around with her arms crossed, intermittently shaking her head.

"No, no, I can't do this. Russian mercenaries. Fucking terrorists. This is not my domain."

John now understood. He took Nia's coffee mug and set it on the table. He then sat on the couch. "Come sit with me, Nia. Please. Let's talk."

Nia eyed her coffee mug. "I'm fine right here."

"All right. I understand your concern. It's a valid one. But I give you my word that I will keep you safe. Even if it means sacrificing my own life."

"You know what would be safer than relying on you for safety? Not making me go toward fucking mercenaries."

"I'm not making you go. I'm asking."

"Well, the answer is no."

John clenched his temples with his hand and rubbed them. "All right."

"All right what?"

"All right, stay here. I'll board you up in your bedroom upstairs with enough food for a whole week. You'll have a bathroom and all the provisions."

"What if you're not back within a week? What if they kill you?"

"Well, at that point you can start making as much noise as you need to in order to break out of that room. You might get lucky and have someone other than the police arrive to help you. Let's consider it a cosmic roll of the dice that will determine your freedom."

Nia went still. Her eyes showed borderline panic.

"No. No way. I can't risk getting locked up again. I can't go back into that basement, slaving away for the next fifteen years."

Fifteen years... That was her *reduced* sentence. No wonder she was panicking.

"I think I'm offering you a better deal," said John. "Come with me on a little road trip." He pointed at the satellite image of the woods south of the hangar-like barn. "You'll be hidden miles away from this house. Easy escape routes in case there's any trouble."

Nia appeared to consider this, though she wasn't quite convinced.

John thought of what might get her there.

"Look at it this way. Best-case scenario, I get killed, and you drive off into the sunset."

Nia couldn't suppress a smile as she shook her head. "You're insane."

John felt his sanity had slowly eroded over the years, so not much to dispute there. "I'll take that as a yes."

Nia appeared to calculate John's offer once more before nodding.

"Good," said John. "One last thing. How do we remotely keep track of your computers in case the Grail fires off the binary signature?"

"I'm going to need a smartphone."

John strode over to the TV stand and opened a drawer. He excavated a pile of phones and spread them on the coffee table.

"When you're a diplomat having multiple affairs, proper hardware to cover your tracks is a necessity. Hopefully one of these will work."

Nia gawked at each phone as if it were a gold brick, a grin forming on her face.

"They'll do just fine."

No sooner had Nia finished uttering her last word, a dull clack came from downstairs. It was the sound of a dead bolt unlocking. The creak of the door swinging open followed immediately. Then came thuds of footsteps on the foyer stairs.

31

John raised an index finger to his lips and motioned with his other hand for Nia to go upstairs.

As she scuttled away, he swept across the kitchen and grabbed a gun taped inside a cabinet. He drew his back flush against the wall, assessing the footfalls sounding from the foyer stairs. Only one person. Heavy trudging. Practically brazen. Entering the living room—

John spun around the corner and pointed the gun. On the wrong end of the barrel stood Bill Fisker, the diplomat that was supposed to be diplomating half a world away. A luxury gym bag hung over his shoulder, as his wide eyes practically inhaled the gun.

"Slowly lay down the bag and put your hands up."

The only movement that came from Bill was the trembling of his hands. The last time John had seen someone this scared, the man had ended up urinating on himself.

"Please, I..." Bill stammered, "it was nothing serious. We were just fooling around."

He thinks I'm the husband of one of his mistresses. John could use this to his advantage.

But then Bill said, "Please, I have a daughter too."

It took John a few seconds to process. This man's sexual exploits were women so young—likely as young as Jenny—that he thought John was an angry father. John could practically see it: this sleazebag scouring bars and coffee shops around DC's college campuses, flashing his credentials, painting pictures of jet-setting flights across the world, photo ops with public figures, luring impressionable and cash-strapped young women with gifts, exploiting fractured relationships with their fathers.

John lowered the gun. In a flash, he leaped and snatched Bill by the collar, slamming him against the wall so hard that every picture around them slid like an avalanche and crashed.

"Imagine another creep saying that about your daughter, you sick fuck."

"I know, I know, I'm sick...please, I'm sick... please, I can't even get it up most of the—"

"Shut up."

John used every ounce of willpower to suppress his anger. *Be smart, John. Focus on the mission.* He put Bill down and went to work.

With the detached attitude of someone handling an inanimate object, John zip-tied Bill's wrist and ankles, blindfolded him with a kitchen towel, and gagged him with a balled-up sock (courtesy of Bill's sweaty left foot). From Bill's person, he took a phone, wallet, keys, and badges. Then he slung him over a shoulder and hauled him into the master bedroom. After tossing Bill on the bed, John strode out, shut the door, and went into Nia's room.

He found her sitting on the bathroom floor, back against the wall.

"I heard—"

"Shhh," whispered John and beckoned her to follow.

Once they were downstairs by the kitchen bar, John whispered a little louder.

"The owner is back much sooner than he should be. I don't know how or why, but it doesn't matter. What matters is that he thinks I'm the disgruntled father of a young girl he's been seeing."

"Gross."

"It is. It's also going to buy us some time. The longer he thinks that, the longer he'll be too embarrassed to report this to the police. But once he sees our pictures, he will report. The good thing is that he hasn't seen you, so he can't corroborate that you are here. Regardless, once the FBI and CIA figure out I was here, they will recalibrate their search radius."

Nia leaned back casually at the news of all this.

"So you're telling me we can't take his Range Rover?"

John cracked a smile, remembering it wasn't her first evade-the-authorities mobilization.

"I'm afraid not. But there will be footage of the Toyota Camry I drove here leaving this neighborhood. We'll drive in the opposite direction and switch for another vehicle to go north." John's eyes swept over Nia's computers. "What about all this?"

"I can upload it to the cloud. It will take time, but we won't have to worry about it again."

"What about his phones? Can you still use them or will they be tracked?"

Nia gave the Jenny-eyeroll special. "Please. By the time I'm done with them, they'll point to street merchants in Bangladesh."

"Good. There is one phone you need to hack first." John slid Bill's cell phone across the counter. "I need access to his calendar. If he's going to be missing an event tonight, I need to know who will ask questions. Most importantly, I don't want any more surprises at the door."

Nia hacked the phone in under sixty seconds. Bill had set his date of birth for the PIN, which Nia read off his driver's license. The correlation between technology getting smarter and people getting dumber rang true to John. He scrolled through Bill's calendar. Nothing today. At nine a.m. tomorrow, his cleaning lady was supposed to arrive. Nothing else was scheduled until seven thirty p.m., when someone named *Meghan "American University"* would come over.

John slid the phone on the counter, having gotten the clarity he needed. It was time to prepare for evacuation while Nia hacked some unsuspecting cloud and uploaded the Grail tracker.

———

At nine sharp the following morning, Zofia Nowak rang the townhouse doorbell twice before inserting her copy of the key. To her surprise, the door was already unlocked. She shrugged and carried her cleaning supplies upstairs to the living room. Muttering a few swear words in Polish, she assessed the mess throughout the floor, particularly the shards of broken picture frames.

"Pijany idiota."

Ever the consummate professional, she composed herself and carried her supplies to the top floor. When she swung open the master bedroom door, she dropped her bucket with a gasp.

Bill Fisker was sprawled on the bed, wearing nothing but his tighty-whities, gagged with a balled-up sock, his wrists zip-tied to the top corners of the bed frame.

Some forty miles southwest, moving at exactly the speed

limit on I-95, Nia and John enjoyed egg-and-cheese muffin sandwiches and coffee.

32

The stolen SUV had been ditched for a stolen RV.

Unlike Bill Fisker, the owner of this vehicle was a retired lieutenant with a more predictable movement pattern—a quiet life in Boca Raton, Florida, with two months in Virginia during the holiday season.

John had chosen the RV for other reasons as well. It was a thirty-five-foot home on wheels—kitchen, dinette, bathroom, bedroom (for Nia), sleeper sofa (for him)—which meant they could remain out of sight of lodging establishments and restaurants. Lastly, he wanted the advantage of RVs being associated with retirees and families, making them inconspicuous despite their size. At the moment, there was even a semblance of a family vibe with Nia sitting in the passenger seat. Except families typically didn't drive toward Russian mercenaries.

"We should put on some music," said Nia as they passed Rockville, Maryland, on I-270 North.

John kept his eyes laser focused between the road, the speedometer, and the side-view mirrors.

"You're in charge of the playlist."

"Aye-aye, Captain."

Nia played the center console buttons with the same dexterity she reserved for her keyboard, the satellite radio stations coming alive through the RV speakers. Classic jazz, no. Contemporary jazz, no. Talk radio, no. Talk radio, no, no, no. Hard rock, *bingo.*

Nia turned up the volume, the surround sound pumping the guitar riffs, drumbeats, and raspy vocals of AC/DC's "Highway to Hell."

John tore his eyes from the road and gave her a look. "Really?"

"It's fitting, no?" she said with a grin.

John shook his head and turned his attention back to the traffic ahead.

"All right, all right, I'll change it."

After she made a few leaps across stations, the intro melody of "Dancing in the Dark," by Bruce Springsteen, filled the vehicle. Nia leaned back and bobbed her head to the beat, and soon her lips synced to the lyrics. John went still. Still as the cold, black night.

"Change it," he said.

Nia didn't seem to hear him.

"Change it."

"What?"

"Change the song."

"Oh c'mon, this is a great—"

"I said change it."

The edge in John's voice sent Nia's hand slapping the radio off button. After that, she remained frozen in her seat. John stared at the road's lane separators, the silence growing more uncomfortable with each streaming dash.

Nia finally broke it. "So it was her favorite song?"

John hardly wanted to get into it. But he felt bad about his outburst.

"No. Claire liked country music. Springsteen wasn't really her thing."

"I wasn't talking about Claire."

John shot Nia a sideways glance. Her perceptiveness felt intrusive. He decided not to engage, instead checking the driver's side mirror before passing an eighteen-wheeler.

"What happened to her?" said Nia.

"I don't know what you're talking about."

"Look, man. If you're going to use my brain for your personal vendetta, then don't play me for an idiot. A man who slides his family photo in front of me and has no qualms about dying has clearly lost it all. I'm just trying to understand what happened to your daughter."

John realized no one had brought up Jenny in front of him in a very long time. People who knew him well also knew that he believed personal tragedies should be reserved for broken hearts, not prying ears. But considering he'd stolen Nia's chance at a faraway path to legitimate freedom, John found her prying equitable.

He summoned his words through a quivering breath and said, "She took her life with a bottle of Xanax."

The hum of the highway took over, undulating to the bounces of the vehicle. Like the rhythm of sorrow.

"I'm sorry," said Nia. "I really am. I've seen too many drug overdoses in my neighborhood. Some were accidental, but many weren't."

The fact that Nia intimately understood such tragedies made John more at ease with the exchange. Plenty of people had given their condolences to him, but they usually rang hollow.

"Your wife must've taken it hard. Being a psychiatrist."

John took in another heavy breath, unclogging emotions that had coalesced for a long time.

"It wasn't just the guilt that she didn't see the signs. There's a history of suicide in her family. She thinks she passed that on to Jenny. I tried to tell her otherwise, but she just couldn't accept it. I tried everything. I tried…"

John's voice began cracking, and he ended it there. There would be no more talk of this, he decided. The silence grew, becoming so heavy that it seemed to slow down the vehicle.

"Is it okay if I put the music back on?" said Nia.

John nodded.

Through the speakers came the sultry vocals of TLC. The song: "Waterfalls."

As John listened to the lyrics, he found them far more pleasing than "Highway to Hell," even though the message seemed to be the same.

Turn back while you still can.

33

John pulled the RV off the road, as deep into the woods as the bulky vehicle could make it. It wasn't far, but enough not to be visible to the passing traffic. He shut off the engine and turned to Nia.

"Let's get some fresh air."

Nia took in the thick forest, masked in the late-evening gloom, and promptly said, "No thanks. I'm good."

"Are you sure? This will be your last chance for a while."

"I'm a city girl, Captain. Woods freak me out."

Good, thought John, needing it to be true for the assurance she wouldn't flee. But just in case, he decided to paint a vision.

"Woods shouldn't worry you. It's the bears that come out at night."

"I'm sorry, *what*?"

"You're fine as long as you stay in the vehicle."

"What if you don't come back?"

"If I'm not back here tonight, wait until the morning, then go to the road and walk five miles south to the juncture."

John popped open the front console, revealing a stack of hundred-dollar bills.

"That's a thousand to get you started. Something tells me you won't even need that much."

Nia stared dully at the cash. "So this could be it."

"It could be it for me," clarified John and strode outside.

Surprisingly, after a few seconds, Nia followed him, like a duckling wary of its surroundings. John smirked as he pulled up the topographic map of the area on his handheld GPS.

To the west of him was the Allegheny River, while the national forest sprawled to the east. Southward, the road meandered to the nearest junction. North of John, past a mile and a half of forest, a clearing encircled a hill. At its peak sat a house next to a barn made of corrugated metal.

The whole property already had all the elements of a perfect hideout, but when Nia had pulled up the tax records to find the property deeded to a person who'd died just a few months ago, John had no doubt left.

He took in a deep breath, the air thick with the earthy scent of birch wood. How many breaths did he have left in him? It was a question he would morbidly ask before every mission, and—considering he was still alive—it had become a sort of superstition. Superstition, luck, the odds. Could Claire really be a few miles away?

Now there was a question John had never asked before a mission.

The night fell over the forest like a blanket of woe. Dressed in camouflage, John stepped out of the bedroom and walked to the front of the RV.

Nia's mouth opened into a gaping smile.

"Busting out the old SEAL gear?"

John couldn't suppress a chuckle. Eight years had passed

since the last time he'd worn a military-issued combat uniform, which made his over-the-counter outfit and gear feel a bit like a novelty. But John had maintained his physique and fitness over those eight years, which gave him confidence he was still relatively the same fighter, no matter how misguided that belief might be.

"It doesn't work like that," he said. "The military owns your life for the duration of your service. They own the equipment forever. But you'd be surprised at what you can buy in stores these days." He shifted his Noveske rifle from behind his back and tapped it. "Not to mention the internet—" John broke off as Nia recoiled at the sight of the gun, stumbling backward.

"Whoa, Nia, relax, it's okay..."

Nia seemed to hear nothing, her chest heaving at a frantic pace. John put the rifle away inside the bathroom. He then sat next to Nia on the sofa.

"I didn't mean to scare you."

"It's not you," she said, slowly gaining control of her breathing. "I just get anxiety attacks when..."

There was no need for her to finish the sentence. She had grown up around guns and violence, and the trauma had clearly accumulated like sedimentary rock. John imagined it could be even worse than the PTSD service members acquired in the field.

"I understand," he said.

"No," said Nia, finally regaining herself. "You don't."

34

OCTOBER 25, 2011

Nia's program was not compiling.

The error message: *subscripted value is neither array nor pointer nor vector.*

"Well, what is it then?" Nia huffed.

She examined the offending line of C code and just couldn't see the issue. The thing was, the whole block of code was a mess. Triple-nested *for loop* modifying a two-dimensional array... that was just sloppy programming. Better to split it into two methods, log the values.

"C'mon, Nia! You can do better."

No sooner than she had uttered her words of encouragement, she heard the creaking of floorboards outside her bedroom. Yep, she'd woken up Mama, and now there would be hell to pay. The rule was bedtime by ten p.m. and absolutely no computer stuff for more than four hours a day. Nia checked the time in the upper right corner of her screen: 11:07 p.m.

Mama will take the laptop away. It didn't matter that Mama worked three jobs to scrounge up the money for it; rules were rules.

But then Nia heard a heavy thud in the kitchen, immediately

followed by her mother's voice in the bedroom. Something was horribly wrong.

Subscripted value is not an array.

Nia's heart pounded to the cadence of her mother's footsteps from the bedroom to the kitchen. Her mother's scream sent a bolt of lightning through her. Yelling. Objects crashing, shattering. Nia looked at her trembling hands. Was the whole world shaking? Her mother cried out, and Nia bolted toward the kitchen and swung her door open.

The light from her room revealed two men in the dining room, pinning Mama to the floor. She was squirming, the corner of her mouth bleeding profusely.

Subscripted value is not a pointer.

"Go back to your room," said the bigger of the two.

"She's got nice shit in there," said the skinny one. His sunken, hollow eyes took inventory of Nia's laptop.

"Leave her alone," said Mama. "She won't do nothing."

"Shut the fuck up," said Skinny, chewing his chapped lips. He was tweaking, Nia realized. His eyes settled on Nia, as though finally seeing her for the first time.

"You a fine little thing, ain't ya?"

"C'mon, man, get the cash from the bedroom and let's get the fuck out of here," implored Big. But Skinny didn't seem to hear him, his eyes in a kind of trance. He stood up and ambled his way toward Nia.

"How old is you?"

Mama screamed and yelled as Skinny crouched in front of Nia. Veiny branches bulged in his unblinking eyes. The stench of sweat and alcohol was thick and musty.

"You wanna go to your room? Show me your computer?"

He brushed the side of Nia's face with the back of his hand. His clammy fingers slithered over her collarbone. Nia went numb.

Subscripted value is not a vector.

Nia heard a crash behind him before she saw the kitchen vase shatter over Big's big head. He rolled to the side, wailing, and Mama charged at Skinny.

He stood up and met her halfway, Nia stumbling backward. She watched her mother bleed and cry and scream and swing, until Skinny brandished a gun from under his hoodie and then... Nia finally figured it out.

Subscripted value is an integer: 1 gunshot.

Her mother slumped to the floor.

She exhaled a hoarse groan. She never exhaled again.

The dog next door barked.

Skinny couldn't stop staring at the blood pooling around his feet. Big stumbled into Mama's bedroom and came out with a fistful of cash. They both ran through the front door, leaving it wide open.

Cold autumn wind entered the house.

35

John felt a sickness in his stomach he hadn't felt in a long time. Nia's story felt more vivid than so many events he'd witnessed with his own eyes. Yet it wasn't just what he now knew about Nia that induced nausea. There was a distinct sense of guilt rising inside him for adding another chapter to her collection of ordeals.

"I'm sorry," he said. "For everything." He looked toward the bathroom, where he'd put the rifle away. "Look, I'll do my best to make this quick. Just turn around while I get the gun."

"Captain, it's fine. I can look at guns. I just get triggered when they appear suddenly."

John wasn't so sure about all that, but Nia produced a smirk.

"Go get the gun and do your thing. Hopefully they shoot you and I'll be on my merry way to freedom."

There was the dark sense of humor John had gotten accustomed to. At least he hoped it was humor; he genuinely wondered how much of it was Nia's wishful thinking.

John took his rifle and stepped into the night.

Using panoramic night vision, John methodically swept through the woods. At the 1.517-mile mark on the GPS, he could see the clearing beyond the trees. Sliding to the edge of it, he lifted his NODs and peered through his night vision binoculars.

The house atop the hill was a two-story cottage. Only two windows on the ground floor emitted faint light. The kitchen. All other lights were external, beaming into the corners of the house and the driveway. No cars. The barn next to the house looked like a giant barrel that had been split vertically in half and laid horizontally on top of the clearing.

Unless someone was watching the perimeter through night vision, there was no way John could be seen as long as he kept low to the ground. He dropped into standard military leopard crawl, his pulling forearms synchronized with his pushing legs. *Been a minute, huh, John?* he thought after twenty yards, his muscles tensing more than he'd expected. He stopped regularly to assess the terrain, listen for any sounds, and ensure there was no tripwire in front of him.

Ten yards from the house, he lifted himself into a crouch, performing a 180-degree scan with the infrared laser of his rifle. All clear. Following the shadows, he crept to the south wall of the house. Grazing the siding as he moved, John turned the corner around the back and climbed the two steps of an elevated deck.

He peered through the glass of the double doors: the kitchen and dining room were empty, barely lit by a small fluorescent bulb beneath the top cabinets. John tried the knob. Locked.

After adhering three strips of duct tape over a square of wood-bordered door glass, John wrapped a rag over his fist and punched. The pane broke with a dull thud, and John palmed the duct tape along with the shattered glass stuck to it, then laid it all on the patio. Hand through the hole, he unlocked the dead bolt, followed by the knob.

John slowly opened the door and entered the dining room. On the far end of the house, he detected more light, intermittent with shifting hues. John lifted his night vision goggles, allowing his eyes to adjust. He cautiously moved into the great room. Clear. An L-shaped couch and two chairs surrounded a coffee table. On it, an ashtray was filled to the brim—one cigarette butt had glowing specks of ash.

John crept through the room, approaching another. The sound of a television show came into focus. John peered from around the doorway. A man in jeans and a white T-shirt was sitting on a couch, watching *Jeopardy!* John slid into the room, his silencer leading the way.

Jeopardy! host: "This Balkan city hosted the 1984 Winter Olympics."

"What is Sarajevo," said John.

The man spasmed, then froze upon seeing the rifle pointed at him.

"Don't move and don't speak," said John, moving sideways in a circular path to the front of the room. He could now see a pistol lying on the couch cushion next to the man. Half-polished bottle of vodka on the floor. The man's left arm was wrapped heavily in gauze. Another block of gauze was visible beneath his thin shirt. *He's been wounded.*

The initial fear in his eyes melted into a neutral expression. John didn't like the look of it. *Don't do it.* But he did, opening his mouth and reaching for the gun—

John fired a silenced shot into his chest, whatever the man was about to yell dissolving into a shrill yelp. *Too loud.*

Footsteps upstairs. John's eyes followed them across the ceiling. He counted only one person. Approaching the foyer stairs.

"Yevgeny? Chto eto bylo? Eh?"

John propped Yevgeny into a semblance of a normal sitting position. But the Russian upstairs was not coming down. *He knows something is off.* John crouched into a corner, aiming his rifle as far up to the side of the stairs as the angle would allow. He was rewarded with the sight of the Russian's right foot. John put a bullet into it.

The Russian shrieked and tumbled down the stairs, his pistol flying across the foyer. He wailed in agony, his hands cupping whatever was left of his foot.

John braced for a stampede of footsteps upstairs.

But none came.

He cautiously approached the Russian, checked him for other weapons before dragging him away from the stairs. He then tied him up and duct taped his mouth. After a careful scan of the staircase leading to the second floor, John began climbing it.

When he reached the landing, a muffled groan came from a room.

Claire?

36

Heart racing, hope rising, John crept through the narrow hallway.

The first door on the right was wide open. He peered into the bedroom. Empty. He entered and swept the room. *Clear.* A stuffy smell of sweat permeated throughout, the bed still warm. This had to be the room of the foot-shattered Russian. John exited and moved farther down the hallway, four doors remaining. He tested the lock of the door on the left, opened it, and found a bathroom filled with nonperishable food, medicine, guns, ammo.

A groan, again.

It came from the room across the hallway. *Calm yourself, John.* He approached the doorway, twisted the knob, and slowly opened the door. Lying on the bed, head covered in blood-soaked gauze, was a man. His breathing was heavy and labored. He mumbled a few words in Russian. *Another mercenary with combat-like wounds. Bizarre.*

John closed the door and moved to the next room. He opened the door, finding another gauze-wrapped Russian, a jug of water and a urine bucket by his bed.

Next room, same thing.

Last room, the master suite, same goddamned thing.

Four badly injured mercenaries. No Claire. No Grail operators.

What the hell happened here?

John strode down to the ground floor. He took a knee in front of the injured Russian and pulled the duct tape off his mouth.

"Do you speak English?"

The Russian answered by shouting in Russian. John understood very little of it, but there was definitely something about John fucking his own whore mother. John shut him back up with duct tape and checked his foot. He was losing blood at an alarming rate.

From the upstairs bathroom, John retrieved an army medical and trauma kit, and did his best to stop the bleeding. He placed the Russian's wrapped foot atop the first stair to incline the leg.

His good deed of the night accomplished, John made his way to the back patio, swiftly moving toward the last place on the property where hopes of finding Claire still existed—the barn.

The whole structure was made of corrugated metal, painted white but rusted throughout, including the massive double doors. Assessing the scene through the panoramic night vision, John judged he would need a heavy-duty bolt cutter. But as his hands probed the chain wrapped tightly around the barn door handles, he realized there was no lock. Of course there wasn't. Why would you need one when the only concern was keeping whoever was inside from escaping.

Claire... please— John came close to asking a favor of God but refrained.

He found the main chain knot and loosened it. Untangling the chain, John knew he made more noise than he should. The metal links finally slithered free, and John balled up the chains and tossed them aside. Rifle in one hand, John pulled the left door handle with the other.

He opened the door half a foot and peered inside.

Two barrels stood to the right, ten feet away. The ground was mostly dirt with intermittent patches of hay. John slid the door a few more inches, taking in the rest of the interior.

An old tractor was parked beyond the barrels. But the tracks in the dirt belonged to a car. John switched his position to get an angle of the other side. There he found the gray SUV that had been making appearances at the nearby gas station in recent days.

White rectangles lay beyond it, wide and flat, stretching to the far end of the barn. John made his move, stalking inside and taking cover behind the barrels. From this vantage point, he could clearly see that the row of large rectangles lined up beyond the car were mattresses.

John went in farther, taking cover behind the back tire of the tractor. He scanned the mattresses. They were all empty, arrayed all the way to a portable restroom at the back of the barn. John slowly came around the tractor, finding another row of mattresses on this side, and beyond them... *What the...?*

A dental chair? No, it was bigger. It had a crane-like limb branching from the back of it, hanging over the headrest.

John made a move toward the chair but halted in his tracks, seeing it clearly for the first time, even though it had been right down the middle of his vision from the beginning.

A person was sitting on a rusted side chair at the very end of the barn, their back turned to John. They wore an off-white shirt that blended into the wall. The sight was so unsettling that John felt his heartbeat spiking.

Approaching slowly, John slanted his path to reach the person from the side. When he was ten feet away, John started to circle around to the front of the chair. Sitting in it was a man.

Maybe late twenties. He was staring into the wall as though he could see it in the pitch black.

Suddenly, he tilted his head. He rotated it clockwise—toward John. His eyes refused to blink.

Through the phosphorus-green hues of night vision, John watched the man's lips snap open with a throat click. From the black hole of his mouth erupted a sound that was wholly inhuman, some synthetic hiss, like radio static wrapped in howling wind.

He leaped at John.

37

Nia heard a burst of wind howl outside the RV, followed by total silence. No. Not total.

There was a rustling. Maybe branches? *Strange.* It wasn't a windy night.

She stood up from the couch and hesitantly approached the front of the vehicle.

Trees enveloped the entire field of view from behind the windshield. Beyond them was a curtain of pitch black. The more Nia's gaze drifted into the darkness, the more certain she became she was hearing an odd hissing sound. It sent a cold chill down her spine. Goose bumps up her neck.

The rap on the RV door sent her falling backward with a shriek.

Two thumps, pause, three thumps.

She exhaled a sigh of relief—it was John, knocking the pattern they'd agreed on.

He unlocked the door with the only pair of keys they had and entered.

"You all right?" he said, watching her collect herself from the floor.

"I'm fine," she huffed. "You scared the shit out of me."

John didn't bother apologizing. "I'm going to need your help," he said.

"With what?"

"Making sense of what a Grail operator is saying."

———

John drove the RV up the winding driveway and parked in front of the cottage.

He got out of the vehicle and led the way to the barn with a flashlight. Nia trailed behind with short, uneasy strides. "That thing looks creepy," she said, taking in the glowing shafts of interior light that traced the barn's double doors.

You have no idea, thought John, but kept it to himself.

He slid the doors apart and went in first. Nia hesitated for a moment before entering.

The bars of fluorescent bulbs suspended from the ceiling gave the whole chamber a lab-like atmosphere. Aside from a few glances at Nia, John kept his eyes on the Grail operator in the chair, who now faced forward. It had taken John considerable effort to wrestle him down, even though he'd already been loosely chained by the Russians, and for a good reason—he had apparently suffered a mental breakdown, the likes of which John had never seen or heard of. But if there was anyone who could make sense of his gibberish about the Grail, John desperately hoped it would be Nia.

"What is *that*?" said Nia, pointing to the contraption that looked like a dental chair from hell.

"I'm not sure yet."

John grabbed two empty buckets and flipped them over in front of the operator. He sat on one and motioned Nia to join him on the other. She slowly sat down, but John had not seen her this tense since she had come out of the sleeping gas stupor in Georgetown.

The man across from them was unnaturally pale in the neon glow, his sunken eyes staring into a place not of this world. He suddenly twitched, the chains slinking around his arms and torso. After he'd lunged at John with the chair tied to him, John had made sure to tie him even tighter than the Russians had.

"It's all right," he assured Nia. "He's not getting out."

Nia didn't seem convinced.

John strobed his flashlight into the man's face a few times. This snapped him out of his trance, his gaze becoming somewhat present in the room.

"Private First Class Jason Hellinger," began John. "Can you hear me?"

Jason tilted his head toward John, as though noticing him for the first time. An unsettling, almost childish smile appeared on his face.

"You know my name?"

"We spoke fifteen minutes ago. Remember, we..." John trailed off with a sigh. "Jason, I need you to tell me again what happened here."

Jason looked around, frowning as though the entire barn seemed new to him.

"They took us."

"Yes, they did. But what happened in this room? What is that chair?"

Jason's gaze drifted toward the strange contraption. "Oh... that's my bed."

"Did they hurt you in the chair?"

"There's no pain in the chair. The pain comes after."

"How, Jason? How did they hurt you?"

Jason squirmed with a whimper. "I don't want to talk about it anymore."

"What the hell did they do to him?" said Nia, her right leg starting to jiggle restlessly.

"They tortured him until he cracked and likely told them everything he knew about the Grail."

"So why doesn't he know what they've done with Claire?"

"I don't think he knows what's real anymore. He claims he never saw Claire and doesn't know what happened to the other operators. He just keeps repeating the same thing when I ask him about the Grail. I need you to interpret this for me." John shifted his focus back to the private. "Jason, do you know where they've reassembled the Grail? Where is the Grail right now?"

Jason stiffened in the chair. His expression reset into something unnaturally vacant, his voice turning eerily monotone.

"Alpha. Charlie. Seven. Ready. Config location is five, seven, point, five, seven, seven, nine, seven, delta, three, four, point, eight, seven, five, three, six. Standing by."

John turned to Nia. "You know what any of this means?"

"No clue."

"Are you sure? Alpha Charlie Seven seems to be a call sign. But the *config* part? It sounds like coordinates. Or maybe an IP address?"

Nia had nothing.

John closed his eyes, pushed down his rising despair, then opened them.

"All right. Come help me with this." He walked over to the strange chair. Beyond it lay a pile of file storage boxes, stacked haphazardly. "Pick a box and go through it. If you see anything that might give us some clues, let me know."

"What exactly am I supposed to be looking for?"

John handed her a box. "At this point, a miracle."

38

The brain CT scan glowed like a black-and-white kaleidoscope image. It was the seventeenth brain image John had taken out of a box and held up to the neon light. *Bizarre.*

"Same here," said Nia, shuffling through scan after scan in her hands. "CT scans, MRIs, all brains."

"They couldn't have taken these images here," said John. "They must've stolen them from a hospital." He turned to the chair, studying it. "Maybe they stole this from a hospital too?"

John walked up to it and examined every inch. The chair had sage green cushioning, gray-painted metal everywhere else. It was more hulking than any dental or medical chair. The crane-like arm that rose from behind and hovered over the headrest ended into a helmet that looked like it belonged in a hair salon.

John looked up into the helmet. Something was in there. He inserted his hand, feeling a mesh, discs of metal... *click*, he pulled the whole thing out.

It was a net made of transparently tubed wires connecting a network of metal discs.

"Electrodes," said John, tracing his thumb over a disc. "This is for taking EEGs." He looked at Jason. "He said this is his bed.

Why would they be taking scans of his brain while he was sleeping?"

"He said the pain came afterward," said Nia.

"They would torture him afterward. But why? What were they looking for?"

"Are you sure this thing just takes scans?"

"I'm hardly sure of anything here. Maybe we can turn it on."

He circled around the chair but couldn't find a single button. He then placed a hand on the swirl of cords coming out of the crane arm's base and followed its path on the ground. In a pile of hay, John reached the end, to find all the cords severed.

He made eye contact with Nia, and they both shook their heads.

John strode back to the chair and crouched below it, examining the bottom. At the very center, he spotted an engraving. John crawled under and shone a light on it. The characters were so small that he had to get his eyes inches from the letters to read them.

"Dividius Technologies LLC."

"What did you say?" asked Nia.

John crawled out and stood up, dusting himself off. "It says *Dividius Technologies LLC* on the bottom."

Nia dropped her stack of brain scans on the ground.

"Impossible."

―――

"Nia, I'm not sure I understand the relevance."

"You don't find it odd that Dividius Technologies is held by LIS, the hedge fund I got busted for hacking? You're the one who said that some things are too coincidental to be coincidences."

"I did. I just don't see what this implies."

Nia stared at the chair, as if an answer would manifest.

"I don't either," she said finally. "But I don't like it."

"What is there to like here?" said John, taking in the whole barn again. "Look at the footprints. There were many more people here. But something happened."

"Maybe the Grail operators staged a mutiny. Aren't they all former soldiers?"

John considered this, then walked over to Jason.

"Jason, did you and your teammates fight back?"

"Teammates?"

"Yes, your fellow soldiers."

Jason appeared to think very hard.

"I am a soldier," he said with childlike simplicity, his throat thick with desolation. All the sadness of all the broken men John had ever known seemed woven into Jason's voice.

"Yes, you are, Jason. You're a good soldier."

"I'm a good soldier."

John closed his eyes and pinched the bridge of his nose, desperately trying to suppress the onset of tears. The thought that the Russians could have done to Claire what they'd done to Jason was borderline crippling.

"I am a good soldier," continued Jason.

"Yes, you are."

"I am a *good* soldier!"

"Okay, Jason. Okay."

"I am a *good* soldier! Hooah!"

"What's happening to him?" said Nia.

"He's having an episode."

"I am a good soldier! Hooah!"

Jason stood up, chair tied to his back.

"Sit down, Jason. Don't make me tie your legs too."

Eyes wide, smile manic, Jason looked off to the side. John turned in that direction but found nothing out of the ordinary.

Jason took John's glance as an opportunity to start run-hopping sideways.

"Goddamn it, Jason! Don't make me tie you to that tractor."

But Jason was hearing none of it, hopping manically in a straight path.

Where does he think he's go— John finally saw it, his gut twisting into a hot knot. He bolted after Jason, but then the horror of what Nia might witness spun him toward her.

"*Look away*," he shouted, then lunged at Jason. His moment of hesitation ensured he was late reaching him in time, and all his warning did was give Nia a front-row seat as Jason hopped to a ground tool rack and drove his face into a pitchfork.

39

Nia was sitting on the RV sofa, knees to chest, when John wrapped a blanket around her.

What had just transpired easily made the upper echelon of the worst things he had ever witnessed. But the fact that Nia had also witnessed it induced a level of guilt he hadn't felt since Jenny died by suicide. To be fair, they were distinctly opposite kinds of guilt. With Jenny it was the guilt of believing he should've done more, whereas with Nia he was desperately wishing he hadn't done what in hindsight seemed so idiotic.

It strangely only now dawned on John that guilt could only come from those two places: you either wished you'd done something or regretted you had. That was Claire's burden—she balanced both forms of guilt like buckets suspended from a pole over her shoulders. She didn't just share John's regret of believing there was more they could've done for Jenny; she firmly believed she had done the unfathomable—cemented Jenny's death by giving her birth.

The kettle whistled on the stove. John poured hot water over a bag of ginger turmeric tea inside a mug. After adding a squirt of honey and mixing it, he brought the mug to Nia.

"Careful, it's hot."

Nia took the tea, barely glancing at it, her gaze lost in what John could only suspect was her mind replaying the horrific scene in the barn.

John crouched next to her.

"I know you don't have a reason to believe me, but I swear to you on my daughter's grave that I will not put you in that position again. From now on you stay in the vehicle and only come out if the coast is clear."

Nia managed half a nod. John took a pair of two-way radios out of a box and handed one to her.

"What's this for?" she asked.

"In case you need to reach me. I have to go inside the house for a bit."

Nia visibly tensed. "Why?"

John pressed the talk button on his radio, ensuring Nia's beeped.

"Trust me, you don't want to know."

———

The foot-shattered Russian was many shades paler since John had left him lying on the foyer floor. His leg was still inclined on the first step, but it didn't seem to matter; the puddle of blood beneath it made John wonder how the man was still conscious.

He peeled the duct tape off his mouth and showed him a pack of cigarettes he'd grabbed from the coffee table. The Russian nodded.

"Not so fast," said John. "I know you speak enough English to understand what I'm saying, so I'll say this very slowly so that there's no misunderstanding. I'm going to light up a cigarette and put it between your lips. If you answer all my questions truthfully, you will get to smoke it. If you don't, I will take away the cigarette and put it out in your wound. I will light it up again and repeat the question until you either give me the answer or I run out of cigarettes." John tapped the pack to emphasize it was nearly full.

The Russian produced a resigned smile. He then nodded.

John lit up a cigarette.

———

John entered the RV to find Nia still on the sofa. She did seem to be in slightly better spirits. He sat next to her and lifted the empty mug from the floor. "More?"

"Sure."

John went to the kitchenette and turned on the heat under the kettle.

"So, how did the interrogation go?" said Nia.

John smirked. Of course she'd figured out why he had gone in. He leaned against the counter and crossed his arms, taking a moment to admire Nia's sharpness before answering.

"There was definitely some kind of mutiny. But it wasn't the Grail operators. His English was poor, so the best I can surmise is that it was internal. It might be another faction, like Yuri's superiors, which can go as high as the Kremlin itself. There was a shootout and Yuri and his men fled back here to regroup." John peered into the void of the empty mug in his hand. "Claire and the operators are with the other faction."

"He saw Claire?"

"No. He claimed he was here at the house during the abductions and had no interaction with the hostages, until Yuri came back with Jason. The only hostage to make it back."

"Did you ask about the chair?"

"I did."

"And?"

"He died before I finished the question."

John pushed away the images of a dying man taking heavy drags of nicotine in his final moments. It was reminiscent of a last meal. John had no delusions that he wasn't responsible for the deaths of countless other men. But all those men died an ocean away, far enough that John could find a way to compartmentalize his guilt.

The kettle whistled, jerking John from the counter. He made Nia's tea and handed her the mug.

"So that's it?" she said. "Dead end?"

"No. He told me where Yuri and his men went."

Nia's face lit up, which John ascribed to wishful thinking that she and John might be parting ways.

"Russia?" she said.

"Ohio."

Nia's cheerful expression faded. She put the mug back on the floor without taking a sip of her tea.

40

The highway was clear; John's head was far from it. Crossing the Ohio line at exactly 1:15 p.m., he entered his home state with a flurry of questions. Why would there be an internal mutiny among the Russians? What could this other faction want? And why would Yuri go to what appeared to be an abandoned water treatment plant in a small town west of Canton, Ohio?

"It hasn't been operational for over a decade," said Nia, scrolling through her phone in the passenger seat.

"It hasn't been operational as a water plant," clarified John, saying it more to himself. After the ordeal inside that barn, he had resolved to expect circumstances beyond his imagination going forward. Jason's final moments haunted him, but it was the chair now that stirred an unease he wasn't able to translate. Who would make such a thing? For what purpose? The answers to these questions had to begin with Nia.

"What did your research into Dividius Technologies reveal about what they do?"

"That they don't want anyone to know what they do," said Nia. "No website. Shell offices. Their business regulatory filings are full of generic mumbo jumbo about auxiliary facility equipment. But they are wholly owned by the pricks at LIS."

Nia's disdain toward LIS was not lost on John. But the root cause certainly was.

"If you don't mind me asking, why did you hack a hedge fund like LIS to begin with?"

"It's the least I could've done."

The bitterness in her voice almost made John drop the subject, but he pressed on. "Care to elaborate?"

Nia sighed and plopped her phone into a cup holder.

"After my mom died, I moved in with my aunt. She was borderline senile, and her condition only deteriorated. I didn't mind. I took care of her, and no one stood in the way of me and my computer. Until one day we received a notice of eminent domain, which stated that all the houses on our block were slated to be razed to make way for some community center."

John scoffed. "They cleared a community to build a community center?"

"It was all just a bunch of bullshit. The whole thing reeked of corruption, palms getting greased for government contracts. So I hacked into the local municipalities, their banks, and followed the trail all the way to the IRS. That was my first big hack. Once I was inside the IRS, I started poking around. It didn't take long to put it all together. Shady government contracting projects throughout the country all had ties to LIS. When I started digging into LIS, things just snowballed."

"I don't know what that means."

"It means these fuckers have tentacles across the globe. A publicly traded hedge fund that hides offshore accounts and has holdings in companies with ties to Russia and China. That's where I came across Dividius Technologies. It doesn't surprise me at all that the Russians would have their equipment, whatever that chair does. I just can't believe it's all a coincidence."

John mulled on this for a bit. An idea started to form, and it was far from a pleasant one.

"Nia, I hate to say this, but if you stole two hundred million dollars from LIS, it is not out of the realm of possibility that they tracked you down and found out about your work with the Grail."

"Wow, really, man? So this is all my fault?"

"I didn't say that. I'm just saying if you're looking for a connection..." *Unbelievable. She gets defensive just like Jenny.* "Never mind, forget it. I'm speculating and it doesn't even matter at this point. If these people are who you say they are, they would have the resources and vested interest in sponsoring the theft of a technology like the Grail."

Nia went silent. Brooding.

You had to say it, John. How did planting that seed help the situation? Smart.

"John..."

Oh, good. At least it's not the silent treatment. "Yes?"

"If LIS is really behind this, then I will find the Grail myself and destroy that thing."

John almost laughed, though he admired her bravado. The zest. Her naivete in this regard reminded him of himself when he'd first signed up for the Naval Academy, raring to fight the bad guys. To do good in this world.

"Nia, you have your whole life ahead of you."

"My whole life?" She leaned toward John with aggressiveness he'd never seen from her before. "They stole my life the day I received the eviction notice at my aunt's house. These people are the reason I spent years in prison, being the government's code monkey for a machine they had the audacity to steal."

"We don't know that for sure."

Nia looked out her window.

John followed her gaze toward the bruise-colored clouds forming in the distance.

"I guess we'll find out," she said.

41

John pulled into a parking lot behind an abandoned building and shut off the engine.

"Any signal from the Grail?" he said to Nia.

"Huh?"

"The binary signature? Has the tracker you uploaded to the cloud sent anything to your cell phone?"

"Oh, no, nothing yet," she said, seemingly distracted by the borderline dilapidated building. "Why did we stop here?"

"Because it's secluded, and we should eat dinner before we get to the water treatment plant."

"The last supper?" said Nia with her trademark wry grin.

The resurgence of her dark humor was an encouraging sign. John was worried he'd crossed one line too many with his insinuation about LIS being behind all this. But the more he thought about it, the more plausible it seemed. And the more he thought about what might lie ahead at the water treatment plant, the more plausible it seemed that this could be his last supper. *How many more breaths?*

"Nia, since this really could be it—"

"C'mon, it was just a joke."

"I know, but still. I want to ask you if there is a way to check my voicemails without getting traced? I destroyed my phone before I began all this, but I would like to hear any messages that might be worth hearing."

"All right, well, the reason behind the request is pretty grim, but I got you, Captain."

―――

It had taken John fifteen minutes to make and serve fettuccine Alfredo, the same amount of time it had taken Nia to spoof the mobile network servers and access John's voicemail.

She laid the phone between the two steaming plates, but John slid it back to her.

"You drive. I don't want to mess up anything."

"Great. I'm also your personal assistant now."

"That's right. I pay you in grub. Eat before it gets cold."

Nia wasted no time swirling a forkful and plopping it into her mouth, her other hand tapping the phone.

"Okay, let's look at the transcriptions and numbers. Lots of voicemails from 703-416—"

"That's my assistant. Play the most recent."

Nia tapped the screen, and Mrs. Simasek's voice came over the cell phone speaker.

"Captain Mitcham, I don't know what else to do…" She trailed off into silence. Then came a sob. "John…" She had never addressed him by his first name before. "The FBI searched your office, and they won't tell me anything. Why would you do this? Why would you disappear… I just don't understand."

The voicemail ended there. So did John's desire for food. Mrs. Simasek's voice snapped him out of whatever mode he'd been in for the past few weeks, pulling him into the vestiges of a life that he now viscerally understood would never exist again, no matter what outcome would result from his search for Claire.

"Maybe this was a bad idea," said Nia.

"I'm full of bad ideas," said John, resetting into mission mode.

"If the FBI searched your office, how come our pictures aren't all over the news?"

"Because they're working in tandem with the CIA. If they went public with this, people would start asking questions. Publicly disclosing the theft of a government cyberweapon would not be in the interest of national security."

"Makes sense," said Nia, scrolling through the phone. "Speaking of national security, there's a long voicemail from an unknown number."

"Probably a marketer."

"No. The transcript says Mason. It's from a while ago, our second day in Georgetown."

John steeled himself. "All right. Let's hear it."

Nia shook her head—"This can't be good"—and tapped the screen.

"John, it's Mason. I'm violating protocol by calling you, but hey, considering the list of things they'll nail me for, this will be a slap on the wrist. I understand what drove you to do this, I really do, but I promise you this is not the way. You are interfering with an active investigation. You're..." Heavy breathing. "John, the FBI found Claire's note. Why didn't you tell me? Do you have any idea how this looks?" Silence. More heavy breathing. "It's not too late to turn yourself in. We can lean on the fact that you are a grieving father who just had a lapse of judgment. With your record and me backing you, we can reduce your sentence. We... please, John. There's still time to turn around."

The voicemail ended.

John waited in silence for the question he knew would come.

"What note is he talking about?" said Nia.

There was a probing look in her eyes. *Choose your words carefully, John.*

"The people who abducted Claire made her write a note that she was leaving me for a fresh start."

"Made her?"

"Yes. Made her."

"How would you know this?"

"Because she ended it with the same thing her father said to her on the day he took his life. *Please take care of yourself.* Claire and I agreed never to use that phrase. Ever."

John could see Nia's mind racing into overdrive.

"Unless she also wanted to take her own life."

John slammed the table, his plate spilling oily white sauce. Nia recoiled, lurching away from the kitchenette. She was staring at John, partly with fear, and partly with pity toward a desperate fool.

Every breath John took grew more intense than the prior, despite him instructing his body to do the exact opposite.

"I know my wife. Twenty-two years of marriage."

Nia just shook her head. John could sense barbed words coming before she said them.

"You thought you knew your daughter, too."

42

Pewter clouds blanketed the sky, filtering the afternoon light down to a metallic haze. Foul weather for John's foul mood.

It was hardly the mental state he needed to be in before infiltrating the water treatment plant. He scanned the beige buildings and gray water tanks through binoculars—for the fifth time and from a third vantage point—and still couldn't find a single vehicle or sign of life. It was time.

John strode through the sparse trees dividing the commercial plots and entered the RV. Nia sat on the sofa, laptop in her lap. She tried masking the judgmental look from earlier, but John still detected traces of her true feelings—the belief that John had truly lost it.

It seemed nothing would ever be the same after their exchange. She thought what she thought, and John felt the effects of what she'd said like a permanent wound to the soul. How could her words be more painful than most physical traumas he'd experienced? Was it because they had truth to them? Because they came from a place of ignorance? Could it be both? How would he have reacted if he'd been in her position, hearing about Claire's note?

You have to let this go, John. Clear your mind, and focus.

"I'm about to gear up and bring out the rifle."

Nia nodded. No *Aye-aye, Captain.* No dark humor. Just an awkward, uncomfortable energy.

John geared up and exited the RV in silence.

Two hours and seventeen minutes later, John rapped on the RV door and entered. He found Nia still on the couch, a blanket draped across her legs.

"Did I wake you?"

She rubbed her eyes and looked out the window at the darkness. "What time is it?"

"Time for you to see something."

John pulled up to a back entrance of the plant, the RV's headlights beaming into an exit door that was rusted, faded, and pried open.

Nia eyed it suspiciously. "Are you sure no one is in there?"

"I swept the whole place twice. They definitely came through not too long ago. I found cigarette butts that can't be more than a few days old. I need to show you what I think they were looking at, and you tell me if it fits with anything you know about LIS."

"What is it?"

John turned off the engine. "I honestly don't even know how to describe it."

He produced a second flashlight and handed it to Nia, then led the way out of the RV.

They entered a dark hall, the smell of stale water and

ammonia immediate. John weaved through a maze of walls with his flashlight, his other hand inches away from the pistol at his hip. They finally entered a cavernous chamber. Three massive, fifty-foot-tall open water tanks lined the length of it. A pipe wide enough to fit an adult ran through the tanks at ground level, seemingly connecting them.

"And I thought the barn was creepy," said Nia.

John found her remark comforting. A step in the right direction after the fight they had in the RV. He took off the climbing rope that he had hung across his torso and tied one end of it around Nia's waist. He tied the other end around his waist, then placed the flashlight between his teeth and began climbing the ladder of the first tank.

"You gotta be kidding me," huffed Nia.

John was not kidding; he scaled the fifty-foot tank like a cat.

Once his feet were firmly on a ramp above the tank, he wrapped the rope around his forearms a couple of times and shouted to Nia.

"Just start climbing and don't worry if you slip. I got you."

Nia huffed once more and started climbing up the rusted ladder, clenching her flashlight between her teeth. When she reached the top, John offered his hand and pulled her up onto the narrow platform. He untied the rope from both of their waists to ensure neither would be dragged down if one of them fell.

"It's the third tank at the end," he said, pointing his flashlight down the narrow ramp that ran above the three open tanks.

"Of course it is," said Nia.

John led the way, carefully threading over the ramp's rusted mesh bottom. He glanced to check on Nia, who kept about ten feet of distance between them, nervously clutching the ramp's rails on both sides. Just as John threw another glance at her, there was a shrill creak.

Before he could even react, the rusted mesh under his feet snapped in a haze of dust.

John was plummeting.

He fell into the first water tank, briefly hearing Nia's scream before it was muffled by the water. Submerged, John looked up to see Nia's flashlight searching the depths of the tank. John broke the surface, spitting water.

"I'm all right," he said. He swam around the tank, hugging its wall, looking for a ladder. There wasn't one. "You're going to have to toss the rope down. There's no other way out."

Nia turned and looked at the rope. "Are you sure there's no other way?"

"No. Look at the tank wall. It rises ten feet above water. I can't climb it."

"Okay, just making sure."

She sat down and shone her flashlight into John's face.

"Nia, please hurry."

But Nia did not hurry. In fact, she did nothing at all.

A hard knot formed in John's stomach. It grew tighter with each passing second of silence. Nia finally broke it.

"Do you believe in karma, Captain Mitcham?"

"Nia, what is this? What are you doing?"

"Answer the question."

"We don't have time for this."

"I have all the time in the world. You, on the other hand... How long can you swim in that tank?"

"Nia, you're making a mistake."

Nia burst into a hearty laugh. "Am I now? That's rich, Captain. You wouldn't say that if you believed in karma."

John kept himself afloat in a fixed place. A wave of dread sent a shiver through him. He looked toward Nia as if to make eye contact, but only his own face was illuminated by her flashlight.

"This has nothing to do with karma and everything to do with you refusing to help me."

Nia's laugh this time was mostly a cackle.

"Help you?" she said slowly, her voice full of resentment. "That's *all* I've been doing. I helped you, I helped the CIA, the FBI, DOD, NSA, everyone got their hands in the Nia Banks cookie jar. You're all the same. You use me to get what you want, dangling the carrot of freedom in front of me. You fucking people, with your wars and weapons and vendettas. At least Mason had the decency to be upfront with me. You don't even know if your wife was abducted at all. You may not believe in karma, Captain, but she's coming for you. And I'm done helping you."

Nia stood up and carefully made her way to the ladder.

"Nia. Nia! *Nia!*"

John kept calling her name, louder and louder as the beam from her flashlight became fainter and fainter.

Soon there was only darkness and the sound of lulling water.

That was how Nia Banks left John Mitcham to die.

43

JUNE 10, 2004

Standing at the edge of an Olympic-size swimming pool, John looked down the row of other men with shaved heads and beige swim trunks, and asked himself: *What am I doing here?*

Ironically, it was the same question that had prompted him to be here in the first place.

During his last deployment in Iraq, the reality had finally sunk in—there were no weapons of mass destruction. The entire narrative for the war—the claims of Saddam Hussein's regime's involvement with Al-Qaeda—had been predicated on a lie. A fantasy so absurd that John might have found it perversely comical had he not witnessed American soldiers die by the dozens, and Iraqi civilians perish by the hundreds. *What am I doing here?*

What *was* he doing there, other than contributing to the lies and destruction? What had started out as a clear mission to eradicate Al-Qaeda in Afghanistan turned into a campaign to eradicate reality in Iraq.

John had no delusions that a certain level of hypocrisy would be necessary for him to justify his career as a soldier. All humans find a comfort zone of hypocrisy—wear sneakers made in sweatshops, use phones built with precious minerals mined by children, charge electric cars with electricity generated by burning coal—and draw beyond it the line of unacceptable. And so, John decided to redraw his line, after the justified became unjustifiable.

When he came home from Iraq, he mulled it over for a few weeks, and finally informed Claire that his days with the navy would be over after five years of mandatory service. To his surprise, Claire had not looked as relieved as he'd imagined she would be. Instead, she took his hand and placed it on her stomach, and asked a simple question.

"That's great, but how will we pay for diapers and baby formula?"

The most humbling parts of life seemed to come whenever John thought he'd figured it out. But *figuring it out* was a continuous dance, one answer giving rise to the next question, forcing him to constantly adjust his footing. As he wrapped his wife in a tender hug, his elation upon hearing the happiest news of his life slowly gave way to trepidation.

It wasn't just about how they would provide for their child. John's body was now pumping chemicals that fueled the desire to protect, and love, and raise, and care for, and whatever else there was—because nothing else suddenly mattered as much, not even John's red line of hypocrisy. For when it comes to our children, our rigid principles become bendable to the contours of their well-being.

After much pondering, researching, and discussing, John and Claire had settled on him trying out to become a Navy SEAL. It was a role that utilized John's acquired skills; it stabilized days of deployment; the missions had clear and reasonably justifiable motives; and the pay was pretty darn good. With those boxes checked, John applied.

And here he was, months later, in Phase 2 of the Basic

Underwater Demolition / SEAL training, asking the same question. *What am I doing here?* What he *would* be doing in a matter of seconds was attempting the fifty-meter underwater swim, one of the hardest tests for SEAL candidates—he'd try to dive into the pool feet-first, perform a front flip near the bottom, swim underwater to the other end, touch it, swim back, and only then break above the surface.

The test was hard to begin with, but at twenty-five years old, John was practically an elder statesman among the other SEAL candidates lined up next to him. Many were a year or two removed from high school. Eager. Hungry. Fit as dolphins.

So when John saw the failure rate of the first batch of men, he became what the instructors told him never to be: tense. Just minutes ago, he had witnessed a nineteen-year-old from Colorado get mouth-to-mouth resuscitation from one of the instructors, after the kid had become unconscious at the bottom of the pool halfway through his swim back.

With that mental image superimposed over his vision, John heard the command and jumped in. He took a slight sideways angle to gain an extra yard, but he overshot it by so much that when he finished his front-flip, he was facing a wall. Precious seconds lost already, he adjusted his path and swam. Double arm pull, dolphin kick. Double arm pull, dolphin kick. It seemed almost easy at first.

But by the seventh stroke, John needed air. By the eleventh, he needed it badly.

As he touched the pool wall on the other side and turned back, his head felt like it was being crushed by the steel clamps of a vise. He heard muffled echoes. His ears were ringing. Shadows quivering, blue fading. Was he even swimming in the right direction? *What am I doing here?*

It was that question that snapped John back to coherence. In the subconsciousness of his fading mind, the answer suddenly seemed so obvious. Obvious, even though it violated the cardinal rule of SEAL training: do not, under any circumstances, start thinking about your loved ones during the mission, because a yearning heart clouds the mind.

But John's mind was clear as ever. He was swimming for the future he'd promised to build for his child. Swimming for all the late-night diaper changes and burping sessions. The giggles and cries and crawls. First steps, first words. The laughs, the outbursts, the teachable moments, the teenage angst, fights, make-ups, more teachable moments, college campus visits, the whole future to be unrolled like a runner rug: all of it depending on this moment of resolve.

Jenny would arrive into the world in a matter of days, and hell had no chance of standing in the way of John being there for his little baby girl.

44

After what must have been an hour of floating in the water tank, John had finally come to terms.

He had built up enough despair to accept that the only sliver of possibility to survive would be to attempt the unthinkable. The three massive water tanks stood in a single row, connected by a pipe at their bottom that was wide enough for him to swim through. John had seen *something* in the third water tank that he might be able to grab to pull himself onto the wretched ramp that ran above the water tanks. But to reach it, he would have to dive to the bottom of the first tank, swim through the pipe, come up to the surface of the second tank to get air, and do it all over again en route to the third tank.

He calmed his breathing. Centered himself. *Easy, John.* He closed his eyes. Jenny's smile flashed in front of him, as compelling as a command. John inhaled as much air as his lungs could take and dove under.

In the pitch black, he had no idea where the pipe was, which meant he would have to search for it at the bottom—and hope it wasn't blocked by anything. His ears were ringing from pressure by the time he felt the tank floor. Tracing the curving corner where the tank's bottom and wall came together, John's fingers finally felt nothing but water.

The pipe!

John torpedoed into it, fusing his arms ahead like a spear while kicking with his legs. The darkness seemed to wipe time away. His muscles succumbed to numbness, his strength dissipating rapidly. Chest crushed, ears screaming, his mouth bubbling air, he started fading in and out of consciousness. Now he wasn't swimming so much as he was flailing. The pipe was wide enough to fit two adults abreast, but to John it felt like an underwater coffin for one.

During the last burst of movement he had left in him, John suddenly felt nothing. He was certain he was dying, until he sensed he was floating upward. But maybe that's what dying underwater felt like? The pressure in his ears eased with creaks and crackles, and John's face finally broke the surface.

He inhaled air with wheezing breaths and exhaled it with water-filled coughs. Colored spots flickered in his vision.

When he regained enough of himself, John assessed his physical state and came to a cold realization. His lungs needed more time to recover, but the rest of his body barely had anything left to give. The wasteful hour of exertion he had spent floating in the first tank was likely going to be his doom.

Stop thinking and get going, you idiot!

With that admonishment, John took another gargantuan breath and descended underwater once more. This time the dive didn't feel as physically painful as it was emotionally draining. Almost two decades ago, John had passed Phase 2 of the Basic Underwater Demolition / SEAL training by conjuring images of his unborn daughter. Now, instead of dreaming of a happier future, John had to conjure his desire to repair the past. He was fighting to find and save the love of his life, and atone for all the things he should've said and done.

As John entered the pipe again, he knew that he easily could have gone the wrong way and now be swimming back toward the first tank. A crapshoot. That's what his life had been reduced to. Compressed into this one moment like his chest and head were compressed by the water. Delirium set in, and John couldn't tell if he was imagining the sensation of rising.

Once his face felt sweet air, John began scream-inhaling it.

It was nothing short of a miracle.

His ascent to the surface had come mostly with him floating up, his brain so oxygen deprived that most of his motor functions had stalled. John regained enough of them to splash to the wall of the tank. Almost as sweet as the air, his hands felt them, and he grabbed two of the whatever-the-heck-was-sticking-out-of-the-wall. The things in the third tank that he'd wanted to show to Nia.

Nia...

Now there was a cold-blooded foe John had not seen coming.

With each passing moment in the darkness, anger swelled inside him. How long had she been playing him? Probably from the very beginning. Waiting for the right moment. All her morbid jokes about John dying had actually been wishes upon a star. *You're a fool, John.* The quickest way to die was to underestimate someone, and John had woefully underestimated Nia Banks.

But she had underestimated him as well.

After regaining a semblance of normal breathing, John climbed up the rods sticking out of the tank wall, grabbed its edge, and pulled himself up. He hung there bent over for a good while, gathering his strength. He finally propped himself up to stand on the edge, then leaped and grabbed that damn ramp hanging above. More pulling, screaming, the last ounce of his strength leaving him with a trail of burning heat through his lats and biceps.

Still, John managed to climb onto the ramp. He passed out cold.

45

Moving through the hallway with his HK416 rifle. Night vision fading into gray. Stepping over dead bodies. *How many lives have you taken, John?* A child giggles behind the corner—but there's no one there when he turns. Just a long, empty hallway. Each step he takes, it stretches farther, like rubber. But then there is a door in front of him. Corrugated metal. Primitive lock. Shotgun blasts fire into it, and a wind from behind swings it open. All doors are wretched. But this...

A wall of boys. Screaming. A chorus of the world's shame and obscenity. There is no God because no righteous divinity would allow so many children to die. John's mother whispers, *Who are you to question the ways of our Lord?*

A soldier shouldn't question, only serve. Like ants marching. The ants *are* marching, crawling into the screaming mouths of the screaming children.

"Save us, John. Please! Why won't you save us?"

They don't let him answer. Black trails are branching across their faces, the ants swarming their heads. A thousand nasty little sounds of chewed flesh—

John woke up, lost in darkness. Until his fingertips recognized the coarse metal of the ramp.

Under the amber glow of dawn, John approached the RV with caution. Even from a distance, he saw the jagged cavity where the passenger side window had used to be. Of course Nia had broken in; she thought their only pair of RV keys would be floating in the tank alongside John's corpse. Pistol drawn, John scanned what he could of the inside of the RV before opening the door.

Shattered glass crunched under his feet as he entered the vehicle. He slowly made his way through it, reaching the bedroom in the back. Nia wasn't there, as he'd expected. But what else was missing? John strode to the very front and popped open the center console. All the cash was gone. No surprise there.

John swept the living area. Then the kitchenette. The bathroom. Closets. Bedroom. She had taken a laptop and all the phones and chargers. Oddly, none of her clothes were missing. But the black backpack was. Claire had bought it for Jenny before her freshman year at UVA. What a perfect touch to this clusterfuck—in order to find his wife, John was about to chase a fugitive carrying his daughter's backpack.

But first, it was time for breakfast and a fresh pair of clothes.

A small chunk of scrambled egg fell between East Canton and Paris, Ohio. John wiped it away with a paper napkin and resumed studying the map on page 76 of *The Great US Map Guide for RV Enthusiasts*. Ohio was his home state, and Akron was his hometown, but the neighboring Canton area was not a place he had spent a lot of time in during childhood.

What he knew: Nia had the cash, the electronics, the cunning, and a ten-hour head start.

What he suspected: she would gravitate toward places with strong cell signal and plenty of Wi-Fi options.

What he counted on: she was in no particular hurry because she believed John was dead.

Very much alive, John stepped outside the vehicle. The morning rays of sun washed over him with velvety heat. How many mornings had he taken for granted? He'd had plenty of brushes with death before, but the water plant was different for some reasons he couldn't quite yet distill, and many he understood all too well.

All other times John had come close to dying in the field were lightning-fast moments, where adrenaline and quick reactions didn't allow him to ponder the death itself. But in the darkness of that water tank, floating for at least an hour, John had the time and the elements to extrapolate his true feelings. Life without Jenny would always be cruel and painful. But life without Claire would not be worth living. That was the honest and ugly truth.

In a way, John felt liberated by accepting that truth, as though a boulder of denial had finally fallen off his shoulders.

He inhaled the morning air and performed a 360-degree scan, a scan he had made countless times on four different continents. A lonesome bus stop in the distance caught his attention. His eyes narrowed. The beginning of a grin teased his lips.

46

Running three minutes behind schedule, bus 122 pulled up at a nondescript station in the industrial section of Massillon, Ohio. John waited for passengers to disembark (no one did) before stepping into the bus with his most charming smile and a five-dollar bill.

"Hope cash is all right."

The bus driver looked John up and down, taking in the military uniform and rucksack over his shoulder.

"Don't even worry about it. Thank you for your service."

"I appreciate that, but I must insist," said John, holding the bill out until the driver lost the staring contest and took it.

After receiving his change, John settled into a seat in the back of the bus and checked his watch. Unless Nia had decided to walk or hitchhike in the middle of the night—highly unlikely—she had taken either the 6:05 a.m. or the 7:39 a.m. bus. This meant that she had, optimistically, a two-hour head start, or, at worst, was ahead by three hours and thirty-four minutes.

Still better than the ten hours John had initially surmised.

What really irked him was the fact that if Nia had taken the later bus, it meant that she had been at the bus stop while John had been inside the RV. He pulled out the RV map guide and flipped to page 79, going over the marks he'd made with a pencil. Lodging, food, attractions. It would've been nice to have a phone and pull this up in real time, considering the map was limited and five years old.

Stop wishing and work with what you have.

What he had was too much and not enough. There were too many options for Nia and not enough insight into her psyche for him to narrow them down. She had taken with her a box of crackers from the RV kitchenette, but John hadn't detected crumbs of any other food, nor had there been anything new in the trash. So she would have to eat soon, and she sure loved her breakfast. But where?

When the bus crossed the Tuscarawas River, the route that had been dominated by houses turned into a landscape of offices, hotels, apartment complexes, and a church. The bus soon entered what appeared to be the main downtown artery.

Nothing stood out until John saw an establishment by the name of Luna Cantina. The curb sign in front of it almost seemed too good to be true: *Serving delicious breakfast tacos daily.*

It wasn't just that Nia had continuously raved about John's breakfast tacos being the best food she'd ever eaten. If John knew anything about her by now, it was that with her dark humor, eating here would be apropos. *A tribute to the captain, may he rest in peace.*

John leaped from his seat and strode to the front of the bus.

"Can you please stop here? I need to get off."

"The bus station is just ahead," said the bus driver, his tone less friendly with John eagerly hovering over him.

Every yard of distance the bus put between the restaurant seemed like an entire mile to John. The driver finally squeaked the vehicle to a halt and opened the door, and John bolted out. His stride bordering on a jog, John had to force himself to calm down. He didn't even have a plan. If Nia was in there, he couldn't just extract her without drawing attention. All she had to do was scream for help. But she was also a wanted fugitive who would want to avoid the authorities like the plague.

By the time John reached the stretch of sidewalk ahead of Luna Cantina, he'd decided that he would peek in, and if he saw Nia, wait and follow her somewhere more private. He peered through the first window. The place was almost empty in the dead slot between breakfast and lunch. Only two patrons—young men sitting together in a booth, working on their laptops. Nia could be in the bathroom. John waited two minutes, but she didn't appear. He decided to go in.

As he swung the door open, the young lady cleaning the front counter seemed surprised. "Oh, hi. Welcome. Just so you know, we stopped serving breakfast. But our lunch menu should be available in about ten minutes." She turned to no one in particular in the back and yelled, "Ronny, you forgot to bring in the breakfast sign!"

I might be glad that you did, Ronny, thought John. Who would've thought a lazy employee could be a lifeline to John's dwindling hopes. He came up to the counter, offering his second charming smile of the morning.

"I just wanted a cup of coffee, if you don't mind. Largest size you have."

"Yeah, sure. Sugar or cream?"

"Neither, thank you."

After she sprayed out the last sediments from the coffee urn into John's cup, the young lady placed it on the counter with an apologetic expression.

"I won't charge you for it."

"Thank you, I appreciate that," said John. "Say, I was supposed to meet someone here earlier, but I got held up at the navy recruiting office. You wouldn't happen to remember a young lady being here earlier? Dark-brown skin, around your height, curly black hair down to here. She had a black backpack last time she and I spoke."

"Hmm, no, sorry. I don't think I can help you. Actually, Ronny was at the register this morning. Maybe he would know. *Ronny!*"

A scrawny, pale, pimple-faced male shuffled out of the kitchen, wearing a Luna Cantina polo that was a few sizes too big.

"Yeah, what's up?"

"Did you see a girl here earlier with curly hair and a black backpack?"

Ronny mused on it for a moment, then shook his head. But a sudden thought lit up inside him and he blurted out, "Oh wait, was she a fine Black girl?"

John had a distinct desire to shake Ronny until the stupid fell out of him. He briefly closed his eyes and centered himself.

"Yes, she would be Black," he said.

Ronny appeared to pick up on John's surly vibes, apprehensively pointing to a booth.

"Yeah, she was sitting right there, with her laptop out the whole time. Man, she ate like five breakfast tacos. I tried to get her number but..."

Ronny trailed off at the sight of whatever John's eyes were beaming.

"You know when she left?"

"Maybe an hour ago. Not even."

47

John's rising heartbeat was spiking into his eardrums. Nia had been here an hour ago. Maybe less. If he didn't catch up to her now, the odds of doing it later would become astronomically low. But where? She had to be headed to the main transit center, where she could take eight different buses en route to the whole wide world.

John was about to turn and run out of the restaurant, but a sixth sense flickered inside him. *Wait.* She hadn't taken any clothes from the RV. Of course she hadn't. That mismatched, ill-fitting garb John had bought. Ugly khakis. Uncomfortable sports bras. She would likely buy proper clothes first before leaving town.

"Thanks for your help, Ronny," said John and turned to the young lady. "Off topic, but what's the nearest clothing store?"

"We really only have one that's walking distance. Take a right around the corner, four blocks down, another right, and you'll see the sign for Helena's Closet on the left."

"Thank you for the tip, and the coffee," said John and marched out as calmly as possible.

Upon turning the corner around the building, he tossed the coffee cup into a trash can and ran.

Four blocks in, he was panting hard, the rucksack far heavier than he'd anticipated. He turned right and looked for Helena's Closet on the left. But it wasn't there. One block. Nothing. Two. Three. Still nothing. Had he taken a wrong turn? His trudging steps felt heavier with each second of being unable to find it. Lack of sleep was taking its toll. John was ready to turn around, but from the corner of his eye, he glimpsed a faded *H* from a distance. He moved closer, finally seeing all the faded letters:

Hele a's Clo et

Approaching carefully, John flanked the store wall and peered around the corner through a window. It was too bright outside and too dark inside to see well. He could make out a few rows of clothing racks. Maybe a handful of women in there. None of them were Nia Banks. John observed for a few more minutes, then finally entered.

From the moment he set foot in the store, he felt like a thorn sticking out. He was the only man inside the women's-only clothing store, clad in camo. A few curious eyes followed him as he moved through the first aisle, but they eventually resumed scanning the clothing racks.

"Anything I can help you with, sir?" said a saleswoman, rising up from behind a clothing rack. Her name tag displayed *Tiffany H.*

"No, thank you, Tiffany. Just browsing."

"Okay. Let me know if you change your mind." She winked. "I know it can be hard to know your lady's size, but we can figure it out."

John nodded with a smile and slid away as quickly as possible, scanning rows of clothing. A total of seven women, and no sign of Nia. This was a mistake. Of course she would leave town as quickly as possible, buy clothes at a large department store, probably in Canton. John checked his watch. She was likely on a bus to Canton at this very moment.

You've made a costly mistake. Now what?

He could run to the transit center. The thought of running a mile and a half with that rucksack drained him just standing there. Or he could first ask Tiffany if she'd seen Nia by any chance. *What chance, John? You had it and you blew it.* Even if Nia had been in this store, she still would have gone to the transit center. All he'd had to do was wait for her there. What a blunder. He closed his eyes and rubbed his face, dejection settling in, heavy as lead.

As he opened his eyes, the dressing room door swung open, ten yards ahead.

Walking out of it, holding an absurdly large pile of clothes, was Nia Banks.

48

John was too stunned to hide behind a clothing rack. Too tired. Too fed up. Too many things.

Nia didn't notice him until she was about five yards away, halting as though she'd run into a wall.

The look on her face. Widening eyes, slack mouth. Utter bewilderment. John savored it, like a delectable treat. It looked like her mind was going a hundred miles per hour. Her chest was rising and falling. Faster and faster.

But then she regained control. Like a computer that had calculated all the possible scenarios on a chess board.

"Impressive" was all that finally came out of her mouth.

"Just karma," said John, with as much sarcasm as his steady voice could muster. He enjoyed the conflicting emotions on Nia's face before his eyes settled on her stack of clothes. "Found anything you like?"

Silence. She was resetting into a superficially calm mode. Putting on a mask. *The easiest thing to hack is people,* Nia had said to him in Georgetown. John had been too naive to realize she was including him.

"Actually, yes. And they're running a fifty percent off sale."

She slid left, into an aisle. John mirrored her movement on the other side of the rack. "To be honest, though," she continued casually, "I mainly came here for bras and underwear. No offense to you and your Frankenstein couture approach."

"None taken."

Nia slid farther left. John mirrored her.

"What do you think of this shirt?" she said, lifting up a faded blue tank top.

"I think it will clash with my dead daughter's backpack."

That stopped Nia, her casual facade melting to reveal a no-nonsense look.

"If you want the backpack, I'll let you have it."

"Let me?"

"Look, Captain, let's not pretend you hold the upper hand here. All I have to do is scream *stalker* and things get very bad for you."

"I want them to get bad. So bad that the police show up and ask you to provide a statement and ID. I might grab popcorn to watch that unfold."

Nia slid left. John mirrored her.

"I don't like this," said Nia, placing a couple of hangers from her pile back onto a rack. "Again, you're pretending, Captain. We both know you wouldn't risk getting arrested. You'd be stuck thinking about Claire behind those bars. Where she is. What she's doing. What *they* are doing to *her*."

She's good, thought John. She knew the exact buttons to push. But John could see her game so clearly now. It was borderline childish. And two could play it.

"I came back from the dead, Nia. I see the world with new eyes." He edged closer to her. "You wouldn't believe what I'm willing to risk."

Nia slid farther left, and John followed.

She now stood at the end of the aisle. Another step to the left and she would be face to face with John, nothing between them except air that felt charged with static.

Nia was calculating again. That look on her face—John didn't like it.

She dropped her clothes and ran left, back, left again, zigzagging between the racks. John kept up with her, but slowed his stride upon seeing there was no way she could get to the exit door without him intercepting her. He quickly realized Nia had no intention of exiting. Not yet.

She caught up to Tiffany H. and spoke fast in a low voice. As John approached, Tiffany's expression grew more alarmed, her eyes darting between John and Nia.

"Sir, I'm going to have to ask you to please leave," she said as John arrived.

Okay, Nia. Let's play this out.

"Of course," said John. "If I could first get the backpack the young lady stole from me."

Tiffany quickly turned to Nia with an appropriate amount of shock.

"He's lying," said Nia. "That's my backpack."

"Oh, yeah?" smirked John. "Then why does it say Jennifer Mitcham on the tag inside the slip pocket?"

"Because that's my name, you creep."

"Sir, please leave," said Tiffany, her conviction swaying toward Nia again.

"With all due respect, you've heard her answer, and I am here to tell you that it was a trick question. The tag doesn't say Jennifer Mitcham at all."

Tiffany's face was sinking into confusion.

"In fact," continued John, "why don't she and I both write down exactly what the tag says, including the contact info, and hand our notes to you. Then you can verify who's telling the truth."

"Don't listen to this creep, he's just playing games. He's been following me all day."

"That's the first thing you've said that's true. I *have* been looking for my stolen backpack all day."

"You know what," said Tiffany. "Why don't I call the police and they can sort this out?"

Nia went still. Finally, with an acting job worthy of an Emmy, she said, "Fine."

"Fine," echoed John.

Tiffany went around the counter and picked up the landline receiver. Meanwhile, John had a staring contest with Nia. This is how a nuclear war would unfold. No winners. Mutual destruction. *Let's see who blinks first.*

"Yes, hi," said Tiffany into the phone. "My name is Tiffany and I'm calling from Helena's Closet. We have a situation here with two customers. One is accusing the other of stalking, and the other claims his backpack was stolen. I wanted to see if you could dispatch an officer to—"

It was the word *officer* that made Nia blink first and bolt toward the emergency exit.

49

Sprinting through the maze of the store's 50 percent off sale—shirts, jeans, blouses, dresses, bikinis—John finally reached the back exit door, blasting through it with abandon. Sun blaring into his eyes, he looked left. No sign of Nia. Right, he caught a glimpse of the black backpack disappearing around the building.

Run, John, Run!

He turned the corner and sprinted to the front of the building, scanning the perimeter. *There.* In the shadows across the street, Nia was running with impressive speed. John started after her, as a car horn blared—

The SUV stopped half an inch too late, its bumper lashing the side of John's thigh. He cried out, staggered, resumed his run, with someone yelling and asking what the hell was wrong with him.

If you only knew, answered John, limp-racing after Nia.

She was about fifty feet away. Fifty-five. Now sixty. *Are you really this slow?*

Of course he was, carrying at least forty pounds on his back.

He had to ditch the rucksack, but where? Nia was sixty-five yards away. *Shit.* John zoomed by an alley, skidded to a stop, raced back into it. He took off his rucksack and hurled it into a mound of trash bags next to a green dumpster. As good a solution as any. *Now run, goddamn it! Run!*

By the time he got back on the sidewalk, Nia was nowhere in sight. John ran in the direction he'd last seen her, the weight off his back feeling like a miracle. But ten yards farther, the adrenaline from the car hit finally wore off, and the bruise pulsed blade-sharp pain through his leg.

He staggered to the first intersection Nia could've turned at. To his right, the road became lined with houses. To his left, more commercial buildings.

John went left.

Running again. Grinding teeth between ragged breaths. Passing by a bank. Auto shop. Fast-food chain. More retail. So many alleys Nia could've easily slipped into. This was becoming a lost cause. *Think, John.* She wouldn't go anywhere with a lot of security cameras. So no banks, no gas stations. John ran, assessing the commercial landscape, panting hard. Losing hope.

Stop.

If he was this tired, she would have also had to catch her breath after a full-on sprint for over seven blocks. At an intersection, John performed his 360-degree scan. The stretch of buildings to the right looked prime for hiding. Family offices. A barbecue joint. A residential house here and there. Plenty of gaps to slide into.

John moved toward them.

He occasionally stopped between sidewalks and alleyways. *No. Not here,* his instincts told him. Now he was passing by houses. A German shepherd's vicious bark jolted him, as the dog charged at him from behind a chain-link fence. John suddenly registered: he had heard the same barking a few minutes ago. It had to have been Nia.

"Good boy," he said to the shepherd. The dog retorted by planting his front paws against the fence and booming a series of barks, saliva drooling from the corners of his mouth.

He *was* a good boy—but also a vicious fucker that put extra pep into John's step.

The pain in his thigh had subsided, but he'd experienced enough blunt-force trauma on the battlefield to know this doozy would sting for days. What stung him more was that Nia had to be so close, it was almost maddening. Where would she go from here? Nothing stood out for an entire block. Until John reached an intersection and his eyes traveled up the road on the right.

About forty yards away, a flock of Harley-Davidson motorcycles sat arrayed outside a single-story building. John approached it with equal parts eagerness and caution. He soon saw a neon beer sign flickering intermittently. *Yeah.* A biker bar. Light on security cameras. Possibly a few former convicts having an afternoon bourbon. Unlikely for anyone to call the cops from this place. *Birds of a feather flock together.*

John crept to the side of the building, but quickly realized the windows were tinted. No peering into this establishment. He had to go straight in and improvise.

John swung the door open and scanned the interior.

The room was L shaped around a bar. A row of pool tables lined the longer side of the L. Chairs and tables were arranged semi-neatly by the shorter side. At the end of the bar, past a row of hulking men wearing leather vests, sat Nia.

John exhaled a sigh-groan.

He walked in, eyes locked on Nia. She was holding a nearly empty glass of water. Could've been a vodka soda for all John knew. That would explain her relaxed posture. She had a calm expression, and there was even an empty chair next to her at the bar. It was perfect.

John ambled toward it, ready to take a seat. Have a little chat with Nia Banks.

As he pulled the chair out, the entire row of long-bearded, vest-wearing, tattoo-covered patrons stood up in eerie synchrony. John knew he had walked straight into a trap.

50

The smile on Nia's face widened as John's eyes narrowed.

He finally pried his gaze away from her, turned around, and faced the biker gang that had sealed him inside a semicircle of leather, tattoos, and ill intent.

He already had an idea of what this was. Nia had the tactical advantage of getting here before him. She'd spun a victim story akin to her performance at the clothing store, and the bearded men had formed opinions that would be as easy to change as it would be to get their tattoos removed.

"Gentlemen," saluted John. "Whatever story she told you, I can assure you it's a lie."

No one said anything at first, their expressions ranging from subtle smirks to malicious grins.

"Thank you for that assurance," said a stocky biker with shades. His beard was long enough for a member of the band ZZ Top. "I'm sure you'll tell us the truth."

"I'll do you one better," said John. "I'll prove it."

"We have ourselves a lawyer," said ZZ Top.

This elicited a few chuckles. John ignored them and went on.

"That backpack on the bar. It belonged to my daughter."

The bikers laughed at that.

"Are you going to rehearse your entire story from the women's clothing store?" said ZZ Top. "You want us to hand you a pen and piece of paper so you can write down what's on the bag tag?"

"Look, I know she already planted her seeds, but this woman is a world-class liar and con artist."

ZZ Top took a step forward. "A mouth can lie." He took another. "Bruises don't."

For a brief moment, John surmised ZZ Top was referring to the bruises he planned to inflict on John. But then John followed everyone else's gaze and turned toward Nia. She lifted her shirt to reveal a strip of bruise around her back and left side of the torso.

"Care to explain that?" said ZZ Top.

"I have no idea where that came from."

"No? So you're telling me you didn't tie her with a rope?"

John came close to laughing out loud. Of course. He had tugged at the rope to help her get up to the platform above the water tank.

"It's not what you think."

The laughs now grew louder among the bikers. John could feel them brimming with pent-up energy, ready to release it.

"No, of course not," said ZZ Top. "I just have one final question." He came inches from John's face. "Yes or no answer... Did you kidnap her while she was unconscious?"

John could see his warped reflection in ZZ Top's shades. The whole world felt twisted. Twisted as the spiral of questions and answers that only had one outcome. Twisted as Nia's cunning. And twisted as the cold hard truth: John was no better than her.

And he was about to hurt a lot of people.

His left eye twitched.

He blinked once, conjuring a prism of complete emotional detachment.

There were only objects, targets, distances, sounds…

With a predatory quality, John's senses sharpened. Slowed down time.

In three heartbeats—

ZZ Top six inches away.

Two men to his left, three on the right.

One bad knee, two stiff hips, three can fight.

A pool stick resting against the bar.

Two tall glasses and an unopened can of beer within reach.

A shotgun behind the bar, the bartender seven feet away from it.

—John calculated.

It was go time.

He drove his knee into ZZ Top's groin, then unleashed his forehead like a cobra into ZZ's face as he fell forward to cup his manhood. The crunch of broken shades mingled with the grind of shattered nose cartilage.

Spearing his arms sideways, John grabbed a can of beer with his right, a glass with his left; he threw the can into the eye socket of Fighter 1 and smashed the glass against the temple of Fighter 2.

Fighter 3 was already charging with a switchblade. John slid the pool stick handle into a bar groove, and Fighter 3 stabbed himself in the chest with the ferruled tip, emitting a horrid squeal.

John tossed the other glass into the face of Stiff Hips 1, propped his back against the bar, and kicked the lunging Bad Knee 1 and Stiff Hips 2 in their chests.

Landing on his feet, he pulled the pool stick to him by the narrow side, and swung it like a baseball bat at the bartender reaching for the shotgun.

The stick snapped in half against his face; he fell, and John rolled over the bar, grabbed the shotgun, and cocked it. He swayed the double barrel between anyone who still moved.

Men were groaning. Bleeding. Swearing. The biker that had run into the pool stick was wheezing morbidly. Probably a punctured lung. *It didn't have to come down to this, Nia.*

Nia...

John looked to his left. Of course she was already gone. It was as though she was leaving a trail of gasoline and John was the fire.

John came around the bar.

"Back up," he said to those who could still move. They did.

John crouched next to ZZ Top. He checked his pockets until he found and pulled out keys, which he jiggled in front of ZZ Top's face.

"Which one is yours?"

"Fuck you. You don't take another man's bike."

John placed two barrels of cold steel against ZZ Top's two bruised balls.

"Would you rather be a man without a bike or no man at all?"

ZZ Top snorted air and spit out blood.

"Suit yourself," said John, adjusting his finger around the trigger to pull—

"It's the red Fat Boy," said ZZ Top with the sadness of someone giving away their child.

John nodded. "Look for it within a ten-mile radius starting this evening. I'll do my best not to scratch it."

John stood up, walked sideways and backward, swaying the shotgun left and right, until his back felt the door.

"Anyone follows me outside and I'm putting a bullet into the nicest bike out there."

Stiff Hips 2 actually gasped, as though that threat was the most egregious thing that had transpired here.

On that note, John exited the building.

51

John tossed the shotgun into a bush and climbed on a gorgeous burgundy Harley-Davidson Fat Boy. He tucked away the side stand with his foot, clicked the run-stop switch with his right thumb. Instrument lights on, he pulled the clutch lever and made sure the gear was in neutral. He then pushed the starter button.

The motorcycle rumbled to life, and John drove that bad boy off the lot.

Wind in his hair and regret in his heart, John slowly came back out of combat mode. But his eyes scanned the streets for Nia as alertly as ever. How far was this going to go? How far was he willing to go? Until he killed a civilian? He had to intercept Nia here and now before this spiraled into tragedy.

He veered the motorcycle left, another left, riding down the street where Nia would have emerged if she'd escaped through the back exit of the bar. But she was nowhere to be found.

Houses and one-story offices streamed leisurely past John. He drove by the building behind the bar, expecting to catch a glimpse of the bikers huddled around their motorcycles, but no one was there. Not a soul was out on the streets or sidewalks. He flipped the left turn signal to do another loop around the three blocks, checked his side-view mirror— *Motherfu...*

Like a cat, Nia darted across the street behind him. John looked over his shoulder. She was already gone behind a building.

The honest-to-goodness thought that crossed John's mind was that Nia could've been a special ops soldier with that kind of speed and stealth. He planted his left foot into the asphalt, revved up the Harley-Davidson into a 180-degree spin, and raced toward the alley she'd entered.

He careened into it with an aggressive lean, just in time to spot Nia turn right two buildings over. He reached it in seconds. John screeched the bike into a hard right turn, finding Nia about thirty yards away. She glanced over her shoulder, then unfurled her stride into an all-out sprint.

Fat Boy roaring, Nia sprinting, John closed in.

She suddenly staggered, as though she'd seen something ahead.

John couldn't hear anything over Fat Boy's exhaust, but when the brown buildings ahead became awash in blue flashes, he skidded to a stop. Nia was fifteen feet away, backpedaling from the blue lights that projected over the brick facade, police sirens now swelling across the alley.

She stopped and looked at John, then back at the lights, then John, the panic on her face rising feverishly. John understood what she was calculating. Was she better off in prison or with him? Such nonsense.

"Get on the goddamn bike, Nia!"

Nia bit her lip, screamed a swear word, ran to Fat Boy, and climbed on behind John.

"Hold on tight and *do not* let go," said John. "You understand?"

He took Nia's tightening arms around his torso as a yes and

peeled off from the oncoming police car. Or cars. It depended on whether the call had come from Helena's Closet, or the bar, or both. Of course it had come to this. Nia, gasoline; him, fire.

In the side-view mirror, John glimpsed a police car turn into the alley, right as he turned onto the first street. Gears shifting, gas pumping, John raced onto a street two blocks over, veered left, rode through two more blocks, and took a right.

Blue flashes faded in the rearview mirrors, until nothing flashed at all. But now what? He had to retrieve the rucksack, otherwise it would be all for naught. John screeched into a hard right turn, then another, and Nia screamed.

"What are you doing? We're going back!"

"I have to get my rucksack."

Nia said nothing, but her arms tightened—in anger or fear or who knows what emotion at this point.

After riding on the outskirts of downtown, John entered a relatively secluded section of the town that led back to Helena's Closet. He passed by an alley before his eyes registered the pile of trash bags where he'd hurled the rucksack. He turned around, shifted the gear into neutral, and shut off the engine. The motorcycle glided into the alley silently, rolling to a stop ten yards from the green dumpster, and John climbed off.

"Come help me find it," he said to Nia. She exhaled with exasperation, slid off the motorcycle, and started rummaging through trash bags.

John ended up finding the rucksack and brushed the debris off it. He took off his camo jacket, shoved it into the bag, pulled out a blue T-shirt, and tossed it to Nia.

"Put this on."

"Why?"

"Because the police are looking for a woman in a white tank top and a guy in a camo jacket."

"I think they're primarily looking for a loud, stolen motorcycle," said Nia, slipping on John's T-shirt, which draped halfway down her thighs.

"Which is why we're leaving it here." John checked his watch. "C'mon, we can still make the two thirty-five bus around the corner."

Nia stared at him without moving.

John's eyes narrowed. "There's also a cop car around the corner I can drop you off at."

That got Nia moving. Her stare remained.

―――

At five past three o'clock, John and Nia exited the bus at the same station they'd started their respective journeys of the day. With a solid clench around her arm, John led Nia for a third of a mile across an abandoned plot, then an equally abandoned parking lot, finally escorting her into the RV.

Once inside the vehicle, John threw down the rucksack, while Nia threw herself on the RV sofa. She emitted a long, deflated sigh that in no uncertain terms conveyed her feelings about the misfortune of ever having met Captain John Fucking Mitcham.

52

Sitting on the RV sofa, Nia stared into the abyss of the dinette across the aisle.

"Okay," said John, making himself comfortable in the dinette seat directly across from her. "Time for a little chat." He knew that she knew there would be nothing *little* about it.

"Let's start from the beginning. When did you start planning your escape?"

Nia rolled her eyes. "You know when."

"When you woke up on that couch in Georgetown?"

"More like once the sleeping gas wore off and I regained my wits."

"Of course." John leaned back and relaxed a bit, his confirmed suspicions evaporating a few of his many burdens. "Why didn't you escape sooner?"

"When could I have? You had me on lockdown in the townhouse. I tried convincing you to let me get some fresh air."

Ah, so that was her game. John had almost fallen for that one.

"What about all the times I was away from the RV?"

"I honestly didn't think you'd make it back from that house, but there was no way I was going to walk from those woods in the middle of the night. And here last night..."

"Go ahead, say it."

"I had everything planned to escape while you were in the water plant, but I missed the last bus. But once you took me there and fell into the tank, it turned out it didn't matter."

"I see. So that was what all the karma talk was about."

"No, John, it wasn't. Are you really that obtuse?

"I guess I am. Please, Nia, enlighten me."

"Fuck your patronizing."

"Well, that wasn't very enlightening."

"You wanna be enlightened? What do you know about my life?"

"Other than what you told me?"

"No." Nia stood up, taking two strides forward to tower over John.

"What do *you* know about *my* life? Huh? Have you ever walked through the South Side of Chicago? You talk about your missions and war zones, but I've had bullets whiz through my window on a random Tuesday. I've seen more death in my own fucking neighborhood, in the good ol' U-S-of-A, than most soldiers see during deployments. And I'm supposed to feel bad for privileged little Jenny and her jarhead father looking for his grieving wife, who probably just wanted to get away from all the grief. Hell, she's the only one I can relate to. As bad as things were in my neighborhood, all I ever wanted was to be left alone. Oh, but no, Uncle Sam and Wall Street had to show up with an eviction notice, like some fucking ethnic cleansing. I had the audacity to fight back, and now *I'm* the criminal here. *I'm* the problem with this world. And my only atonement is to do their bidding, and now your bidding, like a fucking slave. You don't give a shit about me or my freedom. All you care about is your own agenda, what happens to you and your family, and you don't see anything wrong with using me, a civilian, to chase Russian mercenaries who torture people to the point of suicide by pitchfork. What a model citizen you are, John. You're more full of shit than an outhouse. Are you enlightened now, Captain?"

Nia finally broke off.

John remained silent and still.

There was a subtle ringing in his ear, though from what exactly, he didn't know. What he did know was that he hadn't ever been stunned quite like this. In all his years of life, military or otherwise, he had never gotten as good of a verbal ass-kicking as the one Nia had just delivered.

It would take a long time for John to extrapolate all that she'd said, truly take it to heart, and accept it. But he immediately knew that everything she'd said was so true, he almost wished he'd written it down in case he ever needed a reminder of just how full of shit he was. The reality he had convinced himself of. The behavior he had normalized.

Good job, Nia Banks.

John exhaled with a sense of relief, resetting into a clarity paved by Nia's lambasting. He stood up, walked over to his rucksack, and pulled a large rod coiled in insulated wire. It was so heavy that it rattled the dinette table when he laid it down.

"What the hell is that?" said Nia.

"It's what I wanted to show you before you left me to die."

53

The rod was roughly two feet long, about five inches in diameter, and the strangest thing John had ever seen. Coil wrapped with what looked like a thick, gray, thermoset-insulated wire, the rod ended in a small metal disc.

"There are dozens of these sticking out from inside the third water tank wall," said John. "At first I didn't think much of them, figured they were components for water treatment." He tapped the end of the rod. "But look at the tip. It's the same disc as the electrodes we found on the head mesh of that chair."

Nia studied the rod carefully, interested despite herself.

"Why would a conductor as sensitive as an electrode be coiled inside amplifying wire?"

"That's what I thought at first, but look, I made a slit through the whole wire," John said, pointing to the incision. "There *is* no wire inside. The whole coil wrapped around the rod is rubber or plastic designed to reduce electrical currents, not amplify them. It makes sense if you look at the other end. I had to rip the rod off the wall, so the end is all jagged, but notice the wire outlet here?"

Nia brushed her fingertips across the thin wire sticking out of the rod, at the end opposite the electrode. She continued running them across the coil. "It's not plastic or rubber. It's silicone. It can conduct an electrical current and insulate from it. This was designed to control electrical signals at an extremely precise level."

"Exactly. Probably performing the same function as the electrodes in that chair's helmet. And look," said John as he peeled back part of the silicone coil at the base. "You have to get real close to read it."

Nia brought her eyes a couple of inches from the rod. She read aloud, "Dividius Technologies LLC."

She stepped back, shaking her head.

John said, "I don't know why LIS is backing this technology. But maybe it will help you on your journey to get back at them."

"My journey?"

"Yes, Nia. Our paths diverge here. I was ready to show you this rod at the clothing store, or somewhere more private. All I was going to ask in exchange was for you to give me the cell phones and laptops, and show me how to locate the Grail once its binary signature is detected. I thought it was a fair deal. I give you your freedom and a breadcrumb to LIS, and you give me a way to find my wife."

Some unnamed emotion flickered across Nia's face. Was it anger? No. It looked more nuanced to John, as though different feelings were colliding, the conflict playing out on her face.

"I don't believe you," she said finally. "Why would you let me go before you can verify you found the Grail?"

John sighed. "You left me for dead, Nia. And escaped. You'll do it again the moment you have the chance. I can't operate this mission while looking over my shoulder the whole time. The distraction would likely get us both killed. You may not care about me dying, but despite what you've said about me, I do care about your safety. I've already put you in too much danger, and it ends right here. Just show me how to track the Grail and we can go our separate ways. Heck, you can have Jenny's backpack, I don't care. We can end this amicably."

Nia was now palpably shaken. John had never seen her so rattled before. He couldn't tell if it was an acting job or genuine emotion bursting through her facade.

"I can't accept that deal."

John rubbed his temples. "Why not?"

Nia started backing away in a corner.

"Nia, what's going on? Why can't you just show me the Grail's signature tracker?"

In a voice as small as a mouse's, Nia said, "Because I never uploaded it to the cloud."

A tremor ran through John. It felt as though the ground shook beneath his feet.

"That can't be..."

He suddenly felt lightheaded. He plopped down on the sofa. Slumped.

"Why, Nia? Why would you not upload the tracker?"

Nia slowly emerged from the corner shadows. "I'm sorry. I didn't have enough time. It's not as easy as you think. We had to evacuate that townhouse and plus, I figured..."

"You figured I was going to die anyway. Of course." John chuckled ruefully.

"Captain, I'm sorry, I really am."

John couldn't take his eyes off Jenny's backpack.

"So this whole time, the Quantum Grail could've fired off its binary signature and we would've missed it. We could've found Claire by now if..."

"We don't know if we've missed it, all right? But I will stay here for as long as I need to and upload it to the cloud and show you how to use the tracker. I swear to you."

Her voice oscillated in John's head as though someone was

turning the volume up and down. Heavy nausea churned his stomach. He started seeing double.

"I have to lie down. Just go, Nia. Take the backpack. Take whatever you want and just go."

John staggered to the bedroom and fell face first on the mattress.

54

John woke from the nightmare of screaming children.

Shafts of sunlight filtered through the blinds, casting a zebra pattern over the pillow next to his face. He propped himself up. It felt like he'd slept for days. Or at least made up for all the recent nights when he hadn't slept nearly enough. He climbed out of the bed and peered through the blinds. It was morning. He checked his watch: 09:17 a.m.

He'd slept for over twelve hours.

Nia...

John cautiously moved through the RV, scanning and sweeping. Jenny's backpack was gone. The cell phones. The laptops. Cash. All of it was gone, again. Of course. What else had he expected? An unceremonious end to his and Nia's brief, turbulent time together. He wasn't even angry about it. He had told her to take whatever, and that was exactly what she had taken.

He had to count the few blessings he had left. The most immediate was the fact that the police hadn't shown up here by now. But he had to move quickly. He strode to the closet, took out a roll of packaging tape, and promptly got to work.

Within five minutes, the passenger side window that Nia had

shattered with a rock was sealed with a clear film. *Time to get the hell out of here.*

John turned on the engine, shifted the gear into drive, spun the RV around 180 degrees, and—

Slammed on the brakes.

It had to be a mirage.

Because what else could explain that standing in front of the vehicle was none other than Nia Are-You-Kidding-Me-Right-Now Banks?

———

Nia entered the RV with a mix of confusion and annoyance.

"Going somewhere, Captain?"

"Forgot something, Nia?"

"Oh, I get it. You think I ran off. I guess I can't blame you, given my track record. Well, anyway, the cell signal here was terrible, so I had to take the bus closer to town and borrow Wi-Fi. Don't worry, I was in full stealth mode. The good news is that we're all set. It took me the whole night, but the tracker has been uploaded to the cloud." She took out a phone from the backpack and jiggled it. "You hear this bad boy ring, we have a direct hit. The IP address will be triangulated to a physical location down to about a mile radius. I'm assuming that should be enough for you..."

Nia trailed off and tossed the phone into a cup holder.

"What's the matter, Captain? What's that look for? I said I was sorry. We both did some stuff, and I'm just trying to make it right."

The truth was that John was mainly silent because he couldn't believe his sudden reversal of fortune. A minute ago, he'd been down to practically nothing, and now he had the device that gave him the best chance of finding Claire.

"Thank you, Nia. I'm grateful. And quite frankly, stunned." He scanned the wide-open parking lot. "We have to leave immediately. When the FBI gets a whiff of the police report from yesterday and pairs it with footage of us that has no doubt been captured by a camera somewhere, this place will be swarming with agents, and not just the FBI."

"All right, then step on it, Captain."

John nodded and started driving across the lot.

"We need to put ourselves at least a hundred miles from here, but once we're far enough, I'll drop you off at whichever bus or train station is convenient."

"That won't be necessary."

"Not sure I follow."

"I'm coming with you, Captain. All the way."

John screeched the RV to a halt.

He centered himself, digging for the right words.

"Listen to me, Nia. The irony is not lost on me that I'm now telling you to leave me after all that has transpired, but you and I both know that it's the right thing to do. I've thought a lot about what you said yesterday, and you're right. I'm a hypocrite who has been putting you in harm's way. It all ends a hundred miles from here. Do you understand?"

Nia took a few seconds to respond, but it was evident to John she had already made up her mind about what she would say long before this conversation.

"Well, Captain, I've done some soul searching myself last night. So let's just lay all the cards on the table. The truth is, I have been lost for a long time. Even when I was free and running from the law, I didn't know where I was going. I'm unsure about so many things. I honestly don't know what I want out of life. But I am positive, beyond the shadow of a doubt, that I want my vengeance when it comes to LIS. And don't give me some BS about how vengeance poisons the soul. You of all people had your share of it." Nia paused. "Besides, the idea that these people will get their hands on a cyberweapon that can hack indiscriminately and perform god-knows-what simulations should be as frightening to you as it is to me. "

John took it all in. It was strange to hear her voice when she was truly honest, and vulnerable. And smart. John *was* going to give her a quick lecture on the futility of vengeance. More importantly, he was going to tell her that being unsure of your path in life doesn't justify a perilous detour to hurt those who have hurt you. But there were no lectures or words that would move Nia's youthful resolve. John had lost enough arguments to Jenny to learn that much.

So instead, he decided to borrow a page from Nia's playbook. He would pretend to agree with her, take his time, and when the moment was opportune, he would leave Nia somewhere safe and sound—leave her for good.

"All right, Nia. Have it your way."

Nia smiled and turned on the radio.

Beyoncé's "Single Ladies" was just getting started, and her smile widened.

"All riiight. We got the band back together."

She turned up the volume, and John drove the band off the parking lot.

55

At a rest stop a hundred miles west of the water plant, John served Nia her favorite meal—breakfast tacos. He did so even though it was afternoon.

When Nia had informed him that the tacos at Luna Cantina in Massillon couldn't hold a candle to John's "tortilla masterpiece," he pulled over at a farmer's market off Highway 30 and acquired the necessary ingredients. There had even been freshly squeezed orange juice at one of the stands, which Nia now used to wash down the rather large bite of her first taco.

"So, Captain..." she said after swallowing. "Just out of curiosity, where were you planning to go without me?"

John wiped his hands and mouth after a couple of bites. He pulled out a piece of paper from his left jeans pocket and smoothed it over the table for Nia to see what he'd written:

57.57797, 34.87536

"What is this?" she said with a frown.

"Jason repeated these numbers every time I asked him if he knew where the Russians were reassembling the Grail. He would say 'config location' and rattle out the numbers. If interpreted as latitude and longitude, they designate an area that's about a five-hour drive northwest from Moscow. I haven't had a cell phone or computer to look at satellite photos to see what's there."

Nia finished her taco like an anaconda finishes off its prey. She then brought a laptop to the dinette table. "Might as well look it up now." After a few clicks on the touchpad and lightning-fast keystrokes, she turned the screen toward John. "Nothing but woods and farmland."

John roamed around the satellite map via the touchpad.

"There are industrial buildings nearby," he said. "It could be underground. The satellite images could also be outdated. Or they could've built this structure in the last six months, after they stole the Grail parts."

"I haven't heard that many *could*s since I read *The Little Engine That Could*," said Nia. "It could be all those things, or it could be the most logical explanation, which is that Jason was dredging up who knows what gibberish in his state of mind. I mean, just ask yourself, why would the Russians even disclose to him where they rebuilt the Grail?"

John slid away the laptop with a sigh.

"Maybe they got cocky. Overconfident. Maybe Jason overheard them speaking..." John ended his speculation there, each possibility sounding less plausible than the prior. "Look, I didn't say I had a good plan. It was simply my last resort. I'm all ears if you have a better idea."

Nia turned the laptop back toward her. Thinking. Tapping a key every so often.

"What question do we need to answer?" she said.

"What do you mean?"

"I mean, what are we trying to figure out?"

"Where the Grail is, because that is almost certainly where Claire and the operators are."

Nia rolled her eyes, flashing Jenny in front of John. "Okay,

Dad, that's the objective. But what set of questions and answers will lead us to it?"

"Did you just call me Dad?"

Nia recoiled with a frown. *"What?"*

John adjusted upright in his seat, realizing he'd imagined Nia calling him Dad. *Get it together, John.* "Nothing, never mind. Go on."

"Oh-kaay," said Nia, setting aside her befuddled look. "Again, *Captain*, what questions will lead us to finding the Grail? Think smaller questions, building up to the big one."

"All right. Where is Yuri Volkov?"

"Still too broad. It has to be more along the lines of, what does Yuri want? The answer to that will help lead us to him."

"I see where you're going with this. But I've played this out a hundred times in my head. It all becomes another 'could' game. He could be trying to get back at his superiors. Maybe he's trying to atone. Maybe he just went rogue and is roaming around like a wild dog for no reason. And how does LIS play into any of these scenarios? Are they fronting the money to the Russians? Is Yuri simply using their technology? Or is he trying to track persons of interest at LIS by tracking Dividius Technologies? See what I mean? I could go on forever."

Nia slunk down into the dinette seat, as though pulled by the gravity of her racing thoughts. She sat there in silence for over a minute before speaking. "There is one question we definitely need the answer to." She stood up again, strode to the closet, and brought back the coiled rod, placing it on the table. "What does this thing do? Because then we'll know what the chair does. And we'll understand why Yuri used it and why he went to that water treatment plant."

"That sounds all good and well, but I thought you said Dividius Technologies is a black box."

Nia's mischievous grin made an appearance.

"When I researched them years ago, they were able to hide their digital and legal footprint. But now I have a physical object, and tracking where this was manufactured is a lot more doable. Thank you for the tacos." She tapped the rod. "And the breadcrumb."

56

The day had come to an end, but there seemed to be no end to Nia's resolve. If she had stood up even once from that dinette table teeming with screens, John had not noticed—and he noticed most things. After parking the RV off a secluded road in Salamonie River State Forest, he shut off the engine and walked over to her.

"How about a break?"

His answer came in the form of keystrokes and nothing else.

John understood being in the zone and all, but a rested mind was a more effective mind. He walked over to the kitchenette cabinets, took out a bowl, and poured Froot Loops into it. The sound of corn cereal clanking against the bowl finally got Nia's attention.

"Oh," she said, eyeing the bowl.

John smiled and set it on the table along with a carton of almond milk.

"Take a break. Rome wasn't built in a day."

"No," said Nia, pouring the milk over the cereal. "But a lot of it sure burned in a day. And I'm about to make a bonfire out of these laptops."

"Or, alternatively, shut it down for the night and pick it back up tomorrow."

Nia only then seemed to notice it was night, gazing through the window.

"Where are we anyway?"

"Indiana."

"Pretty far from eastern Ohio."

Not far enough, thought John, but kept it to himself. Now was not the time to make Nia worry about the army of federal agents likely closing in on them by the hour. *Better to keep the conversation steered toward the task at hand.*

"What have you got so far?"

"Nothing. I hacked just about every major electrode manufacturer. I've pored over every patent submitted in the past fifteen years that's even remotely related to an electrode. Absolutely nothing fits this."

John leaned back in the dinette seat, his eyes studying that damn rod for the umpteenth time. The electrode at the tip. The same as the electrodes he'd found in that chair's helmet.

"Do you remember asking me at the barn whether I was sure that chair took EEG scans?"

"I will never forget anything about that barn, I assure you."

"Right, well, I wasn't sure then and I'm not sure now. So to borrow your thought process, maybe we are asking the wrong question. What if it's not an electrode at all?"

"What else would it be?"

"I don't know. But thinking outside the box, if this thing doesn't measure brain activity, what else could it do?"

"I guess it could do the opposite. As in send signals into the brain."

An idea began to form inside John's head, so unrefined it was more of a raw feeling.

"Wait a minute," he said. "All those boxes of brain images we saw. CT scans, MRIs..." He noticed a glimmer in Nia's eyes that suggested she might have her own ideas gestating. "What if those were taken—"

"*After* the chair signals were sent into the brain," finished Nia.

"Exactly. To assess the state of the brain afterward."

"That would explain the silicone coil around the rod," she said. "You would need tremendous control to send an electrical signal to the brain. But why the water tank?"

"Let's focus on one question at a time."

"Okay. The number of patents on devices that send electrical signals to the brain would have to be far smaller than what I've been digging through. Let me grind a little more and I'll wrap up for the night."

John appreciated her plans to call it quits, though he knew she would not follow through. He put the Froot Loops away before Nia could add more sugar to her bloodstream.

———

John stirred to life and sat upright on the sofa. He checked his watch: 3:14 a.m.

Nia was asleep in the dinette, her face buried into her folded arms on the table. She had likely put in thirteen straight hours over that table, save the occasional bathroom break, and John felt a sense of guilt.

With ingrained fatherly instincts, he walked over and picked her up. She mumbled a few words but remained asleep. John carried her to the bed and tucked her in. On his way out of the bedroom, he glanced behind him and spotted a subtle grin lining Nia's lips.

Was she awake and smiled that he'd tucked her in? Jenny used to do that. It was the one childhood habit that had never left her, even during her rebellious teenage years. When had been the last time someone tucked Nia into bed? She'd lost her mother at age twelve. Spent her teenage years with a senile aunt. She'd never mentioned her father, and John surmised he'd probably left or died when she had been very young. Perhaps before she had even been born.

What a fighter Nia Banks was, scratching and crawling against all odds.

Standing at the doorway, watching her sleep, John became struck with palpable fear that he wouldn't be able to protect her. Just like he had failed to protect Jenny and Claire.

His greatest failures echoed within him like they were destined to be repeated.

57

John had finished scrambling the eggs by the time Nia came out of the bathroom, showered and appearing rejuvenated.

"What's for breakfast, Captain?"

"French omelet and toast."

"What's a french omelet?"

"Same as any other French food. Loaded with butter."

"Yumm..."

"If I didn't know any better, I'd think this whole 'get back at LIS' initiative is just an excuse to use me for my cooking."

"Busted," said Nia, breaking off a piece of toast. "I guess I won't disclose what I discovered last night while you were snoring on the couch."

John dropped the spatula into the pan.

"Oh, no. Feed me first, Captain. That's the deal around here."

John smiled and put extra effort into what turned out to be the best french omelet he'd ever made. Or certainly the butteriest.

Nia mostly refused to chew, closing her eyes and letting the velvety layers of eggs, cheese, and butter melt in her mouth. Once she finished her omelet, she unfolded one of the laptops

John had set aside to make room to eat. After a few keystrokes, she motioned for John to sit next to her.

"I didn't even have to scour the patent databases. Front-page article of the November 2015 issue of *The American Journal of Neurology*." Nia pointed to a picture. "Look familiar?"

John was looking at a man in a lab coat posing for a picture. In his hands, held the way one might show off a freshly baked baguette, was a coiled rod with an electrode at the end.

John read aloud the title of the article: "Renowned neuroscientist Dr. Henry Langston aims to modernize DBS."

John felt heat rising inside him.

"It stands for deep brain stimulation," said Nia. "It's a minimally invasive surgery to treat neurological disorders, primarily Parkinson's."

"I know," said John, an inadvertent sigh escaping.

Nia shot him a curious look. Whatever she saw on his face made her go quiet. She intently studied John. He could practically see her figuring it out.

"How long, Captain?"

John looked out the window, though he wasn't quite sure why.

"The first time I noticed my right hand shaking was ten months ago. I thought it was related to my stress and lack of sleep after Jenny passed away. When it didn't go away, I saw a neurologist. The diagnosis was immediate."

Nia said nothing for a while. She placed a hand over John's.

"I'm really sorry, Captain."

They sat in silence, until a frown appeared on Nia's face.

"You got diagnosed with Parkinson's and your wife still asked for separation?"

"She doesn't know."

As Nia's face fell, John distinctly felt he shouldn't be encumbering her with his misfortunes. He also hated people's pity more than he cared to admit, which was why it was time to steer this conversation to a more productive place.

"Okay, enough of feeling sorry for me. Tell me how this Dr. Henry Langston was able to modernize DBS. I know what the procedure does, but I couldn't tell you how it's done." He produced the best smile he could muster. "Maybe his invention will save the ol' captain here."

Nia managed a faint smile and collected herself.

"DBS has been around for a while. The FDA approved it back in the eighties. But it requires a neurosurgeon to implant a small wire, often multiple wires, into a specific part of the brain. A few days later, they install a neurostimulator—which is basically a brain battery pack just below the patient's collarbone—and attach it to the wires. Then they send electrical impulses."

"Wires and electrical impulses inside the brain? I'm no doctor, but that sounds…"

"Bizarre? Yeah. From what I've read about it, they don't even fully understand why it's effective, only that it changes brain activity. But the risks from it are pretty serious. It's not just your standard surgery complications like infection and hemorrhaging. Side effects include depression, cognitive dysfunction, even hallucinations."

"That might explain why Jason—" John didn't bother finishing the sentence. "Okay, so Dr. Langston built a better mousetrap for treating Parkinson's. Why would Yuri be interested in this?"

"I don't know," said Nia, "but look." She clicked to the next page of the article. "Langston's procedure involves submerging a patient in a water tank filled with a dielectric liquid compound that insulates from even the slightest electromagnetic interference. The patient's head has to be placed at a specific position relative to the silicone-coiled electrodes, like the one you found. Once the patient is in position, Langston would send electrical impulses targeted at the brain, but the whole tank is basically operating on the principles of cellular biology."

"So you're saying that the water tank I took this rod from was once filled with this insulating liquid compound?"

"It had to be. The whole tank was likely converted into what you see here in the picture. A container that basically mimics the way our cells use ion fluxes to communicate electrically, which allows for pinpoint targeting of the brain without any need for inserting wires. Except the water treatment plant tanks are much bigger, which probably allowed them to fit multiple test subjects at the same time."

"So what's the chair then?"

"If I had to guess, probably a newer version of this. The tank method might be noninvasive, but it's also not really practical to submerge patients in dielectric liquid. Not to mention that the liquid apparently becomes adulterated after a few patients and needs to be replaced. This would explain why they opted for a treatment plant where the tanks could be flushed out with water and kept clean. But the chair seems like the only practical application of the technology."

"Is the chair being used by any hospitals?"

"No, and that's where it gets interesting. Langston's whole project really went nowhere. There wasn't enough interest from the medical community, so the ROI just wasn't there. Once his funding ran out, he moved on to other research at University of Texas at Austin. But a couple of years later, he suddenly resigned from UT, even though he was a tenured professor of over twenty years. Guess where his name popped up?"

"Dividius Technologies?"

"Good job, Captain. The only record of him being there was a mandatory SEC filing Dividius made back in 2017. They gave him a board seat. I looked at the same filing a year later, and he wasn't there. Now he's back at UT, but only as an adjunct professor, teaching part time. But something clearly went down between him and Dividius Technologies."

John carefully considered. "He either quit or was forced out. Either way, it had to be serious if he left after giving up twenty years of tenure at UT."

"So..." said Nia with the beginnings of a grin. "Road trip to Austin?"

"That's at least a seventeen-hour drive. We have to confirm he's there now, given it's summer break. I'm assuming you have his address and landline number?"

"Even you could have googled that one, but yes. You want me to make the call?"

John studied Nia. Her little mischievous grin. How many times had she made calls in this vein to get what she wanted?

"You're the pro here."

Nia grinned even wider and selected one of the cell phones. After she punched the number in and pressed the speaker button, John heard ringing.

"Hello?" came a man's voice on the other end of the line.

"Hi," said Nia. "May I please speak with Mr. Henry Langston?"

"This is him. Whom am I speaking with?"

"This is Alisha Wilson with America's Best Home Warranty. I was wondering if I could have a moment of your time to discuss—"

"No, thank you. Please take me off your calling list."

The call ended there, and Nia slid the phone away. They shared a few seconds of silence before Nia proclaimed, "We're going to Austin."

"We're going to Austin," seconded John.

58

At a dubious RV park in eastern Arkansas, John handed the attendant forty dollars. In exchange he received a parking space with a 50-amp power outlet and a water connection. More important was what he didn't get—a request to show his ID.

John promptly drove the RV to the designated spot and parked. He exited the vehicle and hooked in power and water. As he took a moment to catch his breath, his gaze floated up into the starlit night. Once there, it refused to float back down. It almost seemed as though the crickets were chirping in tune with the twinkles in the sky, a joyous ode to the rhythm of the night.

At first he didn't understand the source of sadness that was brewing inside him. But eventually it dawned on him that the last time he'd seen stars like this was the last time he had camped with Jenny.

"Beautiful night," said Nia.

John only then noticed her standing next to him, her big brown eyes soaking up the universe. He said, "I know what will make it even better."

When the marshmallow was toasted to golden-brown perfection, John pulled the roasting stick away from the hot coals. Nia already had her hand out, holding a graham cracker square with a slightly smaller square of Hershey's chocolate on top. John garnished it with the melted marshmallow.

"Okay, now place the other graham cracker on top and press it gently while I pull out the stick."

Nia did as instructed, and soon she was left with a perfectly made s'more. The first one of her life, she'd told him. John finally grasped that it wasn't just her innocence she had lost when her mother died and she turned to hacking to survive. She had also lost the little fundamental experiences that made up typical childhoods. She had already seen more of the world than most people did in a lifetime, yet a marshmallow and chocolate between two crackers was a novelty to her.

"Just eat it like this?" she said.

"Like a tiny sandwich. But be careful, the marshmallow is hot."

Nia brought it to her lips and took the first bite of her first ever s'more. Her bliss was immediate and palpable, stirring a wave of emotions inside John. Watching the joy play across her face, he became convinced these little moments—fleeting as the flickers in the night—had to be the essence of life. If not this, then what else?

John soaked in the moment with fervor he couldn't quite understand. Was he trying to make up for all the moments with Jenny and Claire he'd never fully appreciated? Had he ever truly lived in the moment? Does anyone? We worry about the future. We regret the past. And all the while the present slips away from us, like water through our fingers.

John fought back the tears, the sum of his life reduced to the elemental: worry and regret. This moment was no different. Coalescing inside him was worry for Nia's safety. Her future. To balance the scale of his conscience, John piled on his regret. The regret that tomorrow he would make good on the promise he'd made to himself. Tomorrow, after getting the information he needed from Henry Langston, John would leave Nia in Austin, Texas.

He would never see her again.

59

Downtown Austin shimmered in the evening twilight.

John made sure to obey the speed limit on I-35 South, but his eyes kept darting toward the streaming buildings. It had been fifteen years since his last visit, and the transformation was stark. If the goal was to still "Keep Austin Weird," the towers sprouting into the sky sure made it seem like the prevailing mantra had become "Keep Austin Employed."

John had no qualms about the inevitability of progress, but he had rising unease about the purpose of Dividius Technologies LLC. Which office in this concrete jungle had once housed Dr. Henry Langston, and what had transpired to make him leave? John and Nia were only minutes away from finding out.

"You seem distracted," said Nia.

"It's just different than I remember it."

"You've been here before?"

"I used to visit often back in the day."

"Huh. Wouldn't have guessed it by how long you studied the city map last night."

John tensed up. Was Nia onto him? She had seen him study maps of previous places they'd been to. But unlike before, John's meticulous assessment of Austin's topography, road networks, and train schedules had been performed not just in case he had to evade authorities, but in case Nia tried following him after he left her behind.

"I've assessed all locations of this mission and created target packages," said John calmly. "And will continue to do so," he added, and thought, *Just not with you.*

Nia held his gaze for a moment.

"Target packages?" She cracked a smile. "You and your Navy SEAL lingo. I have to admit, you're as scrupulous as I am when it comes to hacking."

I'm also starting to become as devious as you, John mused, but he shared an honest truth.

"Being scrupulous saved my ass many a time."

"I hear that," said Nia, nodding. "So, what brought you here back in the day?"

"Claire's mother remarried to a retired corporal who had a house in the Tarrytown neighborhood. Claire and I would take Jenny every summer when she was little."

"Sounds nice."

"It was ninety degrees most days, and I was forced to bond with my stepfather-in-law by playing golf."

Nia laughed. "No wonder you stopped coming."

"We stopped after he died of a heart attack swinging a nine iron."

"Oh... sorry."

"It's all right. At least he died doing what he loved."

"Now there's a silver lining." Nia sighed, taking in the downtown skyscrapers. "Well, how about you make more pleasant memories of Austin. Maybe we hit up a good barbecue joint after we talk to Langston?"

John realized now that most of his unease had more to do with leaving Nia than learning unsavory information about

Dividius Technologies. Despite his attempts to play it cool, he knew he was a bad liar in situations like this. The best he could muster was, "We'll see if we have the time."

He kept his conscience relatively clear by reminding himself that this was the right thing to do. He would leave Nia with enough cash (not that she really needed it). She would be in a town with plenty of transportation options. The Mexican border was less than a four-hour drive. Enough advantages for Nia to be sipping piña coladas on a beach by this time tomorrow.

―――

At 8:37 p.m., John pulled into a quiet subdivision in West Lake Hills, the affluent city embedded within the borders of Austin. Large lots. Large houses. Even the guest houses seemed bigger than the one-story ranch John's former stepfather-in-law had once owned. There was nothing *weird* about this part of Austin. It was just another enclave for the wealthy, easily found in any other major city.

"He's on the next street," John said to Nia. "I'm going to drive past just to assess."

"Aye-aye, Captain."

John took a right and eased the RV into a ten-mile-per-hour glide.

"It's that one," said Nia, pointing to the fourth house on the right.

John slowed down, scanning the entire property. Dr. Henry Langston sure seemed to have done well for himself. Even by the bougie standards of West Lake Hills, his two-story brick house was a sight to behold.

"I see lights on the inside," John observed. "I'll do a loop around to make sure the perimeter is clear, and then we're going in."

"Roger that, Captain."

John cracked a smile, finding Nia's playfulness particularly endearing on their last day together. Once his lap around the neighborhood ensured the coast was clear, he edged the RV next to Langston's oversize lot, parked, and shut off the engine.

"Let me begin the conversation. But if he starts going into ion fluxes and cellular biology, please step in to translate."

"Sounds good."

John exited the RV, and Nia followed. Together they walked across the freshly mowed lawn, emerging on the stone tiles of the walkway to the main entrance. Greeted by formidable oak double doors with translucent glass panels, John rang the doorbell.

He then waited. And waited. After thirty seconds, he gave a double ring.

"Maybe he's not home," said Nia.

"Maybe. But it seems like too many lights are left on for no one to be here."

After another thirty seconds, John pressed the doorbell three times in succession.

Nothing.

"Now what?" said Nia. "We wait in the car? Oh, maybe we get that barbecue and come back?"

John had difficulty looking Nia in the eye given she didn't know they'd already shared their last meal together.

"Maybe he's out in the back, floating in his pool."

"You really don't like this barbecue idea, huh?"

"Nia, we have to stay focused. Follow me."

"Fine, Captain. Copy that."

John swiftly moved around the left side of the house, glancing over his shoulder at Nia. He encountered a black-painted iron fence that seemed to encircle the back half of the property. John checked the gate. Unlocked. He swung it open and motioned Nia to follow.

Peering around the back corner, John saw at least part of what he'd suspected to find. An elaborate pool with a cabana, ground spotlights illuminating the entire backyard like an oasis. But Henry Langston was nowhere to be found enjoying that oasis.

John walked up onto the deck, hugging the brick wall. The french doors allowed plenty of inside light across the otherwise dim deck. John peered in and took in the interior. A well-appointed kitchen flowed into the dining room. *There.* On the far end, in the library, the chair's back was turned at an angle, just enough for John to see a man sitting in it, noise-canceling headphones over his ears.

John shook his head. "He's listening to music in the library."

Nia joined him and looked through the doors. "What do we do now?"

"We go in."

"Great. Break into his house. That'll really get him to open up to two strangers."

"He'll open up all right."

Nia sighed in capitulation.

John tried the handle. Unlocked again.

Some roads have more green lights than others.

He entered the house. Nia followed closely. They slunk across the kitchen, the dining room, into the library. Floor-to-ceiling bookshelves blanketed every wall, burgeoning with volumes that ranged from textbooks on neural systems to Oscar Wilde's collections of works.

John circled around the chair, approaching from the side to lessen Langston's startlement upon seeing him. Whatever Langston was listening to had him spellbound, his eyes fixed ahead. John came closer, waved his hand to get Langston's attention—then snapped his arm back.

"What?" said Nia, approaching from the other side of the chair. She recoiled immediately, a shriek bursting from her mouth. John ran to her and led her into the kitchen.

He silently swore to himself for not acting quickly enough, and now Nia had seen it, that ghastly bullet crater that had once been Langston's left eye socket.

There's your red light, John.

60

John covered Nia's screaming mouth with his hand. He was simultaneously calculating their current predicament, the possible explanations, and the optimal escape route. But Nia had to be calmed down first, or none of his calculations mattered.

He locked eyes with her, their faces inches apart.

"I know it's awful. I know. But right now we need to get out of here safely, no mistakes. You can't make loud noises, you understand?"

Nia blinked, releasing tears, then nodded.

John removed his hand from her mouth.

"I just talked to him yesterday," she whispered, disbelief twisting her face.

"Which means someone was probably listening." Back against the kitchen wall, he surveyed as far as his sight could reach. "They could've been watching us the whole time. Purposely left the gate and back door unlocked."

"You're saying it's a trap?"

"I'm saying we need to run." He cupped Nia's face with his

palms. "Just stay right behind me and I'll get us through this. All right?"

Nia nodded and John pulled out his pistol.

He slapped the kitchen light switch. Darkness. He needed more of it. He killed the deck lights, dousing the backyard in enough shadows to cover their retreat.

"Follow me," he said and opened the back door.

Exiting onto the deck, John moved in the opposite direction from where he and Nia had arrived. He reached the grass, grazing the brick wall with his shoulder. He crouched at the corner and peeked around it. Nothing. Nothing but a hot Texas night.

Through the sparse gaps of the trees dividing the neighboring lot, John could make out the RV. He pointed to it. "We're going to scale the fence and go through the trees. Position one is that pitch-dark section. We run to it and assess from there. Got it?"

Nia nodded, and off they went. Grip firm over Nia's hand, John ran while clocking each source of light and shadow to his right: the AC unit, pathway lights, the street, the house across the street. He dove into the dark section with Nia and crouched. Their heavy breathing was the loudest sound, followed by crickets.

John interlocked his fingers and formed a stepping platform with his palms. Nia planted her foot on it and grabbed his shoulders, and he lifted her up. As soon as half of her body was on the other side of the fence, John jumped and scaled it beside her.

He landed a second after her, drawing his gun and assessing the perimeter.

"We're going straight through the trees. Keep your fingers pressed against the small of my back at all times. I'll tread carefully."

Nia nodded once more; John started moving, and the human

train of two entered a medley of cedar elms and southern oaks. They slid between trunks and branches, an occasional twig crunching under their feet. It was almost too quiet. They reached the edge of the trees.

John performed a perimeter scan, then took Nia's hand.

"We'll both enter the RV together."

A mad dash ensued. John unlocked the RV with the remote, opened the door for Nia, entered after her, and shut the door.

The sound of panting. Sweat pouring down John's neck. He wasted no time getting behind the wheel and was about to turn on the ignition—

"Do you hear that?"

Nia didn't answer. The growing wail of sirens said it all. Lights materialized behind them. First headlights. Then flashes of blue.

John closed his eyes and swallowed a swear word.

61

An unmarked police sedan drove past the RV, followed by another. They halted in front of Langston's driveway, sealing it shut. Two more unmarked SUVs and a police cruiser rolled past John's window.

"They haven't seen us," Nia realized aloud.

"Being in front of the neighboring lot is buying us time, but they'll sweep the perimeter soon enough," said John, eyeing another approaching SUV in the side-view mirror.

"You think maybe a neighbor called the police after hearing a gunshot?"

No sooner had Nia finished the question, doors swung open from all the parked vehicles, and officers poured out. No. Not just police officers.

"Those are federal agents," said John. "They wouldn't be here if someone reported a domestic disturbance. This was all a setup."

Just then the approaching SUV drove by the RV, then suddenly halted. The vehicle's backup lights illuminated. John felt like his chest clenched as tight as his jaw. The SUV reversed, stopped next to the RV's driver window. John quickly leaned back out of sight. "Stay in the back and don't move."

Nia turned into a statue on the sofa.

A cone of light beamed through John's window, illuminating the front of the RV.

Outside, the click of car doors opening. The thud of car doors shutting. Voices murmuring. John's heartbeat spiked. Decision time.

"Nia..."

"Yeah?"

"Store the vital electronics in the backpack, sit in the front, and put the seatbelt on."

"They'll see me."

"They'll see us regardless. We have to drive off before they block us in."

"We can't outrun them in this thing."

"We just need to get to the woods to outrun them on foot."

"I can't believe this..." muttered Nia, sliding phones and laptops into Jenny's backpack.

A rap on the door jolted her.

"Hurry," said John.

Nia sat in the passenger seat and clicked in her belt buckle, as the flashlight outside John's window spotlighted her face.

"Step out of the vehicle," came a muffled shout from outside.

John leaned forward into the light, turned on the engine.

The amount of time it took for the engine pistons to settle into a steady hum felt eternal.

"Hey! I said step out of the—"

John revved the engine—"Hold on, Nia"—and peeled off.

The screeching tires kicked off a chorus of shouts to stop, agents around the RV drawing guns and backing away simultaneously. John veered left to get around the parked cars ahead, slamming the RV's left flank into the SUV on the side. Like homing missiles, the agents in Langston's front yard turned, sprinting back toward their vehicles.

Lights worthy of a Vegas show—beams, strobes, and flashes—erupted in the RV's side-view mirrors, the sirens following immediately. John swerved out of the subdivision, the road ahead straight and futile. He slammed the gas pedal so hard it practically became part of the RV floor.

Engine blaring, RV rattling, the air inside became thick with a putrid smell concocted of melting tires and overheated brakes. Sirens overtook the revving engine, and a police cruiser edged up to the RV's back bumper. John careened the RV along the path of an aggressive curve, making seemingly every object in the vehicle fly from left to right.

Nia swallowed half a scream before John swayed the RV into a semblance of control as the road straightened. Immediately, the police cruiser started passing them on the left, revealing a trail of black SUVs behind it.

"They're trying to block us in, front and back," said John. "Grab the dashboard handle and *do not* let go."

Nia began to say something, but her voice dispersed under the whiplash of the RV slamming sideways into the police cruiser. John wrestled with the wheel to remain on the road, the two vehicles pushing against each other at seventy-five miles per hour. What the RV lacked in speed, it made up with sheer weight, and the police cruiser sputtered, caught up, sputtered again...

Headlights blazed ahead, a trail of vehicles coming around a blind curve. The first oncoming car was seconds away from a head-on collision with the cruiser, and John doubted the police driver could see the traffic from their angle—

He skewed the RV hard left, running the police cruiser off the road, then swerved to get back into the right lane as the first oncoming car blared its horn, screeching and grazing the left side of the RV. Nia screamed.

John caught a glimpse of the police cruiser juddering to a halt in a cloud of dust, the rest of the car's skid unfolding in the side-view mirror, disappearing behind the curve. John told himself no one got hurt, but he knew it might be a lie. He revved the engine hard, surging down the road, and quickly realized it was dead-ending into another.

Left or right?

The SUVs were closing in aggressively.

Left or right?

An SUV separated from the pack, flanking him on the left.

Left or right, John?!

Ten yards from the stop sign, he pumped the brakes—falling behind the flanking SUV and getting slammed in the back by another—then floored it again, threading the space between the two SUVs, veering, skidding into a tilting left turn. Headlights flashed from all sides—horns blaring, cars whizzing, the RV tipping from inertia, with only the right-side tires touching the asphalt.

John braced for the vehicle to flip over, but the passenger side slammed into a cinder block privacy wall, which sent the left side of the RV crashing back to earth. The momentum carried it forward, sparks flying from the friction against the wall—Nia absolutely hysterical—and John floored it again onto the road.

He assessed the scene behind him in the remaining side-view mirror: one SUV had crashed into the wall, another had been T-boned by a pickup truck, and the last was still in pursuit.

Smoke started billowing from the hood, and John came to grips with the fact that the end was near.

A massive intersection appeared ahead: "North Capital of Texas Highway."

The light turned green in time, and John skidded a hard right onto the highway, the SUV sliding in right behind him. The road was double lane in both directions, the wide grass median separated by steel cable barriers.

John saw it then. His only chance. An intersection whose left turn arrow light was red and headlights of oncoming traffic far enough in the distance.

"Nia, you have got to hold on for me one more time."

This time Nia's voice worked just fine. "Fuck you and fuck everything."

John waited until the absolute last moment before careening the RV left at the intersection, across the opposite lanes of surging vehicles, avoiding an oncoming semitrailer by a margin so thin, only Nia's earsplitting shriek could describe it eloquently.

While decades of combat gave John the acute sense of spatial awareness to pull off a stunt like this, they couldn't defy the laws of centripetal force. Careening a ten-thousand-pound vehicle at fifty miles per hour, John couldn't expect to remain on the road—unless he wanted to tip over, which he certainly didn't—so he straightened the wheel, leading the RV onto a sprawling road shoulder.

He was greeted by a rather large mound of construction soil whose incline all too closely resembled that of a gymnastics springboard.

The front wheels of the RV went airborne. Until they weren't.

The world became a thousand fissures of glass.

62

The windshield cracked into a mosaic of spiderwebs. But it remained intact.

Both front tires had popped when the RV nose-landed back to earth, though the back tires fared better. Teeth-rattling gravel stretched ahead, and the RV rumbled across the road shoulder, which finally and mercifully gave way to the paved parking lot of a large church. John regained control of the vehicle, steering it across the lot.

He couldn't find the SUV in the side-view mirror, but his best guess was that his maneuver had been successful—the SUV had missed the intersection and would have to make a U-turn at the next one, which gave him and Nia a precious head start.

The RV's hood was billowing smoke so profusely now that he had to roll down the window and stick his head out to see. Engine choking, John used the remaining momentum to put the gear in neutral and roll the RV to a stop in front of the trees ahead.

He turned to Nia, who seemed to be staring into an abyss.

John stepped to her seat, released her seat belt, took her hand, and led her out. They bolted into the woods.

Twenty yards in, John heard a distant screech of tires and turned. Through the trees, out in the distance, headlights shone.

"They're in the parking lot already," said John. "I'll carry the backpack."

John strapped it on his back and nudged Nia forward.

The two ran full-out into the woods, the rays of headlights already catching up to them.

Heavy panting. Heavy steps. Heavy backpack. Far heavier than he'd anticipated.

"Nia, stop."

"What?" she managed between deep breaths.

John took in the silhouettes flickering between the trees in the distance.

"We have to split up. I'll act as a decoy to help you get away."

"What if they catch up to you?"

John gave her a look. "I'll feel very bad for them."

"Of course."

"Here, take the backpack, and let's agree to meet at a specific rendezvous point."

"I've got one better," she said, taking out a cell phone. "Take this. It tracks the other phone that's configured to get notified of the Grail signature. Just click here. See the dot on the map? That's my phone."

John took the phone and pointed. "Go straight to the clearing beyond those trees, hang a sharp right before Lake Austin. The bridge to the other side will let you escape—"

"Not my first rodeo, Captain."

Flashlights glinted through the trees.

"Go!" John said, and Nia went.

John ran, veering left, deliberately making noise for the flashlights to follow him.

He slid between the trees, the agents' footfalls growing nearer. In his prime, he might have outrun them. But now he needed to conserve energy, especially if it came down to an altercation with people he once could've never imagined would stand in his way: law enforcement.

He leaned his back against the thick trunk of a southern oak, catching his breath. Flashlights searched the area on both sides of him, twigs crunching under outsoles. He counted three people. They steered a bit off course, passing by him. John counted his lucky stars. That was his mistake. A flashlight spun around and blinded him.

"Put your hands behind your back. Now!"

John sighed. He placed his palms on the back of his head. He heard another agent announce their bounty into the comm radio. More agents would be swarming these woods within minutes. Given the trail of destruction John had left, half of the Austin police department would accompany them.

"Turn around and spread your legs," said the agent with the blinding flashlight.

John did as ordered, facing the craggy bark of the tree and widening his stance.

He heard footsteps directly behind him and on either side of him. Guns were surely drawn.

"Do not move, you understand me?"

"I understand," said John, his voice filled with sadness. What a pathetic, unceremonious display to finally make it dawn on him how far he had crossed the invisible line. A lifetime of doing the right thing, null and void. What was one more step in the wrong direction? That was how John would justify his next actions.

His left eye twitched.

63

An agent grabbed John's right wrist from behind, bringing it from the back of John's head down to his lower back. John's eyes flitted side to side, registering the five feet of distance from the agent on the right, four feet from the one on the left.

The cold metal of the handcuff touched John's lowered wrist—

He dropped to the ground with a 180-degree twist, wrapping a leg behind the agent's knee to pull him down. Shielded by the agent on top of him, John pulled out his gun and pressed it against the agent's temple. The other two agents shouted, until John's voice boomed.

"Back off, now! Don't make me paint this tree with his brains."

It was an empty threat, but silence ensued. John continued the act.

"I'm going to count to three. If both of you don't drop your guns and point your flashlights into your faces, I'm pulling the trigger. One..."

The agents started shouting again, instructing John to drop the gun.

"Two..."

Now it got quiet. One of them said it didn't have to be this way. John almost laughed.

"Thr—"

"All right, all right!" both agents yelled, their guns plummeting to the ground. They pointed the flashlights up into their faces.

John finally saw them clearly. They looked young. Early thirties at most. John had little doubt this was the most intense standoff of their careers. He slowly stood up, sliding his back against the tree, pulling the agent with him.

"Toss the guns and earpieces to me. *Now*."

Once the goods were on the ground in front of John, he crushed the earpieces with the heel of his boot.

"Now, take the batteries out of those flashlights and throw them like you're throwing a Hail Mary. Then you're gonna toss those flashlights just as hard the other way."

John was genuinely impressed by how hard the agents hurled the flashlights and batteries into the darkness, the objects clonking against the trees in the distance. With ample darkness now surrounding them, John kicked the guns on the ground and flung them as far as he could in opposite directions.

"What's your name?" John said to the agent under his clench.

"Byron."

"All right, listen up. Byron and I are going to take a stroll through the woods. If I hear or see you follow, there won't be a count to three. Do you understand?" If anyone nodded, John couldn't tell. "Say yes if you understand."

"*Yes.*"

John suppressed a sigh of relief that his bluff had worked.

"Good. Start walking back the way you came from."

John moved past them, watching their silhouettes retreat.

Soon there was nothing but the crunch of John and Byron's footsteps, the woods going eerily quiet. John quickened his stride and forced Byron to keep up. Two shadows in the night.

But soon John felt Byron getting twitchy.

"Don't do anything stupid," said John, reinforcing the barrel against Byron's back. "I know it's tempting, and the idea sounds so good inside your head. But I promise you there is nothing quicker in these woods than the finger wrapped around this trigger—"

The lash over John's hand was so sharp that it detached his grip from the gun like a repelling magnet.

"Find his pistol!" shouted the agent who had disarmed John and was now tackling him to the ground.

John rolled on the ground with the agent, cursing himself for not detecting they'd followed him all along. The rolling halted with the agent firmly on top of him, hailing down punches immediately. John wrapped his legs around the agent's torso and pulled him to his chest.

The moment the agent planted his palms on the ground for balance, John clamped his right forearm, then swung his own left arm across and twisted the agent's arm back ninety degrees counterclockwise. The pop of torn ligaments sounded sickening in the darkness.

The agent wailed as John tossed him aside, bolting up and registering a fist in the shadows at the last millisecond. It grazed his right cheekbone as he jerked sideways, and John used his momentum of evading the blow to spin with a vicious elbow into another agent's temple. It was Byron, who slumped to the ground.

The third agent was frantically searching for John's gun. But John had felt it when he'd fallen on it after getting tackled. He calmly walked over, picked it up, then pointed it at the frantic agent.

"You're the new Byron. Let's go."

As John shoved the agent through the trees, he felt his forty-five years as though each one were a clamp over a muscle in his body. *What do you expect, tussling with a bunch of thirty-year-olds?* His wrist still pulsating from the pain, he pulled out his cell phone to check on Nia. The map showed her in the clearing up ahead, moving east to west under the ninety-degree bend of Lake Austin. John shook his head. She must have gotten turned around and veered too far east before finding the clearing.

"Move," said John, shoving the agent into a trot.

They emerged from the woods almost immediately, John striding toward Nia's dot. He soon saw her in the distance. *"Nia!"*

She turned with a jolt, then started running to him.

"That way!" John yelled, pointing toward the bridge.

They reached each other at the parking lot next to the bridge.

"Sorry, I got lost," said Nia, panting heavily. "I told you I'm a city girl, Captain." A bewildered look formed on her face. "Who's that?"

"He was collateral. We're leaving him here." John took in the bridge, then assessed the woods. "There'll be more agents coming out of those trees any minute. We need to—"

Lights cut John off.

Those goddamn headlights.

So many of them turned on simultaneously in the parking lot that they practically transformed night into day.

John wanted to exhale a cynical laugh. But what would be the point? He was just a fool who'd thought he could evade multiple units of federal agents and local police.

Then he felt an uneasiness rising from his gut.

There was no flashing of blue or red. His ears picked up a chorus of methodical, deliberate footfalls before he saw the silhouettes fanning out, encircling him and Nia and the agent.

The men finally came into view, dressed in SWAT-grade uniforms, holding rifles, fingers over triggers. From the circle of triggers and Kevlar vests, he emerged. Like an apparition. A demon. The spirit of John's greatest sins.

It was Yuri Volkov.

64

Yuri stopped ten feet in front of John. His intense eyes probed every inch of him, yet his expression remained unnaturally calm. No. Not unnaturally. Fittingly. Why wouldn't he be calm after a perfectly executed plan?

Just when John thought he couldn't have been more of a fool, life sadistically mocked him. He traced his missteps in reverse, like rewinding a tape. It wasn't just that Yuri had set him up with Langston's murder. All of it was now so clear to John. Why Yuri remained here instead of fleeing back to Russia. Why he had a falling-out with his superiors. Because even though Yuri had stolen the Grail and abducted Claire and the operators, he'd still failed to get the main prize—the hacker who was instrumental to the entire operation.

And here John was, handing him Nia on a silver platter.

Yuri would get his vengeance.

Volkov casually strolled to John and opened his palm. "Give me your gun, G. I. Joe."

John's heart was pumping acid. Only one thought raced through his mind. One sliver of hope. To shoot Yuri like he'd shot his brother. To cut off the head of the snake and let the chips fall where they may. John was one twitch away from putting a bullet into Yuri's face when it happened—his hand inadvertently tremored. John felt it down to his core.

Parkinson's. John's greatest enemy. The one he could never defeat. The one that would cost him his life—Claire's just as likely. And what would they do to Nia? All because of that little tremor. Misguided synapses firing inside his brain, like the misguided hope John had been clinging to for way too long.

John's shaking hand caught Yuri's attention. At first John was convinced Yuri thought John was afraid. But the look in Yuri's eyes told him otherwise. Raw intelligence brimmed there. His older brother had been a brute, but Yuri was far more cunning.

"Oh, G. I. Joe, you broken. Just regular Joe now. Shame. Come, give me the gun."

He made a "give it here" gesture with a supple movement of his fingers, as though to mock John with their dexterity. With a nudge toward Nia, he said, "If I ask again, I put bullet in her leg. I keep putting bullets until you give me gun."

A spike of nausea reached John's mouth. He swallowed the bile along with his desolation, and placed the gun in his trembling hand into Yuri's perfectly still, gloved hand.

Yuri examined it, feeling its weight.

"SIG Sauer. The preferred pistol of navy SEAL, eh, G. I. Joe?"

He calmly pointed it at the federal agent and shot him in the head.

Nia screamed, her knees buckling. John caught her before she collapsed.

"Not bad," said Yuri, twisting his wrist to examine the gun again. "Good power. Low recoil." He waved it like a lecturing stick toward the agent on the ground. "So, story goes, G. I. Joe shoot agent."

Out in the distance, the wail of sirens caught his attention. John almost laughed at the bitter irony of now wishing the police would get here in time. For the first time, Yuri's face showed genuine emotion. It wasn't concern; it was disappointment. John understood. Yuri didn't have the time to fully savor the moment before avenging his brother.

The Russian looked to his right, at the shore of Lake Austin, before turning back to John. "But then G. I. Joe felt shame for killing agent, like good American patriot. So he go to lake and kill himself. Honorable, no? He float in lake so agents search for him and not us."

A grin so sly formed on Yuri's face, John was almost mesmerized by it. Mesmerized by the effortless shrewdness. Yuri was a chess player who had mapped out his moves before John knew what game was being played. The truth was, John wasn't even playing against Yuri. He was just Yuri's expendable chess piece, about to be taken off the board.

Yuri said something curt in Russian, and John nearly went blind from the blunt force to the back of his head. He fell to his knees as Nia got swept away by two mercenaries. She thrashed and screamed, but the ringing in John's ears was still the loudest sound he heard.

His vision went in and out as they dragged him under his arms, his feet scraping the pavement. Of all the ways he thought he would die, and all the bodies of water across the world he could die in, for his final moments to come at the beautiful Lake Austin—where he had taught Jenny how to swim—felt unspeakably wrong.

Where *had* it all gone so wrong? Had it ever been right? These were the same questions he'd had since the day Jenny had died, and never a concrete answer. The only concrete thing in life was death—his mother had cemented that into him during Sunday church. *Pull yourself up, young man,* her voice echoed. *Life is a trial for eternity, so earn your place by your Maker's side.*

Maybe that was where it had all gone wrong. The day John abandoned God. How could he meet the Maker he didn't believe existed? *Pull yourself up.* Jenny had committed the cardinal sin, so even if he went to heaven, would he see her there? When would Claire join them? After Yuri put a bullet in her, too? *Pull yourself up!* And Nia? *Nia...*

Pull yourself up, John!

As he was dragged to a pier next to the bridge, John took in the lake under a thin quarter moon, thinner than his chances and options. He heard his own pistol being cocked from behind, the sound twitching his eyes to the right. Then he clocked something clipped to a Russian's belt.

At the instant they dropped him to his knees for execution, John regained enough synapses in his brain to snatch the Russian's flash-bang grenade and detonate it behind his back.

65

Heat. A thousand pins raking John's back. Eardrums numb, world mute.

The blast thrust John forward into a staggered dive off the pier—

A midair sting through his lower-right torso spiraled him into a messy entry. Another bullet sliced his left shoulder before he was fully submerged, the pain acutely loud as the rest of the world became muffled. Inches from the lakebed, John gritted through arm pulls and dolphin kicks, swimming with the lazy current of Lake Austin.

Flashlights searched, passing above him, bullets carved contrails of air, their angles flattening—*swim, John, swim*—flattening—*swim!*

Lights soon began to fade.

When darkness enveloped John, it brought more pain with it.

Unable to hear, nothing to see, John's senses funneled his undivided attention toward physical anguish. His chest was heavy as a cinder block, his lungs begging for a contraction. *Swim, John, swim! Swim...* After what felt like a hundred yards underwater, John torpedoed up to the surface, gulped air, and went under again. *Swim, John, swim...*

More kicks. Arm pulls. Pain. Agony. Torpedoing to the surface, diving under...

He started losing all sense of direction. Sense of motor functions. Fading. Light appeared in front of his eyes, dreamlike...

Snapping into consciousness with a burst, John choke-inhaled the air an inch above the surface, needles poking his vision. He could hear only muffled sounds, barely audible, except for the strident ringing in his ears. Disoriented, he slowly regained his eyesight, colors and shapes overlapping, aligning into a streaming panorama:

Decks, piers, waterfront properties, all sliding past him.

Where was the bridge? How long had he been swimming? Or drifting? He spun around, floating backward. He finally saw dots of car headlights gliding over the bridge about half a mile away.

As his senses returned, so did the pain. His back felt like it had been polished with sandpaper. A bullet had grazed his lower right flank, the second his left shoulder. The torso wound hurt exponentially more than the shoulder. Had the bullet hit an organ? How bad could it be, if he'd regained consciousness? His questions floated in the quiet Texas night, the calm otherworldly after the violent ordeal.

The biggest issue was not pain, but strength. Strength was leaving him. Draining away like the blood he was glad he couldn't see. He sensed he couldn't stay afloat for much longer. Through suppressed groans, he swam toward the shore on the right side.

He reached the dock of a house with a sizable boat tied on one side of it. The other side was dotted with mooring buoys, red balls of rubber that looked like party balloons. John reached up for one and halted—half groaning, half inhaling, the pain shooting from his torso. He fell back into the water, spots popping across his vision. He would have to reach for the buoy with his left hand, even though his shoulder was injured.

He sealed his mouth shut, grinding his teeth through the agony as he reached up and grabbed the throat of the buoy. He lifted himself up enough to insert his right foot into a cleft of a wooden beam.

The fingers of his free hand bored into the crannies of the rope knots around the buoy's loop. Fumbling. Loosening. Tugging at the rope. Finally, he untied the last knot and fell back into the water with the buoy floating next to him. He hugged it like an old friend, then pushed off from the beam with his legs. Hunched over the buoy, John kicked with his feet, floating away from the dock. The current did the rest.

John floated for an excruciatingly long amount of time. How much longer could he hemorrhage before losing consciousness and drowning? When would it be safe to swim ashore? Was he far enough from the swarm of federal agents and Austin police? Did it even matter at this point, with the entire city looking for him? What was one more mile down the lake?

———

John woke from a half-fainted state, snapping his head backward.

Up ahead, his vision projected a trail of red buoys dotting across the entire lake. Was he hallucinating? No. He was approaching Tom Miller Dam, the end of Lake Austin. Beyond it was Lady Bird Lake that hugged downtown Austin.

Downtown Austin...

Just thinking the words felt surreal. He had been driving through the city just a few hours ago, reflecting on its progress, anticipating his talk with Henry Langston, dreading leaving Nia behind, all safe and sound. *Safe and sound...* He would've scoffed if he had the strength.

How could the entire world flip upside down so quickly? How could he not have seen any of it coming? Was he truly the world's greatest fool? How could everything—

Stop sulking. You're still breathing.

Willing himself into a productive state of mind, John recalibrated. He had to keep going. He had to get medical supplies.

Kicking, he steered the buoy left, avoiding the lights cast by a large Tex-Mex restaurant overlooking the shore. His hearing returned enough to make out voices on the patio. Intermittent bursts of carefree laughter, the world going on leisurely by him as he bled to death.

He floated into the shadows of boat slips branching from a pier. One of the slips was empty, a rope hanging from it like a jungle vine. John swam to the rope and grabbed it. He pushed the buoy away, parting with it with the respect he would offer to any standard-issue military gear. Now came the hard part— lifting himself onto the boat slip without groaning.

He exhaled all the air out of his lungs and climbed the rope. The pain projected flashes of light into his retinas. By the time he lay on the deck boards, he was borderline knocked out.

Get up, John. Get up now or you die here.

He rolled to his right, onto his good shoulder, making sure none of his torn waist touched the floor. Crawling on all fours, he crept from shadow to shadow, avoiding light like a vampire. He finally entered an alley between two buildings and stood up. Instantly lightheaded, he leaned against a wall, producing moans unlike anything he'd heard come out of him before.

Sliding against the wall, he reached a parking lot that was awash in the amber glow of streetlights.

He finally looked down at the wound on the right side of his waist. It was oozing tar.

66

John compared his split-open love handle to memories of notable wounds he'd seen in combat. On a scale of one (being a scratch) to ten (flesh blown to pieces), his waist was a solid seven.

He examined his left shoulder. Far less serious. It appeared the bullet had grazed the outside of his deltoid. It still bled and hurt plenty, though.

John leaned back against the wall, gritted his teeth, and took off his T-shirt. He tore off a small piece and adhered it onto his shoulder gash, the tackiness of his blood securing it in place. He tied the remaining shirt into a triple knot in the middle and pressed the knotted ball against the wound on his side. The pain was so acute he actually laughed.

As the knots eagerly soaked up his blood, he tied the rest of his shirt like a rope around his waist. He placed a hand over his shoulder to keep the other shirt piece from falling, and began his trudge across the parking lot.

There was enough light that he could be easily spotted, until he got to the road.

He crossed it and melted into the shadows below the trees

garnishing the front of an office building. He crept across the lawn, moving south, until he saw a privacy wall composed of trees and shrubbery. John let out a hoarse laugh, recognizing the property line of Lions Municipal Golf Course, where he'd used to play with Hank Dawson, his former stepfather-in-law.

If his memory served him correctly, a drugstore was on the other end of the golf course, about a mile southwest. *C'mon John, you can do this.* He found the nearest gap between the branches and entered seconds before an oncoming car lit up the area.

A branch stabbing into his injured shoulder welcomed him; his resulting moan ended in a growl. More branches lashed him, but John cared only about protecting his torso at the expense of every other body part.

After getting thoroughly swatted by the local vegetation, he emerged into a clearing to see the gentle contours of greens, fairways, roughs, and sand bunkers. They stretched in front of him under the starlit night, like blobs of a flattened lava lamp. Which one of these blobs had Hank stood on swinging a nine-iron when the blood clot in his coronary artery sent him to his death?

Oh Hank, if you could see me now, slowly bleeding to death...

The possibility of John meeting the same fate in the same place as his former stepfather-in-law was a cosmic indignity that he considered nothing short of God's mockery.

With a burst of energy stemming from defiance to the Almighty, he turned right and plodded through the rough by the fairway. He stayed close to the wall of trees he'd entered through, using their shadows for stealth and their direction for guidance. Cars passed by intermittently on the other side, but Lake Austin Boulevard was quiet this time of the night. Until it suddenly wasn't.

A medley of sirens and horns swelled in the distance, followed by flashes of blue-red.

John sat on the ground behind a large tree, pressing his back against it, the act pushing the tied knots of his shirt straight into the torso wound. This time the pain skipped his vocal cords and dispensed a tear from his right eye.

Even through the thick vegetation behind him, lights from the road slashed into the golf course, the wail of sirens enveloping John like heat in a sauna. Someone had spotted him. Called the police. Were there cameras around the golf course he couldn't see?

He braced himself for the vehicles to park off the road behind him. To hear the officers shouting. Dogs barking. But instead, the entire convoy zoomed by, sirens and lights fading down the road until John was left with silence and moonlight.

He genuinely had a hard time believing something had gone his way tonight.

His adrenaline retreated, leaving behind trembling muscles. He checked his watch: 10:37 p.m. Unless the operating hours had changed since the last time he'd been there, that drugstore would close at eleven. He had at least another half a mile, maybe three quarters.

Moaning himself to his feet, John continued trudging down the golf course. More trees appeared ahead, and John somehow felt the sting of the oncoming branches before he even entered them. Then he really felt them. *Motherfu...* He hissed through his teeth.

By the time he exited the trees and entered another fairway, he was panting heavily. Dragging his feet, exhaustion settling in, John checked his watch: 10:45 p.m.

His survival was reduced to a fifteen-minute countdown. Either he made it to the drugstore in time, or he'd bleed out in front of it. As he staggered on, his vision turned fuzzy. Black spots flickered in random corners of his eyes, shadows that simply weren't there.

Up ahead, shafts of streetlight sliced through the trees that marked the end of the golf course. John floundered through them, his feet finally touching sweet asphalt. He crossed a road and entered a makeshift construction path made of a chain-link fence and red traffic barriers.

He emerged onto a sidewalk, the lights from the gas station to his left so strident that he had to peer through his narrowed eyelids. Like an oasis, the neon sign of the drugstore came into focus.

He cut through the parking lot, one of his hands reaching for the building as though it were a life raft. It wasn't until he was a few feet from the sliding doors that he realized he couldn't enter like this. Shirtless. Bloody. He didn't even want to know what his face looked like.

His gaze slid left, traveling down the sidewalk until it reached a homeless man. He was sitting back against the wall, head drooped over. In his hands, John saw a cardboard sign:

Veteran. Please Help.

John's knees buckled. *Ain't that something.* He trudged to the homeless man and took a knee with a groan. One desperate veteran facing another.

"I also served," said John, his voice cracking through every syllable.

The man looked up. His eyes were glazed and bloodshot. He reeked of sweat.

"Oh..." he managed.

John reached into his pocket and pulled out a stack of wet twenty-dollar bills. He slid one out and showed it to the homeless veteran.

"I'll give you twenty dollars for your jacket."

The man's eyes lit up. He stared at the bill as though expecting it would disappear at any moment. "Okay," he said finally, sliding off his jacket. He handed it to John and grabbed the bill, crumpling it to his chest.

John stood up with another groan, draped the jacket over his shoulders to hide his wet skin, which was now damp more from sweat than from Lake Austin, and walked to the entrance. He got there just in time to watch the store clerk flip the *OPEN* sign to the *CLOSED* side and lock the door with a cold *click*.

67

John locked eyes with the drugstore clerk on the other side of the glass door. Opposing forces of resignation and desperation slammed into him at once. But it simply couldn't end this way.

"Sorry," said the clerk, his voice muffled by the glass.

Panic. Utter panic pulsated through John. The clerk turned away, and John felt adrenaline rip through his whole body. He slammed his wad of cash against the glass.

The clerk turned around with a jolt. His wide eyes grew even wider when John lifted the side of his stench-riddled denim jacket to reveal the blood-soaked knot of the T-shirt.

"I need five things," shouted John. "You can spend two minutes letting me buy them, or you can spend an hour giving a statement to the police after I die in front of this door."

———

Holding a recyclable paper bag, John shuffled out of the drugstore, his still-wet boots squeaking. The clerk couldn't shut and lock the door fast enough behind him.

Light and privacy. Those were the elements John needed to

fix himself up, and not necessarily in that order. He made his way in the direction of the homeless veteran, passing by him with a nod, then turned the corner around the building. The area was perfect.

The back of the drugstore was lit up enough to accommodate the pharmacy drive-through but shielded from the houses across the street by trees. John plodded farther down to the edge of the light's range, where he would have enough privacy. He slid off his jacket and threw it like a picnic blanket over the narrow sidewalk hugging the building.

With groans and winces, he sat down on it, back against the wall.

He opened a bottle of water and drained half of it. He used the rest of the water to wash down a fistful of 200 mg ibuprofen pills down his throat. Then he untied his T-shirt and gingerly separated the blood-soaked knots from the side of his torso.

Under the neon light, John finally took in the wound clearly. It was more ghastly than he'd realized. The bullet had entered from the back at a forty-five-degree angle, carving a path through his love handle. It was a flesh wound, but a deep one. One inch over, and John judged he would've been floating dead in Lake Austin with his large intestine spilling out of him.

John fumbled with his hand inside the bag and took out a bottle of antiseptic. He untwisted the cap and placed it between his molars. It was the best he had to bite down on for what was about to ensue.

Sweet mother of mercy.

The antiseptic flowing over John's puckering torso wound felt like acid.

He howl-growled, his eyes watering, clouding his vision as he tried to focus on properly washing out the wound. He stopped after pouring over half a bottle, the trail of washed blood streaming across the sidewalk, down the curb, onto the asphalt.

Panting like a dog in heat, John took a sewing kit out of the bag. He picked out a medium-size needle and the thickest thread, then blinked twice to clear the remaining tears from his eyes. He bent the needle into a crescent shape and spent almost a minute trying to slide the thread through the needle's eye with his trembling hands.

He exhaled a laugh of relief once he got it through. He then tied a knot and went to work. Starting from the back, John pushed the needle into his skin, through his flesh, into the flesh on the wound's other side, and out. He did it all over again. And again. By the time John finished sewing up the wound, the antiseptic bottle cap in his mouth was mangled into a morsel of plastic.

John took out a gauze kit and placed multiple layers over the wound. They started soaking up blood immediately. No doubt his stitching job was subpar. He wrapped a roll of gauze around his torso and proceeded through the whole ordeal again with his shoulder. It proved to be far less painful. Or perhaps his pain receptors were simply tapped out.

All stitched up, he checked his watch: 11:37 p.m.

He lifted himself up, grunting-heaving in pain, and draped the denim jacket over his shoulders again. Lightheaded, he leaned against the wall, preparing himself mentally for the next stretch. Wait. He had to thank the homeless veteran first. John came around the corner and stopped above the man, who looked up in surprise.

"You're still here?"

"Wanted to say goodbye before I head out. Where were you deployed?"

The man watched John with glazed eyes, seeming uninterested in small talk of any kind, even bonding over military service. "Iraq," he said finally.

John smiled a sad smile. "Me too. Twenty-Sixth Marine Expeditionary. You?"

The man had to think about it for a moment. "Army. Fifth Infantry Division."

John wasn't sure if he had heard it right. "Did you say Fifth Infantry?"

"Yeah."

Was John hallucinating? Was his brain that scrambled?

"There is no Fifth Infantry Division," he said, more to himself.

A sudden, unsavory look passed across the man's eyes.

"Look, man, I just have the sign. All right?"

It hit John like a punch from the inside. The spiking nausea. So many veterans, forgotten and discarded, begging on the street, and this jackass lied about serving. The indecency of it, in this moment, broke down John. Tenderized his will and drained his last ounce of strength.

Ears ringing again. Eyesight fading. He lurched away, grazing the wall as he went back around the corner. He staggered through a patch of grass, under the canopy of oaks, and fell face down into dark oblivion.

68

A pulsating sting stirred John to life.

He blinked through the fog. Shadows swayed above him. That stench. The stench of sweat and alcohol. A face came into focus. The vagrant posing as a veteran.

He was hovering over John, twisting him to the side, rummaging through his jean pockets. John's disgust sent his hand toward the vagrant's neck. He clenched his throat, squeaking a choking sound out of it.

The vagrant reflexively slammed his fists into John's face. But John wasn't letting go.

Until the man planted a knee into John's torso wound.

John howled as the vagrant rolled away, choke-inhaling air with a fistful of cash in his hand.

They lay on the ground a few feet apart, staring at each other, until the vagrant began crawling away like a hyena. With a parting glance toward John, he got to his feet and ran off.

John checked his pockets. The cash was gone. All he had left was Nia's cell phone and his family picture at Montauk for Jenny's nineteenth birthday. He looked at his torso wound.

The gauze was the color of merlot, and a rivulet of blood slid down his side. At best, the stitches had loosened; at worst, the thread had severed. The gauze on his shoulder wasn't doing much better. He checked his watch: 01:26 a.m.

There was still time. Was there? Austin's train routes and schedules he'd committed to memory during his planning were now reshuffling like cards in a deck. *No, it's right, John. Don't doubt yourself now.* The train tracks veered west along the Colorado River before taking a sharp turn north—the sharp turn John had to get to in under twenty minutes.

He willed himself into a crawl over the grass.

Get up. Get up, now.

He lurched upward into a limping walk.

Trudging east on West Seventh Avenue, he stayed in as many shadows as he could find. Houses on his left, an apartment complex to his right. His vision started fading in and out. Colors and sounds blurred, pulsing to the rhythm of his pumping heart. He shook his head to snap out of it, but it only exacerbated the sensation.

Up ahead, the road ended into a three-lane, one-way highway. Beyond it was the mother lode—a spaghetti junction of overpasses, the train tracks on the other side of it. Given his current condition, it was practically an obstacle course.

He checked his watch: 01:41 a.m.

His blurry vision was getting blurrier. Must go on. With no headlights he could see, John crossed the road and entered a pathway that snaked under the overpasses. Was he still going east?

His answer came in the form of a train chugging lazily, approaching from downtown Austin. He quickened his ragged stride. Stumbling. Groaning. Mumbling... *Where're you going, Captain?* said Nia. Or was it Jenny? The train horn blared. Must go on.

John plodded between a few trees before encountering a hill.

The freight train streamed above him under the starlit night, like some celestial serpent. *Are you leaving me, Captain?* He started clambering up the hill, mostly on all fours. *Dad, you're gonna miss it!*

"I've never missed your softball games."

He reached the clearing atop the hill and started running alongside the train.

The shrill clanging of metal—rhythmic *clickety-clack, clickety-clack*—accelerating— *clickety-clack, clickety-clack*—lungs burning—*clickety-clack, clickety-clack*—heat spiking—*Dad, you're blowing it!*—wind roaring—

Save me, Captain!

John lunged and grabbed the edge of an open sliding door, the box rail car tugging him like a rag doll, propelling him to plant his foot on the floor, his pain neurons firing lighting into his retinas as he rolled into the rail car.

Blaring sounds. Blurring vision...

John squinted his eyes, steadied his shaking hand, and pressed the Mode button on his watch. Tap, tap, alarm prompt activated. Tap tap tap, alarm set for *06:55 a.m.*

Is it set?

John couldn't tell anymore, the LED digits morphing into hieroglyphics.

He faded away... came out of it, but couldn't open his eyes, colors smearing behind his eyelids, like swirling rainbows in an oily puddle of water. Vibrating to the *clickety-clack, clickety-clack...*

Fading to black.

Beep-beep-beep...

John spasmed into consciousness, his vision a haze of dull colors.

Beep-beep-beep...

Migraine. Unbearable migraine. His brain was attempting to break free from his skull.

Beep-beep-beep...

He blinked away the blur from his vision. Shapes crystallized: a lush oak tree, washed by the light of early dawn, framed like a picture by the rail car doorway. The train was stationary.

Beep-beep-beep...

He checked his watch and turned off the alarm. He barely made out the time:

06:58 a.m.

I'm here.

He attempted to sit up, the pain from his torso flattening him immediately. He wailed. Groaned. Swore. He looked at his wound. A fly was buzzing around the maroon, caked-up gauze. A small puddle of mostly dried blood was on the floor beneath him. John reached for the gauze and realized his hand was shaking uncontrollably. Fever. He was shivering all over.

He ran his tongue across his lips. He might as well have licked fraying cardboard.

John made three more painful attempts to get up, to move at all, but nothing.

It couldn't end here. Not like this. Just then the train puffed a whistling sound. Seconds later, it started moving. *No. No, no no. Get up, John.* He reached into the depths of his lungs, screaming himself into rolling over once, twice, until his legs were outside of the rail car, the ground sliding beneath him. Faster and faster. *Just get it over with.*

John pushed off the car floor and fell out onto rough gravel.

The last of his sanity seemed to evaporate as the train sped by.

John willed himself up and started limping alongside the train. Soon enough he was limping by himself, the rising sun slowly searing his vision into a spot-riddled kaleidoscope. He could barely make out the feature he was coming up on. It was a fence. It looked like the right one, but it could've been any fence. No, this was it.

You might not even be in the right town, John...

He laughed. Maybe. He thought he laughed. His voice guttered out like a choking muffler. He stumbled forward, clutched the gate. His fingers fumbled around the intercom box. *Is it an intercom?*

John slapped it, manically... a crackling buzz ... the world swirling...

Claire...

Yes?

I love you, honey.

69

Moving through the hallway with his HK416 rifle. Night vision turning gray. Stepping over dead bodies. *So many lives taken, John...* A child giggles behind the corner. Nothing there when he turns. A long, empty hallway, stretching farther with each step. Suddenly there is a door in front of him. Corrugated metal. Primitive lock. Shotgun blasts fire into it, a wind swings it open, revealing a wall of...

No. This isn't right.

Claire?

Jenny on her knees next to her. "Dad, what's happening?"

"You died, sweetie," says John.

"No I haven't, Captain!" says Nia. Has it been Nia all along? *"Save us!"*

The black wall behind Claire and Nia is no wall at all. From a row of men in black uniforms, Yuri Volkov peels off. He holds John's SIG Sauer pistol. His eyes ignite demon red.

"Save us, Captain!"

Claire is silent. John already knows what she'll say.

"Please take care of yourself."

Yuri fires into the back of Claire's head—

John woke with a jolt.

White. White ceiling.

John's eyes traveled the length of it, the ceiling segueing into a wall covered with photos of men in military uniforms. He was in four of them. His eyes settled on the only photo where people wore civilian clothes. It had been taken in Aaron Bradley's backyard, eight months before his death at the hands of Andrei Volkov's mercenaries.

The picture clenched John's chest. Bradley was in the middle of the photo, his right arm wrapped around John, left around Danny Rodriguez. Like a sign from the heavens, a vertical shaft of light beaming between window curtains illuminated only Bradley.

"He was the best of us," said Danny.

John turned his head to the left. Danny was sitting in a chair next to the bed, his gaze lost in the same picture. "And you," continued Danny, sliding his eyes toward John, "are still a stubborn son of a bitch who refuses to die."

John managed a smile. "That's because you're too good of a medic."

Danny waved that off with his hand.

"You're lucky we're both AB positive. You'd be dead if I had any other blood type."

John scanned the nightstand by the bed. There were two empty blood bags with traces of red inside. Hovering above them, hanging from an IV pole, a bag was dispensing clear liquid through a catheter, straight into John's forearm.

"You should see the catheter under your ass."

John shook his head.

"How long have I been out?"

"Two days." Danny sighed, his playful expression turning serious. "I honestly didn't think you'd make it."

"That bad?"

"I had to restitch you properly. Both bullets grazed you, but the one that went through your waist was definitely a higher caliber. Probably a thirty."

"Seven point six two by thirty-nine," said John.

"Russian?"

"AK-47."

Danny leaned back in his seat. The look in his eyes told John he understood the situation was worse than he'd imagined.

"And the shoulder?"

"That was probably my SIG. They were going to shoot me with it in the head."

Danny considered this for a moment, then stood up and walked out of the room. He came back with a stainless steel flask and brought it to John's lips.

"Take a few swigs. And then tell me everything."

John took a swig of stiff bourbon.

He then told Danny everything.

———

The sun began to sink below the trees on the western side of Danny's ranch. Sitting on a front-porch chair, John admired the view the way only someone with a second chance at life could—through a lens that made colors more vivid and the passage of time a blessing.

Perched atop a gentle clearing, Danny's two-story house was surrounded by swaying branches and rustling leaves in every direction. It was a secluded five-acre oasis that could've been mistaken for a place far more rural than Longview, Texas. What made this patch of land unique was not its seclusion or proximity to a freight line—it bordered the Union Pacific Railroad station, where the train crews changed shifts—but the fact that it had belonged to Danny's family long before Longview ever existed.

John had a hard time wrapping his head around generations of people residing in one place for over two centuries, but Daniel Emilio Rodriguez IV came from no ordinary family. His ancestors had fought in the Mexican War of Independence, which freed Mexico from Spanish rule in 1821. Disillusioned by the newly installed Mexican government considering another monarchy, Danny's family migrated to what would quickly become the Mexican state of Coahuila y Tejas. Legend went that Danny's ancestor Miguel Rodriguez had planted his wartime bayonet into the soil somewhere near where John was sitting now, and proclaimed: "We shall move no more, only live and perish!"

That motto was reflected in the headstones on the southeastern corner of the property, where Danny could trace family lineage that had stood in defiance to Comanche tribes, Anglo-American land-grabbers, and the greatest force to impact the area: Coahuila y Tejas becoming part of Texas, the twenty-eighth state of the United States of America. Danny's family had embraced their new nation—a Rodriguez had fought in every American war since World War I—in part because they lived by one simple creed: Borders shift, duty endures.

It was these types of principles that made Danny the most honorable and trustworthy human John had ever known. The kind of friend John might not talk to for a year, yet their conversations would always pick up as though they'd just chatted a day ago. Danny became the only person outside of Claire to whom John would occasionally open up, even about the morbid possibility of Danny being the one to inform Claire if John had died in combat. The fact that John's closest brush with death came on American soil, after all his deployments, was so unsettling that he couldn't quite accept it—or shake off his lingering feeling of disquiet.

"Why didn't you come to me earlier?" said Danny, gently rocking in the other chair.

"I wanted to be sure about the Grail's location before I involved you and the others. Then it would just be an extraction operation. I didn't want anyone getting caught up in the bullshit leading up to it."

"All due respect, John, your bullshit became our bullshit the moment you found out Volkov's brother was behind it. Bradley wasn't just your friend. Hell, Kevin died next to me behind that big-ass steel desk we hauled into the hallway. What a shit show that was. We lost five guys within fifteen minutes. You don't think the rest of the team wants a piece of Yuri Volkov? Those were probably his mercenaries we ran into. Andrei was just an arms dealer."

John sighed. Danny had it all wrong, but John knew him well enough to know this conversation would be an uphill climb.

"I don't care about getting a piece of Yuri. I just want to save Claire."

Danny seemed to get hit palpably by John's words, and lowered his head.

"I'm sorry, man. I'm being selfish with my own shit." He swirled the last of the bourbon and drained the flask. "But it's everyone's shit now."

"No, it's not, Danny."

"John... you show up at my gate torn to shreds. You tell me the craziest story I've ever heard, and I've heard a lot of crazy shit. You tell me that the brother of the asshole responsible for the deaths of our guys is behind all of it. That he still might be here, in the country. And you really think I'm gonna let it end there?"

John said nothing. He stared at the glowing contours of the horizon, amber light flickering through the flitting leaves. The sight of oak trees swaying in the Texas breeze, which seemed majestic just minutes ago, suddenly filled him with a horrible foreboding.

Danny stood up.

"There is only one way this ends. I'll start making calls."

70

"Who all is in?" said John as he took a seat at the kitchen table, thoroughly refreshed after a ten-hour sleep.

"The usual suspects," said Danny, setting down two plates of scrambled eggs and sausage. "Landry, Diaz, Broussard. And get this. I got Luntz."

"Captain Obvious?" John smiled. "I haven't heard from him in over ten years."

"He teaches high school math up in Vermont."

"I guess he has free time during summer break. And the others?"

Danny set his fork down.

"You know, making it, day by day. I don't know. They don't tell me everything."

John slid his plate away, planting his forearms on the table. "How bad, Danny?"

Danny let out a deflating sigh, his eyes drifting through the window. He rubbed his chin like he was pondering a painful memory. He finally turned to John.

"Landry got out of jail a couple of weeks ago. Served four months for public intoxication and disorderly conduct."

"That seems like a long sentence."

"It was his third intoxication and disorderly conduct in the last year. They found him yelling at a dumpster, claiming Osama bin Laden was hiding inside it. He's been in and out of rehab, but it's just..."

Danny trailed off, and John just shook his head.

"What about Diaz?"

"Same old. Never met a bar fight he didn't like. Just angry at the world. You know how it is. They discard you after service like an empty shell casing. Oh, you have PTSD? Go stand in line with a hundred other vets to get ten minutes of therapy and some ibuprofen for your migraine. Broussard might be doing the best out of all of them. Fishes in the Louisiana swamp most of the year, shut off from the world."

Danny leaned back in the chair, taking in his kitchen as though it was brand new.

"Who am I to talk? I'm bunkered here with more ammo than a goddamn armory. I've stockpiled enough guns to equip a whole squadron. Hell, I could build a little retaining wall from all the C-4 blocks I've stashed."

"Jesus, Danny. Where did you get that much C-4?"

"Trust me, Mitcham, you don't wanna know."

John laughed, but the sadness inside him was spreading like wildfire.

Somehow, despite knowing countless struggles of men and women who had served, a part of John had always believed his own difficulties of adjusting to life after combat were unique to him. But there was nothing unique here. It was a pattern. A clear testament to the government's failure to look after those who'd looked after everyone else. The medals, the holidays, the *Thank you for your services* were all noble gestures. But between the gestures were stretches of grueling life. And for so many of America's bravest, that was the hardest battlefield of all.

"Danny, look..." John poked his scrambled eggs, looking for the right words. "I'm just gonna say it. This is not a suicide mission. And it sure as hell won't fix any of our problems. It's a sugar high, at best—"

"I know what this is," interrupted Danny.

"Do you?"

"Do *you*?" said Danny, tossing his fork onto the table.

John rubbed his temples, wishing he had just kept his mouth shut. Too late now.

"All right, Danny, tell me. What is it? What am I missing?"

"Support, for one. Clarity, for another. The fact that you actually thought you could do this by yourself makes you the craziest out of all of us. Then you preach to me about what this is and isn't. Right now, this is a *might as well*."

"Might as well?"

"Yes, might as well do a useful deed before we die."

"Don't talk like that."

"Have you even been listening to me? Landry is drinking himself to death. Diaz is begging to get hurt so he doesn't feel any other pain. Broussard is floating in a swamp, staring at trees. The only time I leave this ranch seems to be to attend someone's funeral. We have no use in the regular world. You wanna know the truth? I'd rather fight a thousand mercenaries than sit on my front porch, waiting to die. And it's not because I want to die, John. It's because I want to have some semblance of a purpose again."

Mist started pooling in Danny's eyes. He placed his hand on John's shoulder.

"Fuck all our other missions. Helping you means more to me than any of the shit they told us was for a good cause. And you know the rest of the guys would follow you into any battle."

"I know they would, Danny. But this is not military service."

Danny finally plopped a bite of his now-cold scrambled egg into his mouth.

"No. This is personal."

Personal. That one little word. Was there any other that motivated people more while simultaneously leading them to their impending doom? John had to rein this in, here and now.

"It might be personal, but we need to treat it like professionals."

Danny straightened in his chair. His eyes narrowed, brimming with focus.

"Of course," he said.

"Good. We need to get a head start before the others get here."

A confident smile twisted Danny's lips. "Already ahead of you. I have contacts at the DMV. They're combing through traffic footage from that night, looking for any convoys of SUVs leaving Austin. If they're anywhere near, we'll find them."

John was impressed. Then he was flooded by memories of him and Nia combing through traffic footage in the townhouse in Georgetown. He had failed her so miserably.

"Nia gave me her phone right before we got split up. It had a tracker for her other phone, but…"

"But what?"

"It got wet when I jumped into Lake Austin."

Danny looked confused. He got up and walked out of the kitchen. He was back within seconds, holding Nia's phone and John's Montauk picture.

John took the creased, faded picture and put it in his pocket. "Thanks."

"You're not going to look at the tracker?"

"I told you, it got wet."

"John, it's a waterproof phone, and it was inside a waterproof case on top of it. I charged it for you last night."

John couldn't believe what he was hearing. "They make waterproof phones?"

"For fuck's sake, John, are you still using flip phones?"

John didn't even bother answering. He unlocked the phone with the pattern Nia had shown him and clicked on the inconspicuous icon three menus to the right.

A map opened.

An orange dot pulsated.

Nia's phone was in El Paso, Texas.

71

In the golden glow of the Texas afternoon, Emanuel Diaz wended his way up the long driveway, the first to arrive at Danny's ranch. He wore combat boots, faded jeans, and a white T-shirt. He carried absolutely nothing.

John stood next to Danny on the front porch, observing his old friend arrive with more emotions than he could possibly untangle. Aside from Danny, John hadn't seen another Teammate from his old squadron for nearly a decade, when they threw him a send-off party at McP's Irish Pub, the famous navy SEAL watering hole in Coronado, California. It wasn't until Diaz came within twenty feet that John noticed the bruise over his left eye.

"You don't seem happy to see me, Mitcham," said Diaz, planting himself directly in front of John.

John examined Diaz's face. The bruises on the left side of his head were all the colors of the rainbow.

John said, "Is this the part where you tell me 'you should see the other guy'?"

"The guy is a girl, and she doesn't have a scratch on her.

Friendly advice: never cheat on a Colombian who keeps a baseball bat in her closet."

John snickered. "You were once quick enough to dodge bats."

"I still am. She heard me mumbling her cousin's name in my sleep, and began her batting practice at four a.m."

All John could do was shake his head.

"Well, she prepared you well for what's about to come."

"No, my friend. Those Russian fucks have no idea what's about to hit them."

That was Diaz. Short fuse and long hyperboles.

———

Andrew Broussard passed through the gate an hour later, methodically marching up the driveway with a drawstring backpack slung over his left shoulder. His beard ran down to his chest, a thick tangle that surely didn't feel good in the ninety-five-degree Texas heat.

Once he was close enough, John realized Broussard's beard was now more salt than pepper. His hairline had receded by half an inch since John had taken shots of Jameson with him at McP's. The rest of him seemed in as good a shape as he'd ever been. Slender, sinewy frame, not an ounce of fat.

Broussard stopped, equidistant from John and Danny, and managed a greeting by way of a grunt. He then walked into the house.

———

Maurice Landry arrived at the gate shortly after nine a.m. the following morning. He walked up to the front porch with a standard-issue rucksack and heavy gait. John stared at his own reflection in Landry's aviator sunglasses, until he finally took them off.

"I can't believe you dragged my ass down to Texas," he said to John and cracked a pearly-white smile.

John gave him a hug.

"I heard you could use a break from Cleveland."

"Brother, Cleveland could use a break from me."

———

Two hours later, a blue Toyota Prius drove through the gate.

"Is there anything more conspicuous in rural Texas than a compact hybrid?" said Landry, watching through the kitchen window as the car rattled over dirt and gravel, leaving behind a trail of dust.

"Yeah," said Danny. "A vegan restaurant."

This elicited laughter from everyone as they watched the Prius park in front of the porch. The driver door swung open, and out climbed Sam Luntz. He stretched out thoroughly, placed his left hand on his hip, his right above his brow like a visor, and took in the property.

"This dude," said Diaz.

Luntz finally walked to the back of the car and popped open the trunk. He pulled out an enormous rucksack. Then a hardshell spinner suitcase with wheels. Then a duffel bag.

"Jesus Christ," said Landry. "Luntz thinks we're going on a cruise."

"You can't say he didn't come prepared," said Danny. "Come on, let's help him out."

John walked out with his Teammates onto the porch, the soreness of his wounds reminding him it was a good idea to let the others help Luntz with his luggage. Luntz was surrounded by Diaz (who grabbed his duffel bag) and Landry (who grabbed his suitcase); he waved at John and said with a straight face:

"I brought a lot of stuff."

You sure did, Captain Obvious.

72

"Why are they still in the country?" asked Landry. "It's been five days since they acquired the target."

A fair question, thought John, although it was the reference to Nia as the acquired target that rankled. Yet, she was exactly that. Which was why John needed to follow his own advice and clear his head of all personal attachment.

"We only know that Nia's cell phone is still in the country," he corrected, pointing at the laptop screen that held the undivided attention of everyone huddled around the dining table. The Google Maps satellite image showed a compound on the outskirts of El Paso, Texas. "But, based on the ranch I infiltrated in Pennsylvania, this fits the exact profile of where they would set up base."

"We think they're coordinating their exit across the border into Mexico," chimed in Danny. "Strategically, El Paso makes the most sense. They're probably working with the cartels to secure a safe passage. I wouldn't be surprised if the cartels are also helping them secure their flight out of Mexico. Which is why we don't have much time."

"How many of them are there?" said Diaz.

"I counted thirteen when they had me surrounded," said John. "But there are likely more. We need to assume we're outnumbered at least three to one."

"Great," said Landry. "Six farts in their forties against twenty mercenaries."

"I'm a better shot at forty-four than I was at twenty-four," said Diaz.

"That's because you were permanently shitfaced at twenty-four."

Everyone at the table erupted into laughter. Except John.

"All right, that's enough. We need to focus. Every second counts."

"Yes, sir," came a few responses.

"Danny, you and Broussard prep the gear and weapons. You know what everyone likes."

"Roger that," said Danny. Broussard acknowledged the command with a spit of his chewing tobacco into a plastic cup.

"Luntz, you're in charge of logistics, to and fro, including all the contingency plans. It's an eleven-hour drive with no stops other than to get gas, so we will need to take shifts."

"On it," said Luntz.

"Diaz and Landry, you're helping me plan out the assault. Danny found the most recent building plans from the county office. Eleven years old, but it's the best we got."

"Copy," said Landry and Diaz in unison.

John looked around the table. Alert faces. Eager.

"Anyone have any questions?"

"I have a question," said Luntz. "Why is her cell phone still on?"

An awkward silence fell over the room.

"What do you mean?" said Danny.

"Nia's phone. Forget where it is. Why is it even turned on?

Yuri doesn't need anything on that phone. He already has Nia. He has everything he wants."

Looking at the blank expressions around the room, John surmised that Captain Obvious had posed a question whose answer should've been obvious from the get-go, yet no one else had realized it until now. John said it aloud.

"He doesn't have everything yet. The phone is on in case I am still alive."

"So he left it on to lure you into a trap?" said Luntz.

Exactly.

———

Danny separated the brisket point from the flat. The glory of the sight was only matched by the mouth-watering smell of a perfectly-smoked-for-twelve-hours Texas-style barbecue.

That glorious sight was obscured when everyone else huddled closer to the meat, like a pack of wolves. And wolves they were, all right. Apex predators with the skills to hunt down the evilest of men. But as John leaned back in his chair, watching his men pile their plates high, he couldn't quell the torrent of guilt and doubt. Had he ever really intended to ask his old Teammates to help him extract Claire, back before he knew Yuri Volkov was involved? His gut told him the answer was no.

The only thing that helped him supplant his guilt for involving them in all this was the orange dot pulsating in El Paso, Texas. That was the compensatory quality of culpability: you can justify a great guilt by covering it with an even greater one. And right now, nothing ate at John more than his responsibility for Nia's predicament. Even though she was too valuable for the Russians to kill, every moment John and his Teammates carefully planned the operation to save her posed a risk that she could be smuggled out of the country in the meantime. What if she'd been moved already? What if the orange dot was nothing but a trap?

"Stop staring at that phone," said Landry.

John looked up to find Maurice holding out a plate with three slices of the brisket flat, two chunks of burnt ends, baked beans, and collard greens. After tucking the phone away into his pocket, John took the plate and set it on the table.

"Thanks."

"What's the matter?" said Landry, his eyes scanning John's face.

John squeezed his right hand into a fist, then released, frowning at it the way one might regard a jammed gun. "You know," he answered with a suppressed sigh.

Landry considered that for a moment. He set his plate on the table.

"Look, buddy, I'm gonna give it to you straight. Right now, the biggest risk to our safety is not the Russians or your Parkinson's. It's your doubt. You need to clear your head before dawn. Otherwise we should call off this mission."

John wasn't so sure about Landry's ranking order of risks, but he couldn't deny his uncertainty presented a clear danger to the men he considered his brothers. Landry seemed to sense John's thoughts, and leaned in.

"I don't mean to make light of your condition. We all feel for you. But at this early stage of your disease, your intermittent hand tremors are no worse than my limp or Luntz's bum hip. Shit, man, Diaz's hands are shaking from alcohol withdrawal far worse than yours."

John managed a faint laugh.

Landry glanced over his shoulder at everyone slowly making their way back to the table with plates full of brisket. He placed a hand on John's shoulder.

"None of us are what we once were. But we are all here and fully committed. We go with you leading us, or not at all."

The rest of the has-beens took their seats, wasting no time wolfing down the succulent meat. Silence ensued. It was soothing under the starry night. The fire crackled ten feet away, casting orange hues over familiar faces that had by now told all the familiar stories. *Remember that time Danny threw a hand grenade instead of a stun grenade? Remember when we got shit-faced before the tug-of-war against the other squadron and still won? Remember the mission in Kabul? Remember Aaron Bradley... may he rest in peace.*

"How come we don't do this more often?" said Diaz through a mouthful of brisket.

"Hunt Russian mercenaries?" said Landry.

This elicited loud hoots. Everyone knew what Diaz meant, yet no one gave the answer—even though they all knew it, in one form or another:

Entropy grows with time.

Acknowledging that, John had a sudden moment of enlightenment. He wasn't fighting the Russians. Or LIS. Or whoever was behind all this. He was battling entropy. Ever since Jenny's death, he had taken on the universe's accelerating disorder. Trying desperately to turn back the clock. To glue back the pieces. But he only seemed to shatter them further, no matter how good his intentions were.

"Here's to Captain John Mitcham," said Danny, raising a toast with his Mexican lager. "His shit show of a life has brought us all closer together."

The men laughed, and John forced a counterfeit smile. It did well to mask his horrible angst that he had brought them all together just to die.

73

The four a.m. alarm went off.

John opened his eyes, slapped the clock. He assessed his state. His side and shoulder were sore despite the painkillers Danny had given him. He felt all the usual nerves before a mission. Tingles rose up his spine, knots formed in his stomach, ringing grew louder between his ears. He ran through his mental checklist, calibrating, recalibrating, all while trying to maintain that elusive equilibrium between too wired and too calm. It was a familiar concoction of sensations that arose from only one reality:

There's a good chance I might die today.

———

Piss. Shit. Shower. Brush your teeth. Dress. Final gear check. Final weapons check. Final run-through. The finality of no turning back. Be ready for things to go wrong. But don't doubt your plan. Don't doubt yourself. Don't be afraid. The first enemy is all your doubts and all your fears and everyone who ever told you that you couldn't do this. You can do this. Remember your SEAL ethos. Recite it, feel it, believe it:

There is a special breed of warrior ready to answer our Nation's call. A common man with uncommon desire to succeed. Forged by adversity, he stands alongside America's finest ... to serve his country, the American people, and protect their way of life.

I am that warrior.

———

Are you that warrior?
    I am that warrior, sir.
    Are *you* that warrior?
    I am that warrior, sir!

———

The gloomy haze of dawn's prelude stretched before a Black Chevy Suburban gliding west on I-20. Shadows on the horizon receded under the rising tide of the sun's rays, six highly trained killers hurtling toward El Paso. Atoms colliding. Cosmic forces set in motion 13.8 billion years ago. There was no stopping this.

74

Danny pulled the Chevy Suburban off an access road twenty miles east of El Paso.

As the SUV rumbled over the rough desert terrain, John checked his watch: 5:47 p.m.

Right on schedule.

After twelve minutes of weaving through a field of fourwing saltbush, Danny entered a valley. Flanked by two steep hills, it narrowed slightly with each passing yard. By the time Danny eased into a dead end and shut off the engine, the hills blanketed the vehicle with shadows. A perfect base of operations.

John opened the passenger door at the same time all the other doors swung open, and the SUV spilled six former navy SEALs clad in desert camouflage. Danny opened the trunk, and as the rest of the SEALs huddled around the back, John remained in front of the car and performed his patented 360-degree scan. He noted all significant slope and terrain variations. He then crouched and ran his hand over the dirt. Scooping a fistful, he rubbed it between his palms and tossed it in the air.

His eyes closely followed the trail of dust until it fell on the ground or dematerialized. The wind was blowing away from the two-story house perched on a hill a mile north of here—an advantage in the unlikely event Yuri had dogs at the compound that could pick up foreign scent. But John knew he would have to check the wind direction again on the other side of the hill. He finally walked over to the back of the car. The gear had already been laid out, courtesy of Danny's paranoid decade of stockpiling for the end of the world.

Noveskes dominated the carbine options, although Diaz and Broussard preferred the Heckler & Koch HK416, John's former weapon of choice. A McMillan TAC-338 sniper rifle was propped against the car for Luntz. Allocated for each of the six members of Operation Nia was a SIG Sauer pistol, an IBA bullet-resistant outer tactical vest, a pair of M84 stun grenades, breaching explosives, a helmet with NODs, and fully loaded ammo magazines for their respective weapons.

Yet among all the lethal and ancillary equipment, one item was more imperative than any other—a high-altitude, ultra-quiet, multi-camera-equipped drone.

John carefully observed the live panoramic footage of hills and flats on a laptop screen.

Luntz piloted the drone, which cost almost as much as the rest of the weapons and gear combined. Price tag aside, this clandestine eye in the sky—built with parts more advanced than anything John had used during his last deployment—was readily available to the general public. It even calculated exact wind direction and speed, rendering John's dust toss utterly obsolete. That fact, more than all the technology laid before him, was what made him feel old.

He had been out of active service for over eight years, yet

advancements in technology made it seem like decades had passed. There was always an unrefined understanding inside him that the moment one felt antiquated was reached when the pace of change struck more angst than awe. No matter how much he tried to shake it off, the image of that chair he'd found in Yuri's Pennsylvania compound kept resurfacing, making him feel out of his depth. And when John began fearing what he didn't understand, his mind leaped to horrible possibilities. If the Pennsylvania compound had yielded the chair, what could possibly lie in El Paso?

No sooner had the question run through his head, the compound came into view on the laptop screen.

"You sure they can't detect the drone?" John asked with slight concern.

"Highly unlikely," said Luntz. "I'm hovering at thirteen thousand feet right now. I'll bring it closer and zoom in."

As Luntz did just that, the SEALs huddled around him, some observing the screen on his remote controller, others watching the same laptop as John.

Perched on a plateau, the two-story stucco was proportional on all sides. Four large SUVs were parked in front of it, the driveway a wide snake of dirt and gravel stretching a quarter mile to the nearest road. The drone orbited around it slowly and precisely, the zoom on the camera so powerful that John could make out imperfections in the stucco—and a man in a window.

The image wasn't quite clear enough to make out his face, but the black uniform was undeniable.

"They're there," said John, just as the man receded into darkness.

As if he had said a command, the chorus of magazines sliding into rifles filled the ravine.

―――

The night had set over El Paso, Texas, and reality had settled inside John: he had never been more nervous before any other mission.

He had tried to convince himself that his angst stemmed from his guilt of putting Nia in this situation. But now, moments from go time, there was no denying it. John felt as protective of Nia as he would have been of Jenny.

Where is your head at, John?

It was a dangerous question to ask before embarking on an operation that required absolute objectivity and emotional clarity. He ran his left hand over the gauze-covered wound on his right side. The damn thing was sore and far from healed, his shoulder not much better. The rest of the Teammates of Operation Nia formed a crescent moon in front of him.

He looked at them with a melancholy that quickly dissolved, leaving a void where no emotion lived. John turned off the only glowing lantern. His left eye twitched.

"Let's roll."

75

Assessing the terrain through NODs, John led five warriors down a hill. Yuri's compound was 1.12 miles from their base as the crow flew, but John and the team had already walked that distance just to get over the large hill. Up ahead, another hill, much gentler, but far more dangerous. From this distance and vantage point, the compound's outdoor lights looked like a cluster of stars on the horizon.

John made sure to follow the agreed-upon path—drawn up at Danny's ranch, confirmed with the drone, and verified with a reconnaissance sweep while there had still been daylight.

The drone flyover had been nothing short of vital to detect tripwire posts on the back side of the property. The findings confirmed John's suspicions about the compound, which was why he was being extra careful with his stride and diligent with his eyes. Still, he could sense the rest of the team was itching to go faster.

As they started hiking up the hill, John raised his right arm vertically, then dropped it, rotating it in circles parallel to his body. The SEALs followed his command, shifting from their wedge formation into a single-file column.

In a matter of minutes, John raised two fingers, signaling they were two hundred meters away. He transitioned into a crouched walk, the infrared laser of his rifle now swaying sideways. More lasers joined from behind him, an armada of invisible searchlights.

A hundred meters away, John halted and raised his index finger to signal the distance from the target. Luntz separated from the column, veering off toward two o'clock. The rest of the team took a knee, patiently observing Luntz as he disappeared behind the plateau of the property.

Then they waited.

The silence grew more tense with each second.

Finally, Luntz's voice came over the comm radio into John's ear.

"Alpha Team, this is Zero-Five. P-1 is secure. I repeat, P-1 is secure."

"Roger, Zero-Five," replied John. "Alpha Team heading toward P-2."

John motioned forward and transitioned into a military leopard crawl. The slope was mild enough to accommodate the movement, and it gradually flattened, but John's wounds were hampering his pace. Each pull of the arms and push of the legs was a pendulum of pain oscillating between his shoulder and waist. Knowing he was not at 100 percent physically strained John's mental focus and confidence. *Keep it together.*

Twenty meters away, he and the team reached a ridge of stones lining the plateau's edge. Slowly and methodically, John weaved between the trip wires, throwing glances behind him to ensure everyone followed his exact path.

Ten meters away, John halted and scanned the house once more. Every corner. Every window. Every inch.

The kitchen windows were emitting a faint light, but all

other windows were dark. The outdoor sconce lights threw blinding triangles in the night vision that John made a point to avoid. He gave another forward motion with his arm and started crawling in the shadows.

The team followed him toward Position 2: the electric backup generator installed five feet from the house's southwestern side. They reached it within sixty seconds, huddling around the unit as though it were a sacred monolith—and they were about to disrespect it like heretics.

Broussard stuck C-4 plastic explosive blocks onto the generator and connected them with a detonation cord. He gave John a nod, and John whispered into the comm microphone.

"Alpha Zero-Five, this is Zero-One. P-2 is secure."

"Copy, Zero-One," Luntz acknowledged over the radio.

John crouch-walked toward the back door, the team trailing tightly behind. As soon as they reached the double doors, Diaz began taping C-4 around the doorway. He soon gave a thumbs-up, drawing himself flush against the adjacent wall on the left side. Broussard joined him while John, Danny, and Landry backed away to the right of the door.

John whispered into the microphone.

"Alpha Zero-Five, this is Zero-One. Alpha Team is in position. Begin the countdown."

The silence lasted mere seconds. But how many neurons fired off in seconds? How many synapses were bridged? How many chemical reactions roiled through the body?

"Good copy, Zero-One," crackled Luntz's voice. "Beginning the countdown now."

Heart racing. *Are you that warrior?*

"Three..."

Adrenaline spiking. *I am that warrior.*

"Two..."

Breath catching. *Are you that warrior?*
"One..."
Atoms colliding. *I am that warrior.*
"Zero—"

76

BOOM. Luntz detonated the C-4 on the power pole transformer.

BOOM. Diaz blew up the backup generator.

BOOM. Broussard breached the back door.

Green. Black. Chaos.

John entered the house at the same time as Diaz, finding two Russian mercenaries frantically searching for handguns on the dining table—John put two bullets into one, Diaz three into the other.

They moved forward swiftly, infrared lasers scanning—*bam bam bam bam bam*—three more mercenaries gunned down upon entering the great room.

Lights emerged from the rooms. *How can that be if the generator is out?* Phones and flashlights, of course.

A chorus of Russians yelling, coordinating. Thundering footsteps above, the ceiling practically shaking. All-out mobilization.

Gunfire from the left, indiscriminate firing in the dark, and Diaz caught a bullet.

Fuck, they're behind the couch.

Alpha Team sprayed bullets into the couch, rewarded by immediate grunts and howls followed by thuds. John and Broussard circled around the couch to find two more mercenaries in a pool of blood.

John and Danny crouched next to Diaz.

"I'm all right," he said.

He wasn't. His thigh was torn with a high-caliber bullet, bleeding so profusely that John had no doubt his femoral artery was severed. Danny dragged him into a corner and opened his med pack.

"Go, go, go," he said to John. "I'll wrap him up and join—"

Flash beams and gunshots cut him off. John ran and dove behind the kitchen bar, joining Landry and Broussard. They all changed their magazines, and Landry wasted no time tossing a stun grenade into the great room.

The flash-bang went off, and the ringing in John's ears felt palpable—evidence enough it was far worse for the mercenaries on the other side. He swung his rifle around the kitchen bar, Broussard brought his over the top, both firing rapidly.

Two mercenaries went down; two more staggered into a side room.

John began charging forward, but then heard them before he saw them—*clank clank clank*—at least two stun grenades tossed from the stairwell, bouncing toward the kitchen. He ran back and ducked behind the kitchen bar, but it didn't matter.

Blur. Nausea. High-pitched ringing.

John barely made out the flashlights scanning the kitchen. Bullets began ravaging the kitchen bar, the wall, and the whole goddamned area strobed with gunfire, amplifying John's dazed state. He did the only thing he could think of to jolt himself out of it: John Mitcham punched himself in his torso wound.

The pain shot a bolt of lightning up his spine, snapping him into a semblance of coherence, just in time to see a gun muzzle in his face—*Oh, Claire*—but the Russian slumped to the ground, a bullet sluiceway in his forehead.

Strong hands pulled John backward.

John looked up to find Landry. He was grinning—until his neck burst open.

Horror made John fire indiscriminately in the direction where the shot had come from. One of his bullets struck the mercenary in the face, and he planted it on the floor, but John kept firing into the dead man's head with blinding fury.

Broussard snatched John backward, pulling him behind the narrow side of the bar.

"Focus!"

Those were the first words Broussard had said all day. They were spot on. John pushed down the anger and sadness of his friend's death, coming back into the world with cold determination.

"We check on Diaz and move forward."

Broussard nodded, and they both peeked around the bar. Danny was in a corner behind a lounge chair, putting finishing touches on the thick wrap around Diaz's leg. More footfalls cascaded down the staircase. John and Broussard emerged from behind the bar and mowed down legs indiscriminately. A pair of mercenaries tumbled down and were finished off by John and Broussard at the landing. John reloaded his magazine, and Broussard followed suit.

Suddenly, intermittent gunshots came from outside.

"It's Luntz's sniper," said Broussard.

"They must've exited out front after they tossed the flashbangs," said John.

Nia...

Danny swept across the room, joining them.

John quickly led the way toward the front. He drew his back flush against the wall, then swung his rifle around a doorway into a bedroom. Empty. Broussard did the same with the room on the opposite side of the hallway. Clear.

They finally reached the front door.

Three dead mercenaries were sprawled on the porch. No sign of Nia.

John became acutely aware of how eerily quiet it had become. He looked at Danny and Broussard, and brought his index finger to his lips. He quietly trod back into the hallway. Broussard and Danny followed, all three of them grazing the staircase rise below the balusters, their rifles pointed upward.

A creak of the floorboards came from above. John pointed to the area of the ceiling where the sound had come from, then gave a hand command. Off they went up the stairs.

John's heart was drumming in his ears, adding a distracting bass to the stun grenade-induced ringing. He reached the top floor landing and saw a long, narrow hallway full of doors. Oh, how John hated those doors. The green hues of his night vision were picking up no light whatsoever. Then Danny pointed to a door on the left, toward the back. John couldn't see it at first, but the faintest trace of light was escaping under the door.

John quickly led the way and assumed position with a stun grenade in his hand. Broussard gave another nod on the other side of the door and violently kicked it in. John tossed the flashbang into the room and backed off. As soon as it detonated, John and Broussard merged shoulder to shoulder at the doorway, scanning the room.

Suddenly, John felt the unholy burn of bullets spray into his back.

77

John fell forward, watching the wall ahead of him get perforated with bullets meant for him.

Broussard had already turned on his back, returning fire at the door across the hallway—or whatever remained of it now that however many mercenaries had emptied their AK-47 clips into it.

John followed suit, turning onto his back, which felt like it had been pummeled with a meat tenderizer. If not for the bulletproof vest, he would be feeling nothing at all right now. He emptied his magazine into the shredded door across the hallway and took cover with Broussard behind a wall in their room.

Only then did John see a flashlight propped on the bed, a perfect decoy by the mercenaries to lure him in so they could fire from across the hallway.

"Alpha Zero-One, what's your status?" said Danny over the radio, although John could also hear his voice from the hallway. John got a thumbs-up from Broussard and spoke into the microphone.

"Alpha Zero-Three, we're good. Lower your voice."

"Copy that," whispered Danny. "I'm going to toss a stun grenade through the hole in the door."

"Copy, Zero-Three," said John, slapping a fresh magazine into his rifle. "We're ready."

John listened as the grenade thud-and-clanked into the room across the hallway, detonating almost immediately. He charged into the room with Broussard, finding four huddled mercenaries stumbling into each other, two of them firing blindly, shooting one of their comrades. John and Broussard finished off the rest in a true fish-in-a-barrel fashion.

After the bodies slumped on the floor, the world went quiet.

The adrenaline began receding just enough for John to fully experience the extent of his pain. His side. His shoulder. His back. His ears. It suddenly occurred to him.

Where is Yuri?

Had he escaped out the front door and taken Nia with him? John was just about to speak into the microphone to check in with Luntz, but then he heard a whimper. He exchanged a look with Danny and Broussard.

They carefully exited the room. The hallway was capped by a door at the very end. The thin space between the door and the doorway was as dark as everything else—until the door's outline illuminated, creating a monolithic rectangle in John's night vision. Like a gateway of solemn inevitability, unearthing his most primal fears. But John was going to open that door, and that would be that.

He plodded ahead, the muzzle of his rifle leading the way. Were the walls caving in on him? His heart wanted to escape his chest. But there was no choice. Was there ever?

John stopped in front of the door and twisted the knob. It was unlocked.

Someone placed a hand on his shoulder. John didn't bother checking whether it was Danny or Broussard. He abandoned all his caution and all his training. He lifted his NODs, the green-hued prism giving way to the gloom of his naked eye. John then swung the door open.

A part of him expected to get shot. No. Almost wanted it. But a far larger part of him knew with absolute certainty what he would find. His greatest nightmare manifesting in a house in El Paso, Texas, in the United States of America.

In the amber-red glow of a rusted lantern, Nia was on her knees.

Over her right shoulder peered the predatory eye of Yuri Volkov, the barrel of his gun planted at the back of Nia's head.

78

Nia's eyes bored into John's core. They weren't emitting fear. Instead, they showed an emotion far more unsettling. Resignation. A helplessness that John could not cure, because no matter how he calculated the standoff—the gun to Nia's head, John and his men blocking the only door, the alignment of the moon and the stars—the final and only card Yuri held was to end Nia's life.

"G. I. Joe," he said.

To John, it sounded almost like a question. As though Yuri was expecting someone else.

"Put the gun down," said John, a useless plea to buy more time.

Yuri scoffed fittingly. "You fucking Americans say stupidest shit. Why you say this?"

"Because it doesn't have to be like thi—"

"More stupid shit. Stop talking and tell your friends to back up."

John waved off Danny and Broussard, listening to their retreating steps without taking his eyes off Yuri.

"You've already taken my wife. Doesn't that make us even for your brother?"

This made Yuri's peering eye narrow.

"What you talking about, G. I. Joe?"

"I'm saying we're already even. So let her go."

"You make no sense."

This fucking monster. John had to reframe his understanding of the human condition, because Yuri clearly didn't operate under the principle of "eye for an eye." It was eyes and more eyes for one eye.

"You have every right to avenge your brother. But she had nothing to do with it. So just let her go and kill me instead."

Nia let out a sob, and Yuri yanked her hair.

"Shut up," he said into her ear. His head emerged fully over her shoulder.

Was that anger in his eyes? No. It looked more like disbelief.

"You killed my brother."

Again, he said it as though it was a question. He started laughing. A sickening cackle. "I fucking hated my brother. Piece of shit. Put cigarette burns into me when I was kid. I should buy you vodka shot."

John couldn't quite process what he was hearing. It had to be a trick. Some endgame Yuri was playing. Anger began to simmer up John's neck.

"Then why did you kidnap my wife?"

Yuri grimaced, shaking his head.

"You make no sense again, G. I. Joe. I don't know anything about your wife."

John felt a weakness in his knees. This had to be a ploy, as sickening as Yuri's filthy laugh.

"Let me guess," said John. "You didn't kidnap the Quantum Grail operators either?"

"Of course I kidnap operators. I paid for job, I do the job. What the fuck your wife got to do with it? Are you crazy? Eh? Head don't work after all the years of fighting?"

John nearly lost his balance. He couldn't tell if the blood was rushing into his head or draining from it. What the hell was going on? This... it couldn't be.

Get it together, John.

"Yuri, who paid you to kidnap the operators?"

Whatever came across Yuri's face was not an emotion John had ever witnessed on another human. It was a combination of dread and... what else was that? John would not have realized it had his eyes not flitted toward Nia, absorbing her resigned state. That was Yuri's other element. Utter resignation.

"Do you believe in God? Eh, G. I. Joe?"

John collected himself.

"I lost my faith a long time ago."

This softened Yuri a bit, a semblance of empathy entering his expression.

"I understand," he said, his gaze drifting somewhere beyond the room. "We see things." Suddenly he was back, and so were his dread and resignation. "But God exists. You know how I know? Because I see devil. I meet him."

Yuri's icy tone sent chills up John's back. He couldn't tell if this was some Russian metaphor.

"Who did you see?"

Yuri shook his head again.

"They call him King of Hearts. But he heartless man. He don't have soul."

"Yuri, just tell me who he is, and I will take care of him."

Yuri burst into his cynical cackle.

"Ohh, G. I. Joe. You either work for him or you stupidest man I ever met. I think last is true. You stupid and you be dead soon." A sudden darkness came over his eyes. The air felt charged with electricity. "I do you favor," growled Yuri, readjusting the gun against Nia's head.

"Yuri, no!"

But Yuri was pulling the trigger—

His right ear exploded and Nia screamed, Yuri's lifeless body slumping to the side.

John ran across the room and swept Nia into his arms.

He closed his eyes and held her tighter than he'd held anything in his life, her sobs reverberating against his body. He finally opened his eyes and looked at the bullet hole in the window. His gaze traveled beyond it, settling on the cylindrical silhouette of the water storage tank. It was too far and too dark for John to make out Luntz lying somewhere on top of it, but he nodded in his direction anyway.

79

"We have to evacuate," said Danny.

John had a hard time letting go of Nia, and she had her arms around him as tight as a bear trap. He stood up with her wrapped around him like that and carried her out of the room.

"Begin SSE immediately," he said to Danny and Broussard on his way out.

He sat Nia down on the floor in the hallway, an ample distance away from the gore in the room. He slowly unwrapped her arms from him and cupped her face.

"Are you hurt?"

She shook her head, tears streaming down her cheeks.

"Good," he said and handed her a flashlight. "You stay right here until we collect your electronics and any other sensitive information. Do you know where your stuff is?"

"It's all there," she said, pointing her shaking finger back at the room.

"Okay. I'll be right back."

John surged into the room to find Danny and Broussard already sliding Nia's laptops and cell phones into a duffel bag. He swept the area and started poring over the boxes lining the back wall. He halted upon opening the second box. It was filled with the all-too-familiar brain scans.

John flipped through a stack of MRIs, CTs, and PET scans. He moved on to the next box. Nothing but brain neuroimaging.

"That shit again," said Danny, standing over John's shoulder.

"Do we take it?" asked Broussard.

"No," sighed John. "Just keep looking."

"What are we looking for?" said Danny.

"I don't know. Just not this."

The three of them kept poring over the boxes, first methodically, then bordering on frantically.

Until Danny stopped and said, "I think I found something. It looks like a transcript."

"Of what?" said John, rummaging through a box in front of him.

"Of you."

John halted, meeting Danny's bewildered gaze.

"And Nia," Danny added.

John walked over, crouched in front of Danny's box, and pulled out a few sheets of paper. He couldn't quite understand what he was seeing. Each sheet contained a dialog-style printout of a conversation between him and Nia.

"They must've spied on you and typed out the recording," said Danny.

All John could do was shake his head. "Put it all in the bag."

They searched the rest of the boxes and found only more brain scans. They swept through every other room on the floor and discovered nothing of interest. John went back into Yuri's room once more for a final sweep, though he had a hard time looking away from Yuri's corpse. It wasn't the body itself that bothered him, but all the words Yuri had uttered before dying. He noticed for the first time a sliver of buff color on the floor, sticking out from under Yuri's torso.

"You searched him, right?" he asked Danny.

"Yeah, he had nothing on him."

John crouched next to the body and tugged at the beige paper. It turned out to be a manila folder Yuri had fallen on top of. John opened it. Inside were three black-and-white photos of a man. It appeared they had been captured by someone surveilling him as he was getting into a car. The strangest thing about it was that he looked familiar to John.

"Do you recognize him?" he asked Danny and Broussard as they huddled around him. They both shook their heads. John sighed, placed the envelope into the duffel bag, and said, "Let's roll out."

The four of them reached the downstairs landing, Nia led by John, her eyes closed at his insistence. The last thing she needed to see was more dead bodies. John took her to the front porch, where Luntz was guarding the perimeter.

"Thank you," said John, pulling Luntz into a hug.

After they released each other, Luntz handed him a pair of keys and pointed to the second-from-the-left SUV parked out front. "That one."

John nodded.

"Never fuck with a guy who drives a Prius," said Danny, emerging from the house and patting Luntz on the back.

"How's Diaz?" asked John.

"He lost a lot of blood, but I think he'll make it. Son of a bitch keeps swearing at me, complaining the bandage is too tight. Can you believe it?"

"That I can believe," said John. "But Landry..."

Danny cleared his throat. "We'll give him a proper burial."

"I know you will."

"John, are you sure you want to do this? We can be on standby."

John gestured around him, shaking his head at the carnage and destruction. "Look around you. There'll be no more of this."

Danny was quiet, and John gave him a hug. Then he hugged Broussard.

"I'll see you when I see you," John said to no one in particular. That way the lie felt less egregious. He turned away in the faint glow of moonlight and led Nia to the SUV. He popped the trunk open and tossed in the duffel bag, followed by his weapons and gear.

Nia was already in the passenger seat by the time he climbed in behind the wheel. It felt as though every emotion a human being could experience was flowing through him at once. John shook his head as if to diffuse the swell inside him, then turned on the engine.

He drove off down the dirt driveway, his eyes staying mostly on the rearview mirror. Like the rest of John's fraying life, the view was swallowed by darkness.

80

In a dated room of a rundown motel in Albuquerque, New Mexico, John heard Nia come out of the bathroom. Her gasp was immediate.

Sitting on the twin bed farthest away from the bathroom, John had his back turned to her, having just taken off his shirt. He quickly slipped into the fresh T-shirt he'd just pulled out of his rucksack, even though it was too late. Nia had seen his back, and no one should see vast stretches of skin that look like a mangled eggplant.

"How much pain are you in?" she asked.

John almost laughed. He'd always had a high tolerance for pain, but that scale had shifted and expanded and twisted, and the truth was that John no longer had an accurate gauge for pain.

"It's not as bad as it looks," he said, finding some truth to it. The other truth was that John was glad Nia had said anything at all. She had been quiet the entire ride to Albuquerque. It was hard for John to tell how much of it was temporary shock as opposed to permanent trauma.

She sat next to John, looking him over with a borderline

skeptic expression, as though she didn't buy that he was in front of her.

"I was sure they'd killed you in Austin."

John placed his palm on the back of her head and gave it a playful shake.

"Yuri knew he didn't," he said. "That's why he kept your phone on."

Nia frowned at this. "No. No, that's not why at all."

"I don't understand. Why else would he keep it turned on?"

"Because he was looking for the Grail himself."

John slid away from her, as though needing the space to process her words.

"Nia, that doesn't make any sense."

"I know. But it's true. He was looking for the Grail, and for the King of Hearts, whoever the hell that is. They grilled me on everything I know. They spoke in Russian the rest of the time, but I can tell you that the entire time they had me, Yuri obsessively kept checking my computer for the Grail's binary signature. And he was worried about the King of Hearts. He thought it was him that stormed the house when you and your SEALs showed up."

John emitted a slow, frustrated exhale. He rubbed his face, searching for an explanation, for the meaning, for anything at all to make sense of this. It finally dawned on him.

"He also said he didn't kidnap Claire."

"Yeah. So?"

"So we know that's not true. We have the footage of the van leaving the area around my neighborhood. I've seen that same van in the security footage at Franklin Medical Center. And Yuri sure didn't deny that it was him and his mercenaries who abducted Claire's patients."

Nia took a long time to digest that.

"Maybe we missed something," she said.

"Like what?"

"I don't know. But the DOT footage is still on my laptop. We can go over it again."

John and Nia had finished an entire pizza and a two-liter of Coke by the third time they reviewed the DOT footage of the van. If there was something to be missed, they sure were missing it. The footage undeniably showed the van leaving John's neighborhood and making its way to Franklin Medical Center, after which the mercenaries had swapped it for a semitrailer truck.

"There is nothing here," said John.

"We can go over it one more time," said Nia, stubborn as ever.

"We're wasting our time. I've looked at this footage so much I can give you the rundown by memory. At 8:05 a.m. the van is clocked at the intersection of South Glebe and Columbia Pike. At 8:09 it's passing exit seventy-one on I-66... wait, I mixed that up. It can't be 8:09. That's only four minutes between the two."

Nia pulled up the footage with a few clicks.

"No, you're right. 8:05, then 8:09. Four minutes apart."

"That can't be. I've driven on that stretch of road a thousand times. It takes ten minutes if the traffic is good. But it was already morning rush hour, so it would've taken even longer."

Nia kept toggling the two images of the van, her brow furrowing deeper with each click of the touchpad. "I don't know what to tell you. The timestamps are correct."

She finally locked her eyes with John. He could tell her mind was in overdrive. Goose bumps rose up his neck. "The van was going west on I-66. Can you pull up footage east of it, a few minutes earlier?"

"You stole my line, Captain."

It took Nia two minutes of furious scrolling through MP4 files before she halted and froze. John already knew what he would find, but he had to witness it with his own eyes.

"The van was on I-66 at eight o'clock," said Nia, pointing her finger at the timestamp below the frozen footage of the van captured with a highway camera. "The same time it was supposed to be in your neighborhood."

John plopped on the bed.

His body felt squeezed from all sides.

In the vein of Luntz, he blurted the obvious.

"They're two different vans."

Nia shook her head with incredulity, gawking at the screen. "Same plates. Even the checkmark dent seems the same. But... I can see a slight difference in their shapes now that I'm closely looking at them."

John regained himself.

"Do we have the footage of Glebe Road, north of I-66?"

"I'm going to have to hack back into the DOT."

Nia went into full Mozart mode on her keyboard.

81

Nia had tracked what she and John had dubbed Claire's van all the way to West Virginia. There she had lost it for good.

John pretty much lost all hope then, staring blankly at the laptop screen, as though an answer would reveal itself in the stale satellite maps of rural vastness.

"We have nothing," he said, more to the screen than to Nia.

"We at least know Yuri wasn't lying about not kidnapping Claire."

John snapped himself out of self-pity, resetting into the state he knew best—mission mode. "Let's assume he was telling the truth about everything else. He said he was paid to kidnap the Grail operators. But he didn't know where the actual Grail was. And he clearly was afraid of whoever this King of Hearts is."

"What kind of a man would a Russian mercenary fear?"

John thought about this for a moment.

"Someone more ruthless than him. Remember all those injured mercenaries at the ranch in Pennsylvania? There was a shootout. It had to be this King of Hearts."

"Which means he was probably the one who hired Yuri to kidnap the operators."

"All right, so let's play this out. Yuri kidnaps the operators. During their handoff to the King of Hearts, he gets ambushed. He escapes with Jason in tow, the only operator that doesn't get handed over to the King. Why would Yuri then track us all the way to Austin and set us up?"

"Maybe he wasn't tracking us at all until we got to Austin."

"What do you mean? He killed Langston and set us up."

"I don't think he was as clever as you think he was. I think he was following the same trail as us. I don't know where he found that chair, but he could have tracked Dividius Technologies to that water treatment plant, which led him to Langston, just as it led us. Our paths just collided, and we fell into his hands."

John leaned in. "Nia, if he didn't set us up, then who did?"

John was close enough to see her pupils dilate by a fraction.

"I think you already know."

The way she said it made the hair on the back of John's neck bristle.

"John, I don't know who this King of Hearts is, but you need to consider the strong possibility that this was all a setup from the very beginning. Why else would there be two seemingly identical vans unless someone wanted you to think Yuri kidnapped Claire?"

John experienced an entirely new flavor of fear—a chilling helplessness, as though he were a puppet at the mercy of a force too sinister for him to even begin to understand.

He stood up and paced around the room. He finally halted in front of the duffel bag, unzipped it, pulled out a box, and placed it on the floor in front of Nia.

"Open it."

Nia didn't move for a few seconds. She then removed the top, peering into the box as though expecting a snake to leap out of it. She stared at the sheets of paper for a good bit before pulling a few out. John carefully observed her expression settling into bewilderment.

"I remember this," she said. "Our conversation at the townhouse in Georgetown. I was explaining to you how a quantum computer works with the Froot Loops."

"Someone was listening."

"But how did they know we were going to be there? They would've had to install listening devices inside the house before we ever arrived."

"I assumed they listened through one of your laptops or cell phones. They still might be."

"No way, John. No way. I know these devices inside and out, the hardware, the software, better than anyone."

"Then it's more disturbing than I imagined."

"I think it's still more disturbing than you realize."

John only then noticed Nia's hands trembling.

"What do you mean?"

"Did you look at the timestamps printed at the bottom of these pages?"

John grabbed a page from the box. He gave a few blinks of disbelief before saying, "It's a typo."

"Is it?"

"It has to be. The date is eleven months ago. What else could it be?"

Nia's breathing was becoming a runaway train.

"I don't know... something's not right... I..."

John anchored his hands on her shoulders.

"Hey, hey, hey, it's all right."

It was not all right. Nia was spiraling into a full-on panic attack.

"I need to... I need to get out of here..."

"Nia, we can't lose our cool now and run outside."

John pulled her into a hug to calm her down, but quickly realized there was no need for it.

Nia had fainted in his arms.

82

John watched Nia stir awake in her bed.

She had slept for a solid six hours, and John for barely half that. He was surprised to see a smile wash over her face.

"Morning, Captain," she said, outstretching her arms. "Sorry about last night."

John returned the smile. "Nothing to be sorry about. It was my fault. I shouldn't have shown you that box so soon. You've been through a lot."

Nia propped herself up on the side of the bed.

"I just needed rest. And you're right. It's probably a typo."

"Don't do that," John said swiftly.

"Do what?"

"Don't bullshit me, Nia. Not you. Not after all we've been through."

Nia stripped her facade, settling into a calm seriousness. "Okay."

"Good. I thought a lot about what you said last night. I asked myself a simple question. Why would someone want me to believe that Yuri Volkov kidnapped Claire?"

"So that you'd follow him. And..."

"You can say it."

"Kill him."

"Exactly. Do the dirty work for the King of Hearts. But then I stepped back. What would I need to do to accomplish that? To track down Yuri?"

Nia crossed her legs at the ankles before answering.

"You'd need me."

"Precisely. If the King of Hearts has the Grail operators, it means he's the one that has rebuilt the Quantum Grail. Which means he has only one person left to acquire to complete his masterpiece."

"I know that."

"Of course you do. But that's not why you panicked last night. Is it?"

Nia shook her head.

"Why do you suspect the timestamp on our conversation printout is not a typo?"

"Because... whoever has the power and the resources to coordinate all this, to set us up, to execute everything with such precision, it just seems unlikely they would miss a detail as trivial as a computer configured with the wrong date and time."

John went quiet for a good while.

"You're very smart, Nia. The smartest person I've ever known. You told me about the power of quantum computers. The qubits, more calculations than there are known atoms in the universe, Froot Loops and all. Back in Georgetown, you looked me straight in the eye and told me you didn't know exactly what the Quantum Grail does. But you did give me the worst-case possibility. So now I want to hear you say it. What do you think the Grail does?"

Nia buried her face into her palms, then slid her hands to the back of her head, where she massaged her scalp as though stimulating her answer.

"It simulates outcomes."

"Like the actions of a grieving father and desperate husband?" John said, his voice thick with sorrow.

"I'm so sorry."

"Don't be. You're the main target of this simulation, I assure you. I'm just driving the vehicle. A dumb brute with a clouded mind and poor judgment. But today, I stop driving."

"What do you mean?"

"I mean we part ways."

"What?"

"Look, Nia. I'm going to come clean. I was going to do this in Austin, after we talked to Langston."

Nia scoffed. "Of course. That's why you were acting all weird."

"My intentions came from a good place. I didn't want to put you in any more danger. Now that we both know that you are the endgame of this thing, it's imperative that you don't follow me."

Nia laughed with a healthy dose of sarcasm, but John detected a note of genuine hurt.

"Let me get this straight. This King of Hearts ran a simulation eleven months ago on the original Quantum Grail. Orchestrated and executed an elaborate plan, down to the death of every last mercenary. And you think I'm safer without you than *with you*?"

"Nia... death follows everywhere I go. Do I have to spell it out to you that I think God has forsaken me?"

"I thought you didn't believe in God?"

John waved off the question. "Only when it suits me."

"Well, how convenient for you. Let's see how this suits you. Has it even occurred to you that this King simulated exactly this outcome? That you would become so jaded you'd abandon me?

Then he can just scoop me up and complete his Grail masterpiece."

John leaned back at that. *Abandon* was a word choice that revealed her childhood insecurity—but setting that thought aside, her point was valid. It was one John couldn't really refute, which only fueled his frustration.

"I just want you to be safe. To get away from all this. Live a semblance of the normal life you've been robbed of. You deserve that much."

Nia studied him curiously. She then stood up and sat next to him. Her gaze was so confident and sharp, it made John borderline uncomfortable. She just kept staring at him, searching his eyes.

"I see the way you look at me," she said. "But I'm not her."

John froze. But under his stillness brewed a storm. He felt utterly transparent with Nia's eyes boring through him. She took his hand, as though sensing his vulnerability.

"A part of me envies her, though. The life she had. I... look, I'll come clean as well. I decided to join you in Ohio because I wanted to get back at LIS. But I also did it because of the way you look at me. I never knew my father. I miss my mother more than I remember her. It just felt good to be around someone who..."

Nia's voice faded, moisture pooling in her eyes.

John pulled her into a hug.

"So that's the backbone of our relationship?" he said. "Misguided emotional attachment and breakfast tacos."

Nia let out a hearty laugh.

"Oh, kiddo, what are we gonna do?"

"Stick together," she replied without missing a beat. "Strength in numbers. Isn't that the basic military principle?"

John wasn't convinced.

"Look, Captain. You have to accept the fact that whoever ran this simulation has the upper hand, and likely knows what we'll do regardless of what we decide. For all we know, this King of Hearts is reading the transcript of this conversation right now."

It was a frightening notion. But John thought he understood.

"So, you're saying we're damned if we do, damned if we don't?"

"Something like that. But what exactly are we doing?"

John walked over to the duffel bag and pulled out the manila envelope. He took out the three black-and-white photos and handed them to Nia.

"We're going to find out if this is our King of Hearts. Then we're going to shove his simulation up his ass."

83

"Where did you get these?" asked Nia, shuffling through the photos of a middle-aged man.

Under Yuri's dead body, thought John, but he said, "It was among the boxes of brain scans and our transcript."

"These look like surveillance photos."

"Exactly. Either Yuri tracked that man or paid someone to do it. Either way, he must be of high importance for Yuri to keep the photos so close to him. The strangest part is, that man looks familiar to me."

Nia shot him a look. "You know him?"

"I don't know if I've met him, but I've seen him before. I never forget a face."

Nia picked out a photo and grabbed a cell phone. She then took a picture of the picture.

"I'll run a reverse image search and see if we get a hit."

———

"His name is Fredrick Memet," said Nia. "He's a quantum physicist."

"Of course he is," said John, staring daggers at the picture of Dr. Frederick Memet that Nia had pulled up on the laptop.

"Guess where he taught physics for a long time?"

"UT Austin?"

"Bingo."

Nia clicked and scrolled furiously, her eyes gobbling the search results.

"Looks like he resigned his tenured position and disappeared around the same time as Dr. Henry Langston. But unlike Langston, I don't see any records of him reappearing."

John didn't even have to say it; Nia was already pulling up the mandatory SEC filing Dividius Technologies had submitted in 2017.

"Yep, there he is," she said. "Fredrick Memet. Newly minted member of the board." She pulled up the 2018 filing. "His name is still there in 2018. Langston's is not."

"Two go in, only one gets out," said John.

"Something went down between the two of them."

"Something that landed Langston with a bullet in the head."

"Why would the two of them join up to begin with?"

"What do you mean?"

"Langston was a neuroscientist. That's a branch of biology. Memet is a physicist."

John considered this carefully. It was a question Nia was far better equipped to answer than he was, but he gave it a shot anyway.

"We know Dividius was interested in Langston's deep brain stimulation mechanism. That thing required silicone and electrodes and coils. That sounds like physics to me."

"It is," admitted Nia. "So maybe Memet was brought in to improve Langston's device. But what does a machine to treat Parkinson's have anything to do with quantum computing?"

"It doesn't. Maybe that's where the rift between the two came from. Memet repurposed Langston's device for quantum computing. You said yourself there wasn't enough interest in Langston's device from the medical community, and he lost his funding. But the entire Silicon Valley is racing to build a quantum computer. Plenty of funding for that."

Nia shook her head. "Dividius Technologies probably never intended to use Langston's technology for Parkinson's treatment to begin with. They just used him to build a quantum computer. Which makes sense as to why he'd leave. He got bamboozled."

"You mean how we've been bamboozled all along?" said John. He picked up a photo of Memet, desperately trying to remember where he'd seen that face before. "If he is the King of Hearts, I have no doubt he approached Dividius Technologies with the idea to build a quantum computer."

"But he must have been missing something," said Nia. "A part he needed to complete his device."

"Exactly. Mason said parts were clearly missing from the burned-down site of the original Grail. So the question is, how did Memet get a whiff that the government had them?"

"L-I-S," said Nia, enunciating each letter with disdain.

John laughed. "I was right all along."

"How so?"

"I said back in Georgetown that someone on the Grail team leaked the information. Someone technical. Back then I thought they leaked it to the Russians, but it was LIS all along. I mean, think about it. LIS works with a vast network of government contractors. It would be easy for them to plant a mole that seemed legitimate. Someone Mason would never suspect. Why would he? They would be vetted, hold the necessary security clearances."

Nia mused on this for a good minute in complete silence. She finally broke it.

"All of that is plausible. But how did they find out about the Quantum Grail project to begin with?"

"Maybe the mole was there from the beginning. Someone who'd worked with LIS before. It's a small world. Heck, I knew Mason from my navy days. It's how I recognized him from the security footage at Franklin Medical—"

"John? John, are you all right?"

John had planted his palm on the wall above the nightstand, as though the room was a swaying ship. "Son of a bitch," was all that came out of his breathless mouth.

He regained a semblance of composure and picked up the photo of Dr. Frederick Memet. If he were staring any harder, his gaze would've burned a hole through it.

"I've never seen this man in the flesh. But I've seen him in a picture hanging on a wall in Dr. Edwards's office."

"Who's Dr. Edwards?"

"Claire's supervisor at Franklin Medical Center. The man who showed me the security footage of her patients getting abducted."

84

John began fantasizing about wrapping his hands around Dr. Edwards's neck.

Whatever showed on his face alarmed Nia.

"Captain, you're scaring me."

Her words took John's boiling fury down a few degrees. He took deep breaths to cool off the rest. A cynical smile appeared on his face, almost against his will.

"It's so perfect, isn't it?" he said. "Edwards had access to all the medical and personal information of every Grail operator. He could go through Claire's notes, see everything that's supposed to remain confidential. Claire has worked with this asshole for almost a decade, and he just used her, then fed her to the lions."

"I understand you're angry. It's diabolical. But we need to be calm and focused."

She was right. "Sorry, kiddo. I just…"

"I know. Tell me about this photo you saw on his wall."

"It was some kind of gathering. He and Memet wore the same jacket. Edwards looked a bit younger, so it must have been taken a few years ago."

"What kind of jacket?"

"An orange-and-black blazer. It had a pattern. Maybe houndstooth."

"That sounds like a college jacket."

Nia's fingers ripped through the keyboard.

"Yep, they both did their undergrad at Princeton. Both graduated in 1991."

It took her only a few seconds to pull up a picture of a blazer.

"Is this it?"

"That's it. Where is that picture from?"

"Princeton class of ninety-one twenty-fifth reunion. Their picture must've been taken in 2016."

John sat on his bed, planted his elbows on his knees, and rested his chin on his interlocked fingers. "He was in front of me from the very beginning. Fed me bullshit without blinking." He looked around the room. "And I kept wondering why he isn't here."

"Who?"

"Memet—the King of Hearts. All he has to do is show up with a bunch of killers, take care of me, and take you. But he doesn't need to. He's simulated a far easier way to accomplish that. Lure me to Edwards and complete his mission."

Nia's gaze seemed lost in the curtains, but John saw she was going far inward, calculating.

"That's a possibility," she said. "Another is that we have deviated from his simulated outcome, and this is uncharted territory."

John smiled ruefully at that. "Which one do you believe is more likely?"

Nia didn't respond. It was all the answer John needed.

"Captain, are we really back to whether we should stick together?"

"No, don't worry. You've planted enough fear in me that the

moment we split up he'll"—John made air quotes—"just scoop you up."

"Good. Now perk up and let's track down this Edwards asshole."

―――

It took Nia less than an hour to hack Michael Edwards's cell phone and pinpoint its location.

"Colorado?" John said with bewilderment.

―――

Within another hour, Nia had unearthed that Edwards was the sole member of a shell LLC that owned a lovely five-thousand-square-foot house on seven acres of land near Aspen, Colorado.

"LIS must be paying their informants handsomely," John said with disgust. "We have to assume Memet is there, waiting with who knows what army."

"We can make a thousand assumptions, each just as likely," said Nia.

John just shook his head. He walked over to the box containing the transcript of his conversation with Nia in Georgetown and started reading it again.

"Word for word," he mumbled. "How is that possible?"

John looked up to find Nia staring at him. The look in her eyes was one of pity. Pity for a flip phone–owning man to whom the ways of the world were becoming incomprehensible.

"Look, Captain. I wrote the programming language they used to run this simulation. The main difference between what I wrote and other conventional programming languages is that mine harnesses the power of the qubits' quantum properties. The rest of it is nothing new. Simulations have been around for decades. Biotech companies create new drugs through protein-folding simulations. The algorithms don't even have to be that sophisticated as long as computers can cram a lot of data, and a quantum computer can cram practically infinite amounts. Imagine a gun that can fire an infinite number of bullets at once."

John smiled, appreciating her efforts to relate to his domain.

"I understand, Nia. But we are not protein cells. They predicted our words."

"Technically, we *are* just a bunch of protein cells. But I know what you mean. What you have to come to grips with is that we —you and I and everyone else—we're all more predictable than we'd like to admit. We think we're unique, and in many ways we are. But in most, we're far more alike than not. Which makes us predictable. Just look at the Cambridge Analytica scandal over a decade ago. The company asked Facebook users to fill out a survey, then built psychological profiles with their personal data, and used it to affect the outcome of our elections with astonishing accuracy. All this with a questionnaire and computers that are ancient technology compared to a quantum machine. I can't even begin to imagine how much data about us they loaded into the Grail. Your military service records, my testimonies to half a dozen government agencies, names of everyone we ever interacted with and all of their records. We are prime targets for a simulation. If ChatGPT, which runs on traditional hardware, can emulate the language of customer support reps and famous authors, the Grail can certainly predict our words down to our colloquial tendencies. That's the whole point of Arthur C. Clarke's third law: any sufficiently advanced technology is indistinguishable from magic."

Nia searched John's eyes, and whatever she saw in them produced a sad smile on her face.

"Captain, imagine a wrinkle on a shirt. How many runs with

an iron would it take to smooth it out? Two? Three? Seven? How smooth would the shirt be if you slid the iron a hundred times over it? A thousand? Let's pretend it's an indestructible shirt that could sustain a million runs. A trillion. A trillion, trillion. That is how many times our Grail simulation was likely run, ironing out the wrinkles until its prediction was smoothed down to every single word we've uttered." Nia leaned in, her eyes electric. "The Grail could've done all that in under a second."

John took Nia's last words like a gut punch. He had used plenty of analogies to explain to Jenny the wicked ways of the world, as parents often do. And here was a young woman, slightly older than Jenny would've been now, explaining to him the incomprehensible, as though he were a child. In a way, his mentality up to this point had been childlike—resistant to accepting what he couldn't believe was possible. But his lack of acceptance didn't make it any less true, and acknowledging that fact was all the acceptance he needed. He would never fully grasp how the Grail did what it did, but being in denial about its capabilities was as dangerous as denying the prowess of any foe on the battlefield.

"Okay," he said. "So how do we outsmart this thing? How do we become unpredictable?"

Nia leaned her back against her headboard.

"I have an idea."

A peculiar grin formed on her face.

"But you're not gonna like it."

85

"You're right, I don't like it," said John.

"How predictable of you," said Nia with a wink.

"Point taken. But you have to understand that no military operation exists without planning. It's just unheard of."

"I'm not saying we shouldn't plan. I'm just saying we shouldn't interact with each other during that planning. The Grail simulation, like any other program, relies on data. Input, output. There is no functioning program without it. So we need to stop providing the input. It might already be too late, and we've provided enough for them to simulate our future actions, but it's all we have at this point."

John closed his eyes and pinched the bridge of his nose.

"So basically, we keep secrets from each other."

"Exactly. The input for the Grail is all of our words and actions. Which I'm sure the algorithm compares to the words and actions of everything we've done before, and of others who fit our psychological profiles. But our thoughts are untouchable. They don't interact with the system. So anything we do that appears spontaneous gives us an advantage."

"All right," sighed John. "What about the other part? The contrarian stuff."

"The actions and words we *do* provide have to run contrary to our nature. It's not just that we have to do the opposite of what we would normally do or agree on. We have to be different. We have to be random. Which, trust me, is harder than you think."

"You don't know what I think."

"Good. Keep it that way."

All John could do was laugh. "Okay. So when do we start?"

"No time like the present—" said Nia.

"—a thousand unforeseen circumstances may interrupt you at a future time," said John, completing the famous words of John Trusler.

He eyed Nia for a good while in silence. She did the same with him. It was as though they were playing a game. In truth, they were. John understood it better than he had imagined he would. He ran through countless ideas, casting aside the most obvious—the ones that followed his training and his instincts—and moving on to the absurd. When he'd calculated the most random and unpredictable and contrarian plan he could think of, a wicked smile twisted his lips. Judging by Nia's face, she didn't like it one bit.

"All right, Nia Banks. Time for you to put your money where your mouth is. Or, should I say, where your thoughts are."

He motioned to Nia to follow him out of the motel room and into a bright, hot summer day in Albuquerque, New Mexico.

———

Two hours later, John reentered the motel room with Nia. He watched her sit on her bed, a swirl of emotions playing across her face. Her eyes were lit up, and John recognized the look. It was one that tore through his memories of Jenny.

He sat down on the bed across from Nia.

"I think it's time we play another round with a more focused purpose."

She nodded, and off they went with a staring contest. Behind their eyes, millions of neurons were firing, synapses bridging, neural pathways forming, information accumulating, constructing fragments that led to thoughts that led to ideas that led to infinite possibilities, all of them collapsing into two individual plans of action. John and Nia smiled at almost the same time.

Both smiles were wiped away instantly by a rap on the door.

John took out his gun and motioned Nia to go to the bathroom.

As she scuttled away, John drew his back flush against the front wall, then slowly slid to the window and peered through the slit of the drawn curtains. If he hadn't held a gun, John would've rubbed his eyes. Splashed water on his face. Anything to ensure he wasn't hallucinating that Dr. Michael Edwards was standing outside of the motel room.

But of course. *They've come for us.* What else could it be? John tried to angle his gaze through the narrow slit to get a glimpse of who was with Edwards, but he couldn't see anyone.

Edwards rapped on the door again.

"Open up, Mr. Mitcham. I know you're in there."

Nia came out of the bathroom, her mouth agape.

John shook his head, waving her back.

"I'm alone and unarmed, Mr. Mitcham. And we're wasting time."

A thousand possibilities, but this one made no sense. John made his decision with no more thought than flipping a coin— he swept to the door, unlocked and opened it, his hand striking

Edwards's collar like a cobra as he snatched him into the room before he slammed the door shut and locked it.

John took cover behind Edwards, exposing the man toward the door like a shield, counting the seconds, sure the door would be perforated by bullets.

But none came.

"There's no one there, Mr. Mitcham," said Edwards.

"Shut up," said John, keeping his gun trained at the door. But with each passing second, Edwards's words rang truer. There was simply no one out there.

John finally dragged Edwards toward the back of the room. Edwards closed his eyes, letting out a whimper as John picked him up and slammed him against a wall. A lone picture of a New Mexico mountain range fell from the impact of Edwards's head thudding against drywall.

"John, stop it!"

Nia's scream jolted John back into reality. He backed off, and Edwards slid back on the bed, clutching the back of his head.

John sat on the bed across from him, the dissipating adrenaline slowly defogging his mind.

"Why did you come here?"

Edwards winced through the pain, blinking a few times to properly see John. When he made eye contact, he spoke as casually as he might to tell the time.

"I came here to die."

86

John was speechless. So was Nia.

It took a few seconds, but John finally blurted out, "This makes no sense."

Edwards grimaced, his hand tracing the back of his battered head.

"It makes perfect sense, Mr. Mitcham. You just don't want to believe it."

"Believe what?"

"That you can't deviate from the simulated outcome. None of us can."

John sneered. "Silly me, I thought you just procured people for your college buddy. But you know everything."

"I don't know everything. But he does. He knows that a moment ago, just before I knocked on that door, you and Nia both had the same thought. You were not going to come to my house in Aspen at all."

John was stumped. He couldn't believe it. No, he didn't *want* to believe this man's words. But as his eyes met Nia's, he knew they were the truth.

"You think you can outsmart this thing," said Edwards. "But

you don't understand. Your attempts to outsmart it were already simulated more times than you can grasp. Your random behavior is only perceived by you to be random. You think you can keep secrets from it by not talking or acting, but humans are terrible at keeping secrets. You've already shared your greatest fears and hopes and regrets with someone at some point. You've already said and done enough for the machine to predict what you'll say and do next. What will be, will be, Mr. Mitcham. None of us can do anything about it."

John began to speak, but Nia grabbed his wrist and put her finger to her lips. He remained silent.

"Bless your heart," said Edwards, his look of sympathy swaying between John and Nia. "You still think you can win. But only he wins."

A thought finally occurred to John, even though it should have been obvious from the moment Edwards had started talking.

"He left you out to dry. After all you've done for him. What a great friend."

"You're confusing me with a willing co-conspirator, Mr. Mitcham. But I've been living in terror for years."

"Of course. It's terrifying to own a multimillion-dollar vacation home in Aspen."

Edwards snickered at that. "You really can't see the forest for the trees."

"Why don't you enlighten me."

"If you follow the trail of money that landed into my bank account to purchase that property, it will lead you to an offshore bank that has direct ties to Yuri and a plethora of Russian oligarchs. The Aspen property was designed to frame me as a co-conspirator to the Russians. The FBI and the CIA already know it was Russian mercenaries who abducted the Grail operators. And they will know why you…"

"Why I what?"

"Why you will kill me."

John was digesting all this on what seemed like an infinite loop. The sheer, diabolical cunning of Memet was frightening. He had done this to his longtime friend. Yuri was right: the King of Hearts truly was a heartless man.

But John was determined not to fall into his trap.

"Well, this is where his simulation breaks, Edwards. I'm not going to kill you."

Edwards laughed. "Of course you will."

"I know what I will and will not do. I'm going to let you walk out that door."

Edwards smiled a peculiar smile.

"No, you won't, Mr. Mitcham. Not after I tell you that Claire and I had an affair."

John froze.

Until his eyelids began twitching. His breathing grew heavy. He slowly regained it, grounded by a single thought.

"You're lying."

Edwards sighed. "I know Nia has already hacked my phone. She can go through my texts, or we can save each other time and get this over with."

"You lie!"

"I know it hurts. But I've been in love with Claire from the day I met her at the VA hospital. She refused my advances for years. But after Jenny's death, she was... very vulnerable. She tried talking to you, but you weren't receptive. So she turned to me, a coworker she thought she could trust. That's right, Mr. Mitcham. I took advantage of your daughter's death to take advantage of your grieving wife. Now it's time for you to do your part."

John growled out a laugh that became a sob.

He wiped a tear from his eye and said, "You're right. Memet

is right."

"John, don't," said Nia. "Please."

"I am going to kill you."

"John, you don't have to do thi—"

John leaped from the bed, wrapping his left hand around Edwards's neck, while the right landed a flurry of blows to his face. Nia screamed, begging John to stop, to not do this. She finally jumped on his back, creating a momentary reprieve for Edwards's face.

John saw the tears streaming down Nia's face, but it wasn't enough.

He slid her off him, took out his gun, and said, "Go to the bathroom, right now."

"John, no, please no, you can't do this, please—"

"Go to the *goddamn* bathroom. I don't want you to see this."

"Stop it. Stop it."

John was entering an out-of-body experience. Memories of Claire and Jenny flooded him, his entire life compressing into this horrible, inevitable moment, like a black hole inside his mind sucking him into singularity.

He cocked the gun and pointed it at Edwards.

Nia shrieked and fell to the floor, covering her ears and shutting her eyes.

She kept crying *no no no*, but there was no stopping this. *What will be, will be,* Edwards had said. But then Jenny said, *Don't be a sucker, Dad*—a random memory of John futilely wasting time and money attempting to grab a stuffed animal in a claw machine, Jenny telling him to let it go, she just wanted to drive a bumper car with him anyway—and why that memory of all memories, John did not know.

But he emerged on the other side of the singularity, coming back into the room.

He lowered his gun.

Nia was curled on the floor, her eyes wet and puffy and utterly afraid. John wasn't nearly as mad at himself for almost delivering exactly what Memet wanted, as he was that he'd been about to do it in front of Nia. A selfish, self-indulgent, deplorable act.

John went to his knees in front of Nia. "I'm sorry, I'm so sorry..."

She just wrapped her hands around him and said nothing.

John stood up. and Nia followed his lead. They packed up their belongings in complete silence.

Without a parting glance, they abandoned that wretched motel room—leaving Dr. Michael Edwards alive and not so well in Albuquerque, New Mexico.

87

John drove north on I-25, even though he had no idea where he was going.

Nia sat in the passenger seat. Quiet. Still shaken.

Nothing felt right about this sunny day, no more than it had felt right the day John Mitcham had buried his daughter under the clear blue sky. He'd hated sunny days ever since, his affinity for them inverted just like Claire had said everything good would be, from family photos to keepsakes.

John was surprised he didn't have more anger toward Claire right now. Toward her infidelity. But the more he reflected on all those months following Jenny's death, the more he felt responsible for pushing Claire toward Edwards. Hardened by years of combat trauma, his reserved demeanor and fix-it attitude were nothing but a hindrance to mending Claire's broken heart. The unfathomable guilt she felt from believing she was responsible for Jenny's suicide.

Now, in hindsight, John saw it all so clearly. He had kept trying to manufacture a semblance of normal life after Jenny's death. And all Claire wanted was to be heard. The day she had asked for a separation at the dining table was the day she told him he was running away from his emotions. But what she'd really meant—what John only now understood—was that he'd been running away from *her*. During the most vulnerable time of Claire's life, John made her feel like she was grieving alone. He had the courage to face any external forces, but his only defense mechanism against grief was to accept and move on. But that's the thing about grief. Closure doesn't come from acceptance. It doesn't come from moving on. It can only come from carrying on. Because no one can truly accept the loss of a loved one. The most they can accept is that it happened, but not that it happened to them.

John had so many regrets in life, yet the most debilitating realization was that most of them had occurred after Jenny's death. Was the road stretching in front of him just another path to another regret? Was he doomed to perpetually feed his previous mistakes into the next? Was there a way to break this loop? Had it already happened when he lowered his gun and let Edwards live?

I let Edwards live...

He checked the mirrors, then swerved the car across two lanes, barely making the exit.

"Where are we going?" said Nia.

"We're getting off this treadmill."

John made a right at the intersection. He drove two more miles, took a left at a forest service road, then ventured another hundred yards before veering the SUV offroad. He eased the vehicle to a stop and shut off the engine.

"Captain, I'm all for randomness right now, but why are we here?"

"Only the Grail knows."

"All right," she sighed. "What exactly are we going to do?"

"We're going to live." He cracked a smile. "Some call it spending quality time."

The sun behind John and Nia lit up the mountain range in front of them. The clash of golden hues and jagged shadows was both stark and striking. They observed the glory while munching on potato chips, sitting on the hood of the car, their backs against the windshield, fresh breeze in their hair.

"Ain't this something," said Nia, emphasizing the point with a crunchy bite of a potato chip.

"It sure is," concurred John with a crunch of his own.

"I bet I can make it even better."

John shot her a look. "Go for it."

Nia cleared her throat.

"Millions of years ago, two continental plates collided, neither budging, the two having nowhere to go but up, forming the mountains in front of us. And a little over eight minutes ago, the sun discharged electromagnetic radiation, the light traveling ninety-three million miles across our solar system. A small, very special fraction of it reached its final destination, creating this magnificent panorama of amber and shadow, just for our viewing pleasure."

Wow...

"Well done," John managed to say.

No one would ever call John a wordsmith, that much he knew. But the feelings Nia stirred inside him were all too reminiscent of the ones he'd felt in another special place and time. He reached into his pocket and took out the picture he'd been carrying ever since he'd started his journey to find Claire.

"This was taken in Montauk," he said, bringing the picture up for Nia to see. The photo had been in a nearly pristine condition when he'd first showed it to her in Georgetown, but now its creases and faded colors felt to John like a reflection of his battle scars and fading hopes of ever reuniting with Claire. He pointed to a lighthouse in the photo's background. "We've been to so many beaches as a family, and I could make the argument that they are just as pretty, if not prettier. But this lighthouse... the way it's perched at the very tip of Long Island, like some sentinel at the edge of the world. You stand there and the ocean feels infinite. Like you can go anywhere. Do anything..." John's voice began quivering. He ran his thumb over the photo, as though attempting to feel the moment with his skin. "She was such a good kid. Could've done anything..."

The heartbreak of happiness frozen in time.

John collected himself and said, "If you could go back and change only one thing in life, just that one thing, what would it be?"

Nia's eyes were firmly ahead. She was silent for so long that John began to think she'd forgotten about the question. But she finally spoke.

"When I was growing up, there was this boy who was supposed to go to a summer camp with a couple of his friends from our neighborhood. But at the last minute, his mom saw his final report card, realized he failed half of his classes, and grounded him. So two of his friends went off to the camp without him, but on their way there, the car they were in got struck by a semi, instantly killing everyone. Imagine the relief his mom felt that he wasn't in the car. That she made him stay at the last moment. Two weeks later, she decided to cheer him up and took him to a White Sox game. On their way back, crossing a street three blocks from their house, they got hit by a drunk driver and died."

John mulled this over. "So you wouldn't change anything because it might make things worse?"

"Yeah, it can fix that one thing at that moment but end up making things worse down the line. So if you ask me, the best you can do is learn a lesson if one can be learned."

"Don't repeat the same mistake sort of deal?"

"One would hope."

"You want to hear something strange?"

"As long as you don't think it will provide relevant input to the Grail simulation."

"I doubt it, because what's strange is that I don't know. I don't know what I would've done differently with Jenny. Neither did Claire. And that was somehow more maddening to her than anything else. It was the catalyst for her to blame herself, her genes, her family history."

Nia studied John with unfiltered sadness. She took his hand and curled up next to him.

John turned to the mountains and exhaled a long, heavy sigh. As he finished, he heard a faint pinging sound.

"Do you hear that?"

Nia jolted upright.

"It's the phone," she said.

"The phone?"

"My cell phone inside the car. The Grail binary signature has been detected."

They jumped off the hood simultaneously, each opening the opposite back passenger door within a second of each other. Nia rummaged through her backpack, fishing out the phone. John realized the folly of his position and ran around the back of the SUV, planting himself over Nia's shoulder as she tapped through the phone.

"And?" he said eagerly.

Nia said nothing. She simply brought the phone up to John's eyes.

The map was showing a red dot in the Sonoran Desert in southwestern Arizona.

88

"Are you sure this is the location?" said John.

"Positive," said Nia, her tone suggesting she was insulted by the question.

John nodded, more to himself than her.

"What were you expecting?" Nia asked.

There had once been a seed planted in John's mind that he would have to journey to Russia, back when he had naively thought Yuri and the Kremlin's military apparatus were behind all this. But as his fingers pinched the satellite map, zooming in and out, sliding it this way and that, it all made perfect sense. LIS was a domestic entity that had chosen the perfect location for a cyberweapon. They had a reliable power grid and broadband access of the United States, but were far away from a populous area to avoid scrutiny. John sighed with admiration at the ingenuity and practicality.

"Something like this," he said.

"I wish I could tell you that they're firing it up to recalibrate the simulation or hack. But this is likely just the final trap to lure you in."

John looked at Nia the way a parent might look at a child

before imparting words of wisdom. He firmly believed Nia already understood what he was about to say on some basic level, but he said it anyway.

"The greatest power is not the ability to make someone do whatever you want, but to give them a choice knowing they will willingly make the wrong one."

With that revelation, John scanned the world around him, spinning 360 degrees. He scooped a fistful of dirt and threw it into the air. Once he determined the wind direction, he picked up three random rocks and tossed them into the dirt as if he were throwing dice at a craps table.

By this point Nia was looking confused, but John didn't stop there.

Just for good measure, he plucked a potato chip out of the bag and held it in front of her. "Break off the other half," he said.

Nia grinned, finally catching on, at least to an extent. She grabbed the other side and broke the chip into roughly equal halves. John collected them and silently counted the total number of ridges along the severed edges. He conjured a few images, performed more math in his head, and plugged it all into the final formula.

Finally, John opened the trunk of the car and took out his trusty duct tape. He tore off a piece, approached Nia, and sealed her mouth shut.

She rolled her eyes at that, evidently finding the measure a bit over the top. But when John taped her wrists together behind her back, Nia jerked around, her eyes wide as saucers. They quickly narrowed in anger. She had realized what was transpiring, though it was too late.

John carried Nia, kicking and muffle-screaming, to the trunk, where he taped her ankles together with the efficiency of a shipping store clerk. He made a point to avoid eye contact, but he still caught her staring daggers at him a few times. Despite the ample amount of duct tape over her mouth, John could make out enough profanity to fill up a swear jar.

He lowered the trunk door and closed it shut.

———

In the shadows of a secluded parking lot in downtown Albuquerque, John cradled Nia into a large hard-shell suitcase. Seeing her contorted into a fetal position, he couldn't help but reflect on his first encounter with her. He had placed her into a large bin in a similar fashion back at the CIA safe house, so perhaps it was only fitting that he was returning her to the world in much the same way he had taken her—against her will.

There was only sadness in her eyes now, the anger long gone. It tore John apart.

But, ever the consummate professional, he stayed focused on the mission.

He double-checked the metal timer lock that connected the two zip ties around Nia's wrists. The timer was set to release the lock in seven hours and thirty-three minutes. John had come up with that number by adding the estimated linear distance (in inches) between the three rocks he'd tossed and the number of combined ridges in the broken potato chip, then multiplying the number by a random bowling score he had once seen a guy get in his now-defunct league. This had yielded the total number of minutes currently counting down on the lock that secured Nia's hands behind her back.

When the lock released, Nia would be inside the suitcase, which would be in the overhead compartment of a San Bernardino–bound train, which John calculated would be approaching a station in Needles, California. It was a convenient location for Nia to head any direction from there; Las Vegas to the north, Mexico to the south, or continue westbound in California.

John checked the duct tape around her ankles, ensuring the end of it was already peeled off so that she could easily remove the rest once her hands became free. He tried to imagine the faces of stunned passengers as her fingers sprouted from the gap he would leave in the zipper, watching a human climb out of a random suitcase. As for the duct tape over Nia's mouth, John came very close to removing it now, just for a moment so that she might give some parting words. But he thought better of it. Or maybe he just couldn't bring himself to hear her voice.

He had imagined he would have a few meaningful and worthwhile things to say when this moment arrived. But John only said what remained in his depleted heart.

"I'm sorry, kiddo. For everything."

Nia mumbled something. It was either "I love you," or "Fuck you."

Hoping it was the former but figuring it was the latter, John closed the air-hole-perforated suitcase, zipped it up (but not quite all the way), tilted it onto its wheels, and started rolling it toward the train station.

———

Five minutes later, John lifted the suitcase into the overhead compartment with considerable effort and an audible grunt. A passenger walking by asked him if he needed any help. He shook his head and politely said, "No, thank you." He watched the man continue walking down the mostly empty train car. Once the coast was clear, John strode out of the car.

———

Two minutes later, John watched the train depart the station, heading west, which was the opposite direction of the wind that had carried the dirt John had tossed in the air a few hours earlier.

―――

One minute later, John Mitcham started crying, praying to a God he didn't believe in that his actions were random enough to never see Nia Banks again.

89

The warehouse-like structure swam in the quivering heat haze of the Sonoran Desert.

Perched on a hill and covered with camo, John brought the binoculars to his eyes for the tenth time since he'd taken up the position. As with the previous nine scans of the structure and its surroundings, his conclusion remained the same: penetrating the building looked too easy.

Despite the sprawling chain-link fence and barbed wire securing the perimeter, there was a plethora of blind spots with no cameras. Despite the camp of mobile homes on the western side of the building, there were plenty of shadows to hide in. Despite the entire facade consisting mostly of corrugated metal, there were a great deal of windows on the ground floor.

It just seemed too damn easy.

What wasn't easy was the sweltering heat clenching John's very soul. But waiting for nightfall would not be advantageous. The entire compound appeared to be powered with enormous fields of solar panels, which meant energy was stored for overnight electricity, eliminating the option for John to cut off the power and execute the mission at night.

But as for all the rest, it just looked too damn easy.

———

At 3:05 p.m., John began his slow and methodical crawl down the hill.

At 3:47, he reached flat ground.

At 4:52, he breached the fence with a bolt cutter.

At 5:03, he was melting into the darkness under the solar panels.

At 5:16, he was crawling toward the shadows of the northeastern corner.

During this crawl, John began to feel something was off. He froze, lying on the ground, all his senses acutely absorbing his surroundings. There was wind. There were shadows cast by the structure. A distinct hum emitting from the building. But what else was that?

From the corner of his eye, he caught the first movement. The ground. Was a patch of ground moving? His eyes flitted to the next patch. And the next. Within three seconds, John knew it was not ground at all. Like they were rising from graves, men stood up, clad in custom Ghillie suits that perfectly matched the dry soil and sparse vegetation. Each was holding an AR-15 rifle.

John didn't bother looking behind him. The swooshing sound of Ghillies in the desert wind was more than enough for him to know he was completely surrounded.

Of course it had seemed too easy.

"Put the rifle down and get on your knees," said a Ghillie. "Hands on the back of your head."

His accent was American but very neutral. John guessed Midwestern. He slowly put down his carbine and propped himself to his knees. As he placed his hands behind his back, he closely observed the movement and formation of the men. Tight. By the book. They were former military.

"Which unit did you serve in?" John said.

"Don't talk and don't move," growled the only Ghillie who had spoken so far.

No charming these fuckers with patriotic kinship.

With six rifle barrels pointed at him, just from what he could see, John's left hand was placed into a handcuff, pulled from the back of his head down to his lower back, upon which his right hand was also lowered and cuffed. It was so procedural that he began wondering whether some of these men were former law enforcement.

"Up," said the man who'd placed the handcuffs, pulling John to his feet.

They took his carbine and started stripping the weapons, ammo, and equipment he had on him. They did so with a precision that finally removed any doubt they were former military. The United States military. That got to John.

"You gentlemen still remember the Pledge of Allegiance, or do you just parrot LIS's HR manual?"

"I told you to be quiet," said the growling squadron leader. "I won't tell you again."

John locked eyes with him, but the man couldn't quite hold his gaze, which said more to John than any of the words he'd growled so far. He wished he could see his face behind that camo point. But then he no longer saw the man at all, as a pair of hands shoved him from behind into a trot.

John slugged his way in the middle of what he could best describe as American mercenaries. They turned the corner, emerging in the front of the building. John saw three silhouettes undulating in the heat, standing next to an entrance fifty yards away. As John came closer, he saw that the two silhouettes flanking the one in the middle held rifles. Even without being able to make him out, John already knew who the man in the middle was. With each step, a dread grew heavier inside him. Ten yards away, John finally saw him clearly.

Dr. Frederick Memet, the King of Hearts.

The entire escort of mercenaries halted, forcing John to stop, both of his arms clenched firmly from behind. They held him as Memet came forward with the two guards. He stopped six feet away in front of John.

John studied him like an aberration. His face looked older and more worn out than in any of the pictures John had seen. Fraying salt-and-pepper hair danced in the breeze, and his expression was as cold as John had imagined it would be. Memet checked his watch, a subtle frown on his face.

"You're late, Mr. Mitcham," he said. "In one way, at least." He looked up at John before turning his head to the left. "But right on time in another."

John followed Memet's gaze up the dirt road. The main artery of the grounds led to a chain-link gate. It slid open, and a convoy of three black SUVs passed through.

John watched it approach with rising trepidation. The column of cars fanned out into a row and parked. All the doors swung open around the same time, the cars spitting out men in black suits. John finally saw it, the confirmation of his sixth sense.

Nia was dragged out of the middle SUV.

"Reunited after only three days," announced Memet in a casual tone.

John's eyes closed, as though his eyelids were being tugged by gravity.

He opened them just in time to see Nia's despondent face, two men in suits presenting her to Memet.

"I have to give it to you, Mr. Mitcham. You did well. Whatever randomness you pulled would've been enough for us to lose her forever. But unfortunately for you, no matter what you did and where you sent her, the simulation always collapsed on the same result. Nia was going to come here to help you." He studied her for a brief moment, more as an inanimate object than a person, then turned to John. "The most predictable actions are those born out of love."

John scoffed.

"Yuri was right. You are a heartless motherfucker."

Memet burst into a hearty laugh.

"Mr. Mitcham, you flatter me. Yuri wasn't referring to me, even though it was me he was surveilling. No, I am not the King of Hearts. He's waiting for you inside."

John went numb. As hard as he tried, he was unable to process what he'd just heard.

Memet made his way through the wide cavity of a hangar-style doorway and was swallowed by the shadows. The men led Nia in first, her eyes staying on John the whole time, her lips repeating *I'm sorry*, until she too disappeared inside.

At last, John was escorted into the building. Shadows gave way to fluorescent lights. Beneath their glare, flanked by more men in suits, stood one man.

Mason Hartwell.

90

Waves of denial cascaded through John, as though his whole body were rejecting the cruelty of Mason's deceit.

"Don't look so morose, John," said Mason. "It's a reunion, for goodness' sake."

John couldn't find the air in his lungs to say all he wanted to say.

"Why?" was all that came out.

Mason chuckled.

"Ah, why? My kids' favorite question. They ask it in perpetuity without even understanding the answer they seek." He paused and looked John over. "I doubt you understand either. Are you asking why I did it? Why you? Why this way? All equally relevant questions from your vantage point."

"Why did I not see it?" said John, seething. "Hartwell... King of Hearts."

Mason's expression changed. His eyes appeared sharper. His lips thinner. It was as though he'd turned off a filter that obfuscated his true self.

"Because most people can't see what's in front of their nose. But the real answer, John, is because I am the best at what I do."

His eyes darted toward Nia, and, as though realizing he was scaring her, he put on his mask of mild politeness. He turned and started casually strolling away.

"Come. Let's go somewhere more proper to sit down and talk."

The bewilderment on Nia's face told John that she was equally as blindsided as he was.

Someone shoved him into a trot again, and this time John glanced over his shoulder and clocked the man. It was the growler. He had taken off his Ghillie suit like the rest of his men.

John followed Mason as he led him through a maze of hallways. His heart was pumping chemicals that seemed hellbent on detaching his consciousness from his flesh, making the entire walk feel dreamlike. He was eventually escorted into a large, windowless conference room in the belly of the building.

The men sat him a few chairs away from Nia. Mason and Memet sat on the other side of the long table, exchanging occasional glances.

"All right," said Mason. "Which of the aforementioned *why*s would you like me to address first?"

John got the sense that he and Nia were being looked over like a lab experiment. In truth, that's exactly what they were. Mice in a maze. A maze in which John's path would end sooner than Nia's. That realization sprouted the most logical why of all.

"Neither," said John. "I want to know why I'm still alive. You already have Nia. I've done all your dirty work. What's the holdup, Mason?"

Mason smiled with some sadness.

"Whatever you may think of me, John, I still wanted to give you the courtesy of knowing you didn't die in vain. You deserve closure in your final moments. It can only come from grasping what an important role you've played in this mission. Because, unlike all the bullshit wars we fought, this is one cause that is not only worthwhile, but will truly alter the course of history."

John's laugh was long and unadulterated.

"Do you even hear yourself, Mason? Dictators have delivered addresses less grandiose. Which answers the very first why. You did all this for the power, like every other asshole with delusions of grandeur. It also answers why I'm still alive. You want to show off your masterpiece. Like a true narcissist."

Somewhat to John's surprise, Mason seemed to take this rather well.

"There might be some truth to that," he said. "But I'm more of a pragmatist and altruist than you give me credit for."

John let out what was unequivocally the most cynical laugh of his life.

"All right, Mason. Walk me down the pragmatism of ruining your own career and the altruism of destroying what was left of my family."

"Honestly, at this point I just want to run the exercise of attempting to get through that thick skull of yours, so you understand that not all wars have to be fought with guns." He settled himself into his chair. "Dr. Memet and I started working on the Quantum Grail in 2017—"

"How could Memet work on the Grail?" interrupted John. "He was your competition."

"He was never the competition. He was the Grail's architect from the beginning."

John exchanged an incredulous look with Nia.

Mason found this amusing enough to smirk.

"Nia had never met anyone associated with the Grail other than myself, but she and I go back longer than she realizes. You won't find my name on any of the official documents, but I am the purveyor of all government contracts for LIS-owned entities.

Including the procurement of Dividius Technologies equipment for the CIA."

The revelation made Nia twitch in her chair.

John's reaction was internal, a simmering anger that was rising with each heartbeat.

"My, my, Mason. How well you've done for yourself. Double-dipping on both ends."

"Oh please, spare me your self-righteous rhetoric. Most contractors in Northern Virginia do what I do. I just do it bigger and better. And when you expand as quickly as LIS"—he shot Nia a look—"you eventually ruffle a few feathers."

He leaned back, looking at Nia with a certain nostalgia.

"Nia Banks, the little girl from the South Side of Chicago. What a pain in the ass you were. Hacking through us like a knife through butter. That's how I knew you were the missing piece of the Quantum Grail project. We'd nailed down the hardware, but no matter how hard we worked, we couldn't write the operating system to interface with it. Trust me, I tried. I paid a pretty penny for Stanford's and MIT's best, but no... it was the brilliant girl with no degree who cracked the code."

"If she cracked the code, then why do you still need her?"

"Nia figured out the operating system, but the Grail simulation software is far from complete. As remarkably accurate as the system is in predicting most things, it also has a few glaring blind spots, exposed by your own simulation. I have to give it to you, John. That little stunt you pulled in Albuquerque with potato chips and rocks made us think we'd lost Nia forever. We got lucky in a sense, because even though the event was a blind spot for the Grail, the simulation's probabilities always merged into Nia coming back here of her own volition. I'd like to think it's the universe's way of saying she belongs here to finish the job."

"Fuck you and your universe," said Nia.

Mason turned to Memet. "You'll have to deal with this, but it's a small price to pay."

The idea of Nia spending the rest of her days here as an indentured servant sent a hot rush into John's head.

"Why did you build this facility? Why put us through all this?"

Mason looked almost puzzled.

"Me?"

He leaned in, as though about to share a secret.

"John, you misunderstand. The Quantum Grail is the architect of all this."

91

John leaned back, even though all he wanted was to lean forward and put Mason into a chokehold.

"I've seen a lot of finger-pointing in DC circles, Mason. But blaming a computer is on another level."

"I'm not blaming it. I'm trying to explain to you that the entire orchestration of you ending up here was fully thought up by the Grail algorithm. We just followed the plan for its self-preservation."

"Self-preservation?"

Mason sighed.

"I didn't think it would ever come to this, but some of the CIA's top brass started asking questions about the Quantum Grail project. More specifically about the approach we took to build a machine that tech companies haven't fully figured out yet."

"Let me guess, the same approach Dr. Langston questioned?"

Mason's eyes narrowed.

"Langston didn't like the direction we were taking with his

invention, and I could hardly expect the CIA and oversight committees on Capitol Hill to be any more understanding. They would've killed this project if they saw our unorthodox methods."

John had a sudden jolt of unease thinking about what unorthodox methods could possibly lead the CIA—an agency that had no qualms about using nefarious means to achieve objectives—to draw the line with the Quantum Grail and shut it down.

"I tried stalling the CIA's top brass for as long as I could, but the end was inevitable," continued Mason. "So, once Nia completed the operating system, we loaded data about everyone and everything even remotely associated with the Quantum Grail. Then we loaded some more. Petabytes of data, from weather patterns, to medical records, to everything humanity has learned about the human condition. We then ran Quantum Grail's first production program. We asked it to simulate an answer to only one question: How do we save it?"

With a premonition, John felt Mason's words lodge inside his chest.

"And wouldn't you know it, of all the possible answers, of all the possible outcomes, it was you. Claire's association with four of the Grail's operators led us to a grieving father desperate to salvage his life and get back with his wife. A man who would take matters into his own hands because he's jaded by years of bureaucracy and mistrustful of the government. A former special ops soldier capable of executing things very few people on the planet can. Your navy SEAL records led the Grail to Yuri, the remaining Volkov brother. He was paid to burn down the original Grail site in Virginia. I did my part by leaning on the budget committees to cut the funding for the VA hospital so that Claire and the operators would be transferred to a low-security facility at Franklin Medical Center. Six months later, Yuri abducted the Grail operators. And I abducted Claire—"

John leaped across the table, slamming his forehead into Mason's face.

He was pulled back immediately by the guards, fists raining onto his head.

"It's all right, it's all right," shouted Mason. "He's fine."

Mason took a fistful of tissues from the table and wiped the blood from his nose.

John was held to his chair by two guards, borderline growling.

"I understand your anger, John. Believe me, I do. But I hope you can find solace in recognizing the Grail's achievement. The level of detail." He leaned in slightly, a peculiar excitement emerging on his face. "Would you believe it if I told you that you wouldn't have gone through with it all had I not poured Lagavulin Sixteen in my office?"

Hearing that opened a valve, and John's anger was doused by a torrent of sadness.

"You... you used one of the fondest memories between me and my wife..."

"The Grail used it, John. You and Claire had told that story a hundred times. The Grail simply calculated its emotional score."

John felt himself sinking into the chair.

"So that whole conversation between us in your office was scripted?"

"I rehearsed every word. I even let you tail me." He scoffed. "You really think you fooled me with a different rental car every day? You were just too blinded by desperation to notice the little things. That was the point. All the evidence suggests the Russians are behind the theft and abductions, but you are the desperate husband who went off the rails and went after them.

And you did, John. *You* infiltrated the CIA safe house and extracted Nia, a feat even Yuri wouldn't dare attempt. *You* and your buddies eliminated Yuri and his men. You were the bull in the china shop, just like the Grail predicted."

John absorbed a surge of shame. As diabolical as Mason was, John had to take accountability for the deaths of all the people the Grail had needed to silence. All except one.

"I didn't kill Edwards."

Mason fused his fingertips together.

"No. But you did leave your DNA all over him. Two hours after you left that motel room, Edwards was found dead by the Albuquerque Police Department. The ballistics will show that the bullet in his chest matches your pistol. We call this a contingency plan."

John shook his head with disgust.

"I guess it's not all just the Grail's plan, huh, Mason?"

"It is, actually. We just had to recalibrate the final phase of the simulation. It's why the Grail sent out the binary signature that Nia detected. We've done it before. The Grail recalibrated the exact moment I had to kill Langston and send an anonymous tip to the FBI so that you would end up running into Yuri in Austin."

"How? Nia's phone would've detected the Grail's signature."

"You forget, she didn't upload the tracker to the cloud after you left Georgetown. There was a gap between then and when she finally did it in Ohio. The period the Grail predicted would happen." Mason sighed with impatience. "You need to come to terms with the astonishing accuracy of the simulation. It predicted that Yuri would steal the transcript of your conversation with Nia that we purposely left at the initial Grail site, along with the brain scans and the chair. Yuri didn't know what he was looking at, but he knew it didn't smell right, so he took it with him to hedge his risk. If he hadn't stolen that chair, he and you wouldn't have had the breadcrumbs that led you both to Austin. He arrived just in time to see you and Nia leave Langston's house, then followed the shit show." Mason leaned in with glee in his eyes. "Just. Like. The Grail. Predicted."

Resignation started settling inside John. And yet, there were still dots he couldn't quite connect.

"Why would brain scans and the old prototype chair be at the Grail site?" said John. "You could've left any other part of the current Grail hardware with Dividius Technologies written on it."

At that question, Mason went silent.

"Perhaps it's better if we just show them," interjected Memet.

Mason sighed, considering.

"All right," he said finally. "Might as well get it over with. It's time for Nia to finally see the hardware for which she wrote the operating system. And you, John..." He shifted in his seat, almost uncomfortably. He seemed to have a hard time looking John in the eye, but he steeled himself and finally said it.

"The main reason you are still alive is because I want you to see Claire one last time."

A searing wave ran through John. Its aftermath left his hands trembling. John genuinely couldn't tell if it was due to adrenaline or Parkinson's. He took solace in knowing no one could see them with his wrists handcuffed behind his back, the chair obfuscating them. But they were shaking mightily. No matter how many times he had considered this very possibility, that Claire actually might be here, he couldn't control his emotions. Mainly because he couldn't process what exactly he was feeling.

The most he could ascertain was disbelief and fear. The disbelief that Mason was telling the truth, and the fear of the very same. With that assessment of his mental state, all John could do was make his final plea.

"My wife has done her part. She served as bait. I took it and did your dirty work. But if you are, as you said, the best at what you do, then find a way to let her be."

Mason studied John with a mixture of pity and condescension.

"Her part is far greater than you could ever imagine."

92

Following Mason and Memet, the guards escorted John and Nia out of the conference room.

They led them down a hallway, which led to another. With each turn, the hallways became narrower, looking less like an office and more like a lab. As John took in the drop ceiling and fluorescent lighting, the hermetically sealed steel doors with tempered-glass windows, the glossy linoleum floor, he liked nothing about it.

He finally saw the last door at the end of the last hallway, and knew they would take him there. Of course they would.

There was no tempered-glass window on this beige hunk of steel. Only a fingerprint panel next to it, where Memet placed his hand. The door unlocked with multiple clangs, and Mason did the honors of opening it. He and Memet went in first. Then Mason waved John in like he was a welcomed guest.

As John crossed the threshold and walked a few steps, he soaked in the details as though assessing his surroundings upon waking up. He then went down to his knees.

The gasp Nia let out fueled his ragged breaths. He bowed over toward the floor, borderline dry heaving.

"Breathe," said Mason. "Just breathe. It's all right."
All right?

The room looked like the dome of an unholy temple, its concave walls blanketed by countless blinking lights of blade servers stacked like bricks. Cords sprouted from them on the floor, like tendrils of mold merging into a large circle of bed chairs in the center.

Each chair was exactly the same as the gray-green contraption John had found at that forsaken barn in Pennsylvania. Except that now a person lay in each chair, tied with belts, twitching intermittently, the backs of their heads swallowed by the crane helmet, a medical tube running into each mouth. The sight itself made John nauseous, but what did him in was that one of the people in a chair was Claire.

John started hyperventilating.

Claire's face was pale, her eyes closed, locks of red hair spilling from under her helmet. She looked like a patient that had been put under anesthesia, dressed in what appeared to be a hospital gown. John for the life of him couldn't recall the last time he'd seen her sleeping, his memories scrambled by the surrealness of the sight in front of him. It felt detached from reality, dreamlike in the hazy beams of spotlights. Every other person in a chair was dressed the same as Claire and appeared to be in the same condition.

"What..." was all that came out of John's wheezing throat. He wheezed more before regaining a semblance of breath. "What did you do?"

"I know it's a bit much to take in the first time," said Mason. "But she's not in any pain, I promise you." He motioned to someone behind John. "Help him up."

Two guards lifted John to his feet, but he felt like he'd left most of himself on that floor. Along with whatever faith he had left in humanity.

"You're being overly dramatic, John. You know damn well these chairs initially had medical purposes."

John couldn't stop shaking his head at the sight of Claire.

"What is happening to her?"

"She is part of the quantum error correction," chimed in Memet, his voice upbeat and dopey. "Her brain is literally part of the Quantum Grail's memory."

Like a shot of adrenaline to the heart, this asshole's tone and words spiked so much rage that John came out of his shell-shocked state. He located Nia. Her face was twisted by disbelief.

John centered himself and turned to Memet.

"What the fuck are you talking about?"

"John," started Mason, "if you're not willing to listen—"

"I'm listening. I want *him* to explain it. It's his invention."

Memet gave a casual *It's all right* look to Mason and came a bit closer to John.

"It's not my invention, Mr. Mitcham. That distinction belongs to Dr. Langston, even though he had no idea what he actually discovered. When he asked me to be part of the peer review for his deep brain stimulation project for treating Parkinson's, I was glad to help. What caught my eye was not his paper, but an extraneous, seemingly innocuous table of data. It showed that when the device sent electrical impulses to the neocortex part of the brain, it would receive far more data back. Langston thought it was just false feedback due to the sensitivity of the device. I would've thought the same had the feedback data not correlated precisely to two to the power of N!"

Memet stopped there, seemingly expecting some sort of *aha* reply from John. And something *was* percolating inside John. A memory he couldn't quite recall.

"Why does two to the power of N sound familiar?"

"Because Nia demonstrated it for you with the Froot Loops, Mr. Mitcham. The power of qubits. That is the crowning achievement of Langston's device. Harnessing the quantum properties of billions of neurons in the brain's neocortex. We still don't understand exactly how it works, but they don't suffer from the quantum decoherence of the traditional hardware used for quantum computing. The scientific community has known for a while now that our brains use quantum computation, but we are the first to achieve practical application."

"Practical application?" huffed John, his gaze floating to Claire. He began shaking his head again. "No. No, no, no... this can't be." He looked to Nia, searching for a semblance of a hint in her expression that this was not as bad as it looked. But all he saw was the same level of disgust that roiled his own insides.

"This is a fucking horror show. You people..."

Mason now stepped forward, patting Memet on the shoulder, like they were a tag team.

"What about it exactly offends you, John? Talk to me."

John laughed out something horrible from his gut that sputtered into a sob.

"Oh, you sick fuck. My wife ... my wife... Why? Why her?"

"We were running one short after Yuri escaped with Jason Hellinger."

"Jason even gave you his configuration coordinates for the quantum error correction scheme," said Memet. "The circle you see is actually a sphere as far as the Grail sees it."

Memet's dopey voice injected another dose of rage into John. He turned to Mason.

"Jason planted his head into a pitchfork. The sound that came out of him when I first saw him..."

"John... I said Claire wasn't in pain. I never said there are no side effects from being in that chair."

John came close to throwing up. But with every ounce of willpower, he regained himself.

"No, the pain comes afterward. Isn't that what Jason said? I thought he was talking about being tortured by the Russians."

Mason sighed, a semblance of guilt finally in his expression.

"I'm not going to bullshit you. We never ran the Grail for this long, and the side effects are…" He didn't bother finishing, glancing briefly at Memet. "We'll take good care of her in her final days, John. You have my word."

John bellowed a cry to end all cries.

He looked up to the ceiling, staring at that dome, the massive propeller in the center of it sucking the heat out of the room, and whatever hope remained in John's broken heart.

He lowered his head and took in Mason. He finally understood every word Yuri had said.

"You were never going to let her live. The CIA and oversight committees weren't the only ones asking questions, were they, Mason? Claire must've had suspicions about what was happening to her patients. She's just another loose end to tie up."

Mason had the courtesy to remove the counterfeit politeness from his face.

"Now you see me."

John laughed bitterly, the cruel irony finally coalescing inside him. He locked his eyes with Mason and said it.

"I saved your fucking *life*."

93

John expected remorse from Mason. Shame, at the very least. But the man exhibited the opposite, anger igniting in his eyes.

"Saved my life?" he said, almost contemplatively. "My life..."

He approached John. So close that John could see every line and pore on his face.

"Let me tell you about *my* life, Mitcham. Not a single night has passed since the day you carried me out of that ditch that I haven't woken up in sweat. I hear children screaming like they are next to me. I get the shakes. The spasms. I swallow enough pills to keep the pharma industry in business by myself. I'm living a fucking nightmare while awake and relive my nightmares in my sleep. And it's all thanks to you. You gave me the gift of living with a sickness. A prison between my temples I can't escape. Believe me, I tried. I've put a gun into my mouth a hundred times." He scoffed, spittle spraying from the corners of his mouth. "I'm just too much of a coward to pull the trigger. But I made myself a promise a long time ago. I would find a way to never send another soldier to war. You are looking at the fulfillment of that promise. It's not pretty. Not yet. But it works. You being here is a seminal moment, regardless of whether you're too obtuse to see it."

John let every word of Mason's soliloquy seep into him.

It cleared up a lot of things.

Not just the disdain Mason harbored for John, but his contempt toward life in general. Those who see the world through the prism of gloom and cynicism, those who believe the default state of a human being is when they are at their worst, those who assume we are all as ugly as they can be on the inside, they have no qualms justifying their atrocities to shape the world in their image. Mason truly was a delusional narcissist, and like all narcissists, he wanted to convince others of his greatness.

John decided he was going to let the man talk. Talk for as long as it took for John to pull out the pin he'd duct-taped inside the back of his waistband and unlock his handcuffs. He leaned his back against the wall, creating space between him and Mason. "Do you really believe I wanted you to suffer?"

Mason's lips twitched, as though his synapses had fired off a rare wave of compassion.

"Of course not," he said, taking a step back himself. "You did a good thing. The right thing." He looked pensively around the room. "Even though it might not look like it, even though the cost seems great, we are doing something special here, John. We will improve the device to eliminate the side effects. Then we will have a flawless machine. Think of the possibilities. We can simulate optimal outcomes of treaties, geopolitical conflicts, end wars before they even start. We can hack any computer, feed the data back into the Grail, having it constantly learn and improve."

An unsettling, borderline manic glimmer appeared in Mason's eyes.

"We live on the precipice of a new age. The birth of AI is

upon us, and we approached it from the hardware end. That's the beauty of it. Our algorithms don't even have to be that sophisticated when we have this much computing power."

The word *beauty* almost made John lose his cool, but he managed to slide the pin into the handcuffs' key post.

"How are you going to achieve all this if your career with the CIA is over?"

Mason grinned, basking in self-adulation. "Privatization, John. It's the wave of the future. How much of our military industrial complex is already contracted out? I'm just switching teams. I belong on this side anyway. Can't stand the bureaucracy." Mason clapped his hands once.

He then turned to John, the way one ends a lecture.

"Now you know. And it's time."

John nodded. "Don't do it in front of Nia."

"Of course."

"I would appreciate one last request," said John rather loudly to cover the sound of handcuffs unlocking. "Let me see Claire up close one last time. Please."

Mason sighed and threw a glance at Memet.

Memet nodded and walked by John, making his way toward the unholy circle.

Two guards grabbed John, one from each side. The guard on the right was the growler, and John almost took pleasure in that.

He slipped back and spun around him, pulling out the pistol from his holster. The maneuver was so quick that John put a bullet in each guard's head before they had a chance to fully turn around.

The gunfire spun Memet around, and John leaped at him like a tiger, the sound of rifles drawn by other guards rumbling through the chamber.

But they had no target, because John was already using Memet as a shield.

"You fucking idiot!" growled Mason, taking cover behind a handful of guards.

John retreated farther, inching toward Claire. The guards started following.

John's voice was swift. "Anyone takes another step forward and I shoot the good doctor."

"Stop stop stop," Mason rattled off.

The room got eerily quiet.

John could only make out the hum of the servers and Mason's frustrated huffing.

"John, what do you think you're going to accomplish here?"

"What's the matter? Your flawless machine didn't simulate this?"

"No. I guess it didn't take into account how big of a fool you are. So I'll ask again. What do you think you're doing?"

John didn't hesitate for a millisecond.

"I'm getting Nia out of here."

94

"John, you are dumber than I ever imagined," said Mason. "We are in the middle of a fucking desert. How far do you think she's going to get?"

"I'm too dumb to know. Now here's what's going to happen. One of your goons is going to slide his bone mic to me. Another is going to give his to Nia. Then you are going to open that door and instruct everyone outside to let her get into your SUV and drive through the front gate. If I don't get confirmation from her that she's out, I'm shooting your partner. If someone tries anything, follows her, lays a hand on her, I'm shooting your partner. Does everyone understand this, or do I need to repeat it?"

John cocked the gun behind Memet's head.

"Okay, okay," blurted Mason. "Motherfucker. Give him your mic," he said to a guard.

The guard took off his mic and tossed it to Memet's feet.

"Pick it up," John said to Memet. They both crouched in unison, Memet picking up the mic and handing it behind his back to John. John placed it in his ear as Mason took off a mic from another guard's ear and handed it to Nia. She put it on with trembling hands.

"It's okay," said John.

Nia turned and walked toward him.

"Wrong way," he said, and she halted. "You have to go. Now."

She inhaled a quivering sigh. "Captain..."

Her gaze tore John apart. But he said it, because he had to say it, because there was no other way.

"Please take care of yourself."

Nia finally understood. Tears spilled from her eyes. With that, she turned and ran out of the room.

Silence was all that was left, besides the ceaseless hum of the servers.

"Captain, I'm in the car," said Nia through the radio after a minute.

"Copy that. Let me know when you drive through the gate."

"Captain, I'm through."

"Copy."

"I... just want you to know—"

The rest of Nia's voice was lost in the bittersweet crackle of the fading signal.

Mason, who had been listening to their exchange on an earpiece, finally handed it back to a guard.

"Congratulations, Mitcham. You've delayed the inevitable, you stubborn son of a bitch."

More guards now poured into the room; clearly, chasing Nia wasn't the pressing issue of the moment.

"Who knows what's inevitable," said John.

"I thought by now you'd realize the Grail does."

"Does it? I believe the world is still full of wonder and the unknown."

Mason sighed with equal parts frustration and resignation.

"Look around you, John. The world you know is already gone."

Those words hit John like a sledgehammer.

"You know, Mason, something Edwards said stuck with me. He said the Grail knows everything because I've already shared all my greatest fears and hopes and regrets with someone at some point in my life. But that's not true. I've been holding something inside for a long time. Never told it to anyone. Not even Claire. I don't even know why. I've shown the footage of our botched mission in Karbala to over a dozen navy SEAL classes. You blowing that doorknob with a shotgun. Us storming in, seeing those nine boys. The messy extraction when I carried you out of that ditch. And not once did I ever mention it was me in that video, let alone the regret I carry for not doing more."

Mason emerged from the wall of guards.

"What are you saying?"

"I'm telling you I knew those kids were going to die anyway. And we let a hundred and eighty-seven more people die with them three days later."

"John..." Mason bit his lip, his eyes frantically searching John's. "What have you done?"

What *had* John done? Now there was a question.

What exactly does it mean to go against one's nature? To do the random and the unexpected. To reach deep into the void left by heartbreak, and touch the unexplained, extract that little something no algorithm could ever quantify or simulate or emulate. Is that not what we all hope is possible? That we cannot be scored or replaced by zeros and ones, bits and qubits, because you can't write an algorithm that describes the things we cling to in our soul.

That was John's hope as he confronted his worst fear—the fear of becoming an obsolete old man with no place in the world. A world he no longer understood. A world that no longer seemed to have a place for him. Stripped him of all he'd ever loved. Discarded him like so many men and women after they gave themselves to their country, though not always to a good cause.

And so, John gave himself once more, this time to a good cause but not to his country, a flip phone–owning man braving his most formidable enemy: an online instruction manual to synchronize two dozen drones, scheduling them to take off three hours and forty-five minutes later, lest he pressed a button on his smartwatch (and oh what a feat to learn that had been!), which he hadn't pressed, and so now a swarm of drones carrying enough explosives to level a medieval castle was hurtling its way through the air, less than sixty seconds from striking the warehouse-like structure that housed the unholy temple of the Quantum Grail.

"Sir, we have bogies incoming," said a guard.

The panic and incredulity and despair on Mason's face were a sight to behold. So was the mad dash of men trampling over each other to exit the room.

John tossed Memet into the wall of rack servers, and the doctor of philosophy slumped on the floor with a groan.

John went to Claire. As unnaturally pale as she was, she was still the most beautiful woman he had ever known. As he watched the love of his life, his hands began shaking. John felt as though his disease was being triggered by his heartache, and maybe it was. He had clung to Claire for emotional support throughout most of his life, so who else would be the anchor for his physical failings? He unstrapped her belts, removed the tube from her mouth, and pushed away the helmet from her head.

John then lifted her, his trembling hands steadied by her body, but not as much as she steadied his racing heart. "Oh, honey," was all he said, holding Claire in his arms in much the same way as he'd held her at the altar of that little chapel in Durham, North Carolina. *We'll do a proper wedding when I get back,* he had said—another unfulfilled deed in the sea of John's regrets.

He sat on the floor and kissed her.

Finally, Captain John Mitcham closed his eyes.

Like all good sons, he heard his mother's gentle voice tell him it would be okay.

The Montauk wind washed over him.

95

SEPTEMBER 9, 2024, 1:05 P.M. EST

REUTERS
Quantum Grail Congressional Testimony Begins

WASHINGTON, Sep 9 (Reuters) — The CIA deputy director, David J. Bohen, testified during an emergency session called by the US Senate Select Committee on Intelligence, addressing the continued fallout from the Quantum Grail project that has rocked the nation. Bohen confirmed that medical experiments were performed on American soldiers and veterans in order to build a top secret cyberweapon, a shocking admission that caused the chamber to erupt. Testy exchanges followed between Bohen and the committee members.

"It's a dark day in our nation's history when the agency in charge of national security betrays the men and women who secure our nation," said the committee chairman, Michael Wagner, a senator from Virginia.

The purpose of the Quantum Grail supercomputer still remains classified, as do the exact details of how American military personnel were used before dying in the explosion of the building that housed it. Among the casualties of the blast that sent a plume of smoke above the Sonoran Desert is Mason Hartwell, a CIA deputy who spearheaded the initiative. Bohen reiterated that Hartwell was a rogue actor, hiding the project's inhumane practices from oversight, a claim that was met with skepticism by most members of the committee.

Bohen maintained that Hartwell's ability to pull off such a stunt stemmed from his previously unknown ties to LIS, the secretive hedge fund that has seen no shortage of scandals over the last decade. Multiple board members of LIS have been arrested over the last two weeks, and the firm's stock price has cratered to an all-time low.

When pressed by the committee to answer how the CIA learned of Hartwell's ties to LIS, Bohen declined to comment due to an ongoing investigation. But that did not stop Chairman Wagner from speculating that the source of information is Nia Banks, the notorious hacker who has a long history of crusading against LIS.

After her arrest in 2021, Banks became a government asset and worked on multiple projects as part of her plea deal to reduce her sentence. Bohen confirmed she was used in the Quantum Grail project but would not confirm whether she died in the explosion.

"The dead don't send anonymous tips about LIS," said Chairman Wagner, drawing the only laughter of the day in the room.

The week will be a busy one for Bohen, as he is slated to appear before three more committees by Friday. Multiple senators and members of the House have already called for his resignation.

A bipartisan bill is quickly making its way through the US Congress to increase transparency of government contractors like LIS. The bill is named the Mitcham Act, after the late John Mitcham, the navy captain who is believed to have destroyed the infamous facility, and his wife, Claire Mitcham, a psychiatrist who tragically perished with her patients in the explosion.

96

SIX MONTHS LATER

At 7:05 p.m. local time, Mason Hartwell entered his penthouse suite at the Paxton Hotel in Ha Long, Vietnam. Crossing the foyer, he noticed from the corner of his eye that the desk lamp in his office was turned on. He distinctly remembered instructing housekeeping to turn off all the lights after cleaning.

He shook his head and strode into the office, mumbling something about drawing unwanted attention as he reached for the lamp switch—

"You can leave it on."

Mason shut his eyes, lowering his head with an exhale. He then opened them, lifted his chin, and steeled himself before turning toward the chair in the corner.

"Hello, Nia."

"Have a seat, Mason."

———

Mason unbuttoned the only buttoned button of his tragically outdated white blazer, and sat in the faux-leather chair behind a laminated-surface desk.

The Quantum Grail

"How did you find me?"

Nia studied him for a moment.

"That's the thing about you old dignitaries with lavish ambitions. You claim you understand the changing world. You build monstrosities to prove to everyone just how much you understand. And yet, you still ask that question. Despite knowing that with each new microchip, each new network, each new stream of ones and zeros, your world slowly becomes *my* world. So, allow me to borrow your own words. I found you because I am the best at what I do."

Mason nodded, though Nia was not quite sure to which part of her answer. Perhaps all of it. As he moved his head, his scarf slipped down a bit. Nia glanced at his neck.

"I see you're healing well," she said.

Mason readjusted his scarf, veiling the splotches of third-degree burns.

"Day by day," he said, picking up a bottle of painkillers from the desk and rattling it.

"You're a survivor, that's for sure," said Nia with slight admiration. "Slithered your way out of that fire, got patched up in Mexico, then flew to the other side of the world. To a stunning destination, if I may say." She threw a perfunctory glance at the tree-covered limestone islands speckling Ha Long Bay. "Great view from here." She locked eyes with Mason. "Of course, the lack of extradition laws to the US is a lovely perk."

After holding Nia's gaze for a few seconds, Mason said, "I appreciate you stopping by, but we could've had this little chat without you pointing that gun at me." He planted his forearms on the desk. "The theatrics are unnecessary."

Nia chuckled.

"That's rich coming from a man who orchestrated one of the most elaborate performances in CIA history. But I assure you, there is nothing theatrical about me holding this pistol. It has a full magazine and one in the chamber. The Obsidian Forty-Five suppressor attached to it is the quietest there is, but you already know that."

Masoned leaned back in the chair, which creaked as though he'd transferred his own tension into it. He studied Nia for a good while before speaking.

"Let me tell you what else I know. I know PTSD better than most. I know all your childhood trauma. I know that guns are your greatest phobia. I also know how it feels to look someone in the eye and kill them. I know those scars stay with you, forever, like a splinter in the back of your mind. Which is how I know you won't pull that trigger."

Nia tilted her head slightly, taking in Mason as though she'd never fully seen him before.

"Wow, Mason. You know so much. But you know something else, don't you? You learned it when you reran the Grail simulation six months ago. It seemed like a trivial thing that happened between my and John's silent brainstorming sessions out in Albuquerque, New Mexico. In retrospect, it was trivial as far as the Grail was concerned. But that was the thing about the Grail simulation. It only attempted to calculate its own self-preservation." Nia's eyes narrowed.

"But not yours."

97

OCTOBER 26, 2019

"Dad, I'm not strong enough," said Jenny.

John smiled and said, "You're plenty strong. It's all about the grip."

He took her right hand and readjusted the pistol.

Jenny said, "Look how much bigger your hands are than mine."

"Your hands are big enough. You just have to grip it as high as you possibly can."

He pressed the V formed by her thumb and index finger high against the gun's backstrap.

"There you go. Now put the flat part of your index finger on the trigger and wrap the other three around the handle."

"Like that?"

"Just like that. Take your other hand and place it against the other side. Rotate it so that your thumb is parallel to the frame—no, that's too high—a little lower—that's it. Now wrap the fingers over the hand on the other side."

"How's this?"

"Perfect. Just make sure your thumb on the firing hand is away from the barrel."

She didn't listen, so John gently placed her right thumb over her left hand.

"Square up to the target and extend your arms. A slight bend of the elbows to absorb the shock. There you go. Is the barrel at your eye level?"

"Yep."

"Great. Just relax. Focus on the target. Fire when ready."

Jenny pulled the trigger and missed the empty soda can twenty yards away.

"How did that feel?" asked John.

"Much better."

"Okay, try again."

She did. And missed. And missed some more.

"I just can't hit it."

"How many shots have you fired so far?"

"Four. Five?"

"It took me seventeen to hit my first can from this distance."

"Yeah, but you were twelve."

"Is that the point I was trying to make?"

"No, Dad. I get it. It takes time, like everything else."

Time was exactly what it had taken. Just like all things worth learning. Like all lessons worth imparting. But eventually, Jennifer Ann Mitcham hit that soda can in fifteen tries.

Four years and nine months later, on the outskirts of Albuquerque, New Mexico, with far more patience from John and courage from her, it had taken Nia Banks only nine.

EPILOGUE

The first wave lapped her bare feet. She wiggled her toes upon its retreat, relishing the texture of wet sand beneath them. Another wave wiped away her marks, a quick reminder that nothing is permanent. The lighthouse stood in the distance to her left, defiant to the ocean and indifferent to her. Nia's gaze sailed into the horizon, where water became sky. She closed her eyes and took a deep breath. The scent of seashells and seaweed. The sound of lashing water. A gentle breeze playing across her face.

Somewhere, a seagull said, "Ha, ha, ha."

ACKNOWLEDGMENTS

I am firm believer that crafting a great novel takes a village. That is why I must first thank my developmental editor, Elizabeth Kulhanek, whose keen eye and sixth sense are simply remarkable.

A huge thank-you to my copy editor, Stephanie Chou, who went above and beyond her duties to catch some glaring mistakes and omissions.

Finally, thank you to James T. Egan of Bookfly Design. The idiom "don't judge a book by its cover" might hold water in a metaphorical sense, but in reality, your world-class cover design skills are the portal to this novel's success.

ABOUT THE AUTHOR

J.D Redvale is a former software engineer who substituted writing code with writing prose. He lives in New York City with a standard-issue cat that is hellbent on contributing to J.D.'s novels by zooming across the keyboard. *The Quantum Grail* is his debut thriller. For more updates on J.D.'s work (and his cat), visit him at jdredvale.com, Instagram @jdredvale, and Twitter @jdredvale.

Printed in Great Britain
by Amazon